An Evening at
Almack's

TIMELESS *Regency* COLLECTION

An Evening at
Almack's

Sally Britton
Elizabeth Johns
Sarah M. Eden

Mirror Press

Interior Design by Cora Johnson
Edited by Jennie Stevens, Kelsey Down, and Lisa Shepherd
Cover design by Rachael Anderson
Cover Photo Credit: Period Images

Published by Mirror Press, LLC

An Evening at Almack's is a Timeless Romance Anthology® book

Timeless Romance Anthology® is a registered trademark of Mirror Press, LLC

ISBN: 978-1-952611-07-0

TABLE OF CONTENTS

The Heart's Choice

Sally Britton

Chapter One

March 1814

"Do stop dawdling, Matilda."

One would think, given her sister's tone, that Mattie was a delinquent child rather than the elder of the two and quite firmly the more responsible sister.

"Stopping to greet our neighbors, especially those of respectable age and rank, is not dawdling," Mattie corrected, attempting to keep up with her younger sister.

"It is when we have better things to do." Beatrice sniffed but finally slowed her rather unladylike stride. "And when the person you stop to speak to is that horrid Lady Fenlock. You *know* she delights in spreading rumors about me."

Rumors that were, Mattie knew, very well founded. Beatrice had something of a reputation for being a flirt.

"She is also someone we need if we hope to be invited anywhere this Season." Mattie looked at her younger sister from the corner of her eye, studying the artful way Beatrice's sun-gold hair escaped her bonnet in playful ringlets. Her sister truly was as lovely as Aphrodite and a contrast to Mattie in almost every way.

Mattie was older by four years, and at age twenty-six she didn't mind being considered on the shelf. Her hair was darker, her eyes muddier, and her complexion not so faultlessly pale as her sister's. Beatrice was tall and willowy, Mattie of an average height and shape. Beatrice could command a room with ease, and Mattie much preferred being an observer on the edges of most parties.

1

"As long as we have vouchers, we will do well enough," Beatrice argued. "We do not need old, gossipy geese to beg us invitations, Matilda. We are attractive young ladies, daughters of nobility." She narrowed her eyes. "Our family has commanded respect for generations." Beatrice tilted her nose into the air and walked at a faster clip again.

It took a firm hold on her tongue to keep Mattie from replying to that remark. Managing her family's estate was far easier than managing Beatrice. The Granthorne barony had meant something for nearly a hundred years, but Mattie knew that in a single generation it could crumble like the ruins of their ancestors' castle. And should people discover their father's ailment, Beatrice would not even be completely to blame.

Mattie's steps on the walk slowed as she considered her father's condition, one for which his doctor could give them no cure. Her heart ached at the thought of losing the man who had been her hero all her life. Her sister didn't seem to notice when Mattie fell behind.

If Mattie could persuade Beatrice to focus long enough to marry her off, she just might salvage the family name, her father's dignity, and her mother's pride. Beatrice must stop being so stubborn about everything to do with marriage. Many of her worthier callers had disappeared after the previous year. Her sister, at twenty-two, didn't command the devotees she had at eighteen and nineteen. But there was one man who might do.

Mr. Arthur Redhurst, a gentleman of means if not in possession of a title, would make a fine husband for Miss Beatrice Rayment, younger daughter of the sixth Baron Granthorne. They would do well together. Both mothers—and Mattie—thought so.

While Mattie had been thinking, Beatrice walked ahead of her by nearly twenty yards, but Mattie refused to run to catch up. They were on the street of their townhouse, after all, and she could at least see her sister well enough to stop any real trouble from happening. Or so she thought, until she saw a gentleman had stopped on the walk, doffing his hat to speak with Beatrice.

Narrowing her eyes, Mattie maintained her even speed and tried to determine who the man was. He was tall and dark haired, and his words carried to her clearly in the air, in a voice as unexpected as it was familiar.

"Miss Beatrice, good afternoon. It is a pleasure to see you after so long."

It cannot be. Mattie's heart lightened, a feeling suspiciously like hope stealing into her heart. But that was ridiculous. Seeing an old acquaintance, even if it was *him*, ought not cause such sensations.

Beatrice curtsied, and Mattie slowed her step, only a few feet away now, waiting for her sister to identify the gentleman.

"Good afternoon," Beatrice said as she returned to her full height. "Pardon me, but how do you know my name? I do not believe we have met."

Beatrice raised a hand to her cheek, batting her eyelashes in her most coquettish manner. Mattie ground her teeth together. No. Beatrice must *not* be allowed to toy with this man's feelings, innocent flirtation or not.

"Oh, we've met, Miss Beatrice. In fact, I've known you for years. You do not know me?" He spoke with a lilt to his voice Mattie had always found rather charming. What on earth was he doing here, on their street? And how could Beatrice not recognize the man who had grown up practically on their doorstep?

Beatrice shook her head, tilting her head coyly. "Sir, I would remember meeting someone such as you. I never forget a handsome gentleman, and it is really too bad of you to pretend to know me. We must be properly introduced, or there will be gossip."

As one of their near neighbors was peering out her front window in that instant, Mattie knew there was a great deal of truth in that statement.

Mattie stepped forward, between her sister and the gentleman. "Oliver, how lovely to see you again." She curtsied, keeping her eyes on the nephew of their steward. "Forgive me. It is Mr. Bolton now we have all grown."

Oliver had come to live with his uncle after the deaths of his parents many years ago, thus forming an acquaintance with the Rayment sisters out of a polite sort of necessity. He'd been a sad, kind lad then, but he had matured into a handsome man. With him standing before her for the first time in years, grown into his new role of gentleman, Mattie decided he'd aged excessively well.

Beatrice, her eyes wide and lips parted in surprise, seemed to be thinking much the same.

"Oliver Bolton? The steward's nephew?" The younger woman gasped. "I hardly recognize you."

Although he'd matured, all his former features remained much the same. If her sister didn't recognize the man, it was likely because she'd never paid him much attention in the first place. Oliver's slight frown seemed to indicate he might think the same.

Luckily Mattie had years of practice when it came to smoothing over her sister's manner. "It is very good to see you, Mr. Bolton. I had no idea you were in London. It's going on five years since you went away from us." Mattie kept her smile merely polite, though her words were said with kindness. "How are you settling into your new life? I understand your estate in Lincolnshire takes up a great deal of your time."

The man's dark-green eyes glanced from her to Beatrice,

but they settled more firmly on Mattie again when Beatrice continued to gape at him. "Westerwind did not take to me as quickly as I wished, but presently the lands and farms are doing well. Have you spoken to my uncle?"

Mattie was the only member of the family who had spoken to the steward in quite some time, and he was forever telling her of his nephew's successes.

"He is very proud of you, Mr. Bolton," she answered. "Of course he mentions you from time to time. It is good that you have such a source as Mr. Hapsbury to guide you. Our family would be quite lost without him."

Mattie chanced a glance in her sister's direction to see if Beatrice had composed herself yet. The speculative gleam in Beatrice's eyes made Mattie's stomach clench. Mattie knew that look. She'd seen it all her life, from the time Beatrice was a child and discovered a toy she coveted.

"Beatrice, darling," she said, hoping her tone was warning enough for her sister that *this* was not a man whose affections were a plaything. "We ought to return home and see if Lady Sefton has replied to our request for vouchers." Mattie had received hints from the patroness that they would be permitted to enter the upper ballroom, where they had been denied the previous year for reasons unknown to any but the patronesses themselves.

"Yes, of course." Beatrice adjusted the reticule on her wrist but looked up at Oliver through her eyelashes in a manner that rather reminded Mattie of a puppy begging for scraps. Unfortunately, the men of London seemed inclined to like puppies. "Will *you* be applying for vouchers to Almack's, Mr. Bolton?" Beatrice asked.

Mattie nearly panicked but tried to remain composed. Oliver's smile diminished.

"I am afraid not, Miss Beatrice. But I do hope you enjoy

5

yourself at the balls. If you will excuse me, Miss Rayment, Miss Beatrice." He bowed and replaced his hat with an air of gravity. "I hope to see you again soon."

"Good day, Mr. Bolton," Mattie said, giving Beatrice no time to ask more questions. She took her sister's arm and tugged her down the walkway, fixing her eyes on their front door.

Hopefully that would be the last they would see of Oliver Bolton. But a strange premonition made her think that wish was in vain. Oliver had always been a well-mannered boy, and he would likely come to the house to call on their father. Even a gesture as well meant as that could be disastrous.

"I wonder if Mr. Redhurst has sent you flowers today," Mattie said, as cheerily as possible, in an effort to divert her sister.

"He sends flowers nearly every day," Beatrice responded, boredom coloring her words.

This will never do. Mattie took in a deep breath and launched into speaking with excitement about Almack's, Mr. Redhurst, and the last few months of the Season. If Beatrice became distracted by Oliver Bolton before being properly engaged, it may well ruin her standing in Mr. Redhurst's eyes. Before their return to the country, she *must* see her sister safely married. The family depended upon it.

Chapter Two

"TELL ME AGAIN: WHY must I attend this party with you?" Oliver asked his friend for the second time in as many days. "I am not certain this is the correct place for me to begin my foray into London society."

"It is the perfect way to begin, Bolton. An intimate card party, only the most well-connected guests in attendance, will give you the right sort of introductions." Robert Dunwilde, heir to an earldom, grinned across the coach from Oliver. "And it's a little late to bow out now, isn't it?" he asked as their carriage arrived at the house of the party in question.

Oliver folded his arms across his chest, tucking his hands beneath them. If he didn't force his hands still, he knew he'd fiddle with his cravat, a nervous habit his recently acquired valet despaired over on nearly a daily basis.

"They will think me an upstart."

Dunwilde waved away Oliver's concerns. "It is the perfect place to find elegant young ladies to keep you company. You worry too much. Enjoy yourself a little."

It was easy for Dunwilde to say. The man was heir to a fortune, a title, and a standing in society Oliver could never hope to obtain. Oliver Bolton, on the other hand, was the son of a deceased merchant and the nephew of a steward, had never gone away to school, and bore the new gilt of a country gentleman.

Oliver followed his friend through an entry hall, relinquishing his hat and greatcoat to a waiting footman. He tried to meet the servant's eye, wondering if this man in his livery could guess how similar their lives had been but five years before.

The servant accepted Oliver's things, bowed, and departed without a word.

Dunwilde had vanished, and the other guests were making their way up the main staircase to the first floor, where they would play cards and drink as though nothing in the world could ever trouble them. He sucked in a deep breath, trying to draw courage from the empty air around him.

The large upstairs parlor he entered was full of tables, laughter, and no sign of Dunwilde. Oliver looked from one side of the room to the other, desperately seeking someone he might know, but—

The warm glow of honey-colored hair attracted his eye, and he took in the young woman with surprise.

It couldn't be. Twice in the same day.

Perhaps the fabled Fates of the ancient world were smiling upon him after all. Miss Beatrice stood near a window, looking out over the party with her bewitching blue eyes. Years before, at seventeen, she had danced across his romantic daydreams. She'd been a delightful child, four years his junior, an enchanting youth with an easy laugh, and then she'd burst into womanhood and stolen his fancy.

Five years ago, she'd been beyond his reach. But now, seeing her twice in one day, he wondered if such might no longer be true.

She met his eyes from across the room, and it was as though a challenge had been issued.

Without further thought, he went to her. He wound his way through the tables, taking notice of nothing else. Her lashes dropped as he drew nearer.

"Good evening, Miss Beatrice." He held his breath,

waiting, watching her closely. She returned his bow with the slightest dip of a curtsy.

"Mr. Bolton, what a pleasant surprise. I hope you are not offended by my lack of recognition this afternoon." She studied his face a moment, her eyebrows furrowing in a most adorable manner.

Initially, that had disappointed Oliver. But he chose to view it as a compliment. He stood taller and tugged at his sleeves.

"Oh, I suppose I have grown rather dashing."

She fluttered her eyelashes at him, and a coy smile appeared. "I absolutely agree with you. You are quite changed for the better."

"Mr. Bolton," a voice said at his elbow, startling him. He turned, looking down into the solemn eyes of another woman from his past. It would be easy to resent Matilda's sudden appearance, given the manner in which she'd led Beatrice away earlier that afternoon.

"It is wonderful to see you again," she said, her words and look at odds with each other. She certainly didn't *appear* delighted to see him.

Matilda turned away before he could respond, addressing her sister. "I understand Mr. Redhurst will not be attending tonight. He sent a note that his sister is unwell."

Although immediately curious as to who this Mr. Redhurst was, Oliver couldn't help being gratified when Beatrice showed no disappointment at the news.

"I suppose he is a very attentive brother." Beatrice hardly reacted and, without another word on the matter, focused on Oliver. "Mr. Bolton, won't you join me in a game of whist?"

Flattered to be the object of her focus, he extended his arm to her. "It would be my great pleasure, Miss Beatrice." He didn't give a thought to Matilda until they'd taken two steps away, then turned to see her staring after them. "Would you like to join us, Miss Rayment?"

Beatrice laughed. "Matilda isn't a great hand at cards. She's far too serious to enjoy the game." When Matilda's only reaction to her sister's words was to arch her eyebrows, he took that as indication enough she would not mind them stepping away.

Oliver quietly admired Beatrice and the way her curls framed her pretty face, counting himself fortunate to spend an evening in her company. Years ago, she'd hardly known he existed.

Perhaps stepping from one rung on the social ladder up to another wouldn't be as difficult as he'd thought.

Mattie watched her sister all evening with concern. In Beatrice's first Season, she had gathered male admirers as a child gathers daisies in a field, whimsically and without much thought. Her father declared her too young to marry, and Beatrice hadn't minded the idea of another Season of such entertainment and admiration.

During Beatrice's second Season, Mattie had been the only one in the family to disapprove of her sister's more calculated tactics in attracting the attentions of unattached young men. Father and Mother had both been certain their darling daughter would make a match most brilliant, for everyone thought Beatrice to be lovely and charming.

Mattie, therefore, was the only one unsurprised when Beatrice declared she had no wish to marry any of her swains and even *turned away* two serious proposals of marriage to perfectly decent young men. Her reason?

"I have no wish to settle into the dull existence of a wife when I could be dancing every night," she had explained.

Watching her sister flirt with Oliver Bolton, a handsome man if Mattie had ever seen one, left the elder sister slightly nauseated. And she could not shake the feeling, as he gave Beatrice his full attention and made her giggle at the card table, that a disaster brewed before her very eyes.

While Beatrice had been oblivious to Oliver in the past, Mattie had, in fact, always admired him. Mattie had often observed the unfortunate boy, taller and finer looking than the sons of the surrounding gentry, and thought his circumstances quite tragic. He was as clever as his uncle, their steward, and always had a kind word for everyone. Yet he was an orphan, uneducated, and without many prospects for his future.

She recalled he had always looked out for her sister with a great deal of earnestness. Protectiveness, perhaps, when they were younger. But what if it had been more? It certainly looked like a different sort of emotion at present.

Oliver gazed at her sister with an admiration she had seen on many a gentleman's face. Mr. Bolton, nephew of their steward, was enamored with Beatrice.

It would not do.

Beatrice had built a relationship with Mr. Redhurst, a man of wealth and consequence.

Mr. Redhurst, Mattie thought, might even be persuaded to marry her younger sister. He'd paid her every attention and seemed to understand her nature enough to make allowances for her behavior.

Beatrice absolutely *had* to marry, and soon. With their father's failing health, and the entailment of his properties to his second cousin, the Mrs. and Misses Rayments could soon be without a home.

Mattie turned over her sister's character in her mind. As long as Mr. Redhurst didn't see evidence of Beatrice's somewhat fickle nature, and if he attended the next event with them, likely Beatrice's attention would focus back where it ought to be.

Oliver Bolton's deep-green eyes, dark, curling hair, and strong jaw might amuse Beatrice for a short while, but Mattie hoped that was all he would be. A brief distraction.

Lady Granthorne came across the room, smiling at her acquaintances as she went, then stood near the wall with Mattie. She opened her fan and spoke, low enough only her daughter could hear.

"Who is that young man with Beatrice?"

How could her mother not recognize him? Mattie had known him at once. She expected Beatrice to be unaware of people below her in social standing, but not her mother.

"Oliver Bolton. Mr. Hapsbury's nephew."

Her mother's mouth turned downward in a severe frown, hidden from all but Mattie by her fan. "The steward's nephew? The one who went away to inherit something?"

"An estate, Mother."

"Dear me. And what is he to Beatrice?"

"An inconsequential conquest, I'm certain." Mattie forced a smile, even as she heard her sister's laughter ring as clearly as a bell. "Beatrice has Mr. Redhurst's interests. She will not forget him easily."

"Let us hope," her mother said, narrowing her eyes.

Mattie nodded, distracted by Oliver's pleasant laugh and the fond way he gazed at her sister.

As much as Mattie had always liked Oliver, she could not allow him to distract Beatrice. The flighty young woman needed stability, and their family needed to maintain a level of respectability that a man in possession of a small estate in Lincolnshire could not hope to attain. Beatrice, used to living in a grand style, would not do well with a man whose fortune required a more moderate outlook.

"Of course," her mother continued in an airy manner, "you could always marry, Matilda."

Mattie didn't deign to reply to that absurd suggestion.

"Oh look, Lady Topley is here. Excuse me, my dear." Her mother glided away, a picture of grace despite her forty-six years. No one in their social circle would ever suppose the baroness to be suffering through the difficulties that plagued their family.

Chapter Three

OLIVER CAME TO PAY a morning call to Miss Beatrice, a true spring in his step. He'd hardly slept the night before, busy as his mind had been in conjuring up Beatrice's delightful laugh and the way she'd looked up at him through her eyelashes. The attention she'd lavished upon him the previous evening, speaking to practically no one else, had done much to encourage him.

The last time he'd had the privilege of Beatrice's company had been just before her seventeenth birthday. Her dancing instructor had despaired over the young woman's lack of ability with the minuet and enlisted Oliver and Matilda to practice the forms. Oliver, barely a passable dancer himself, added to the confusion in the family's music room by stepping on Beatrice's hem and nearly knocking Matilda over.

The dancing master had railed at him, calling him an oaf, but Beatrice had laughed the matter away, and Matilda whispered the correct steps to him the remainder of their practice.

Did Beatrice remember that day?

He presented his card to the butler and waited in the hall, wondering if he would be shown upstairs or if the family were not yet receiving callers.

The steady clop of shoes on marble made Oliver straighten, but it was Lord Granthorne who appeared from the corridor, looking about as though searching for someone.

Oliver's interactions with the baron had been infrequent.

He'd spoken to Lord Granthorne in his uncle's office when they'd discussed estate matters, and never in a more informal setting. If his uncle had spoken to Matilda of his letters, he must've mentioned Oliver's progress and prospects to the baron as well.

"Where are they?" the baron muttered, barely loud enough for Oliver to hear. "They must be around here somewhere."

Oliver cleared his throat, realizing the baron remained unaware of his presence. "Good afternoon, my lord."

The baron's steps halted, and his forehead scrunched, dim blue eyes narrowing. "Who's that?" he asked, voice accusing rather than curious or welcoming. "What do you want?"

Oliver, taken aback, bowed deeply. "I beg your pardon, my lord. I am Oliver Bolton. I've come to call on your daughters."

The older man came forward, his steps swift, and held his hands out in greeting. "Yes, yes. Welcome. Mattie is an exceptional young lady. She will be pleased you've come to see her. Wasn't she stunning last evening? The ball. It was a spectacle, was it not?"

"The ball?" Oliver's forehead wrinkled, and he studied Lord Granthorne, confused.

"Yes. Mattie has a fine pair of feet for dancing, does she not? I must say, she has me to thank for that. We've been dancing together since she was a tiny thing." The baron chuckled, then raised a hand to his forehead and rubbed at it, his eyes dimming. "She isn't small any longer, is she?"

Uncertain as to what response he ought to make, and hesitant to correct his lordship, Oliver began to nod his agreement when a voice from above called down.

"Papa, there you are." Matilda, holding the rail at the top

of the steps, seemed to take in the scene in the entryway before she came swiftly down to the ground floor, speaking all the while. "Mother was looking for you. She needs your opinion on the menu for your birthday."

"My birthday. Yes." Lord Granthorne's expression altered from thoughtful to surprised. "I had best tell her not to serve fish." Without another word to either of them, he hurried up the steps, calling out as he went, "I cannot abide fish most days, but certainly not on my birthday."

Matilda watched him go, her dark brows drawn together and a wistful sort of gleam in her eyes. Her bronze hair, pulled up and away from her face in an intricately twisted chignon, had a tiny white feather caught in it that momentarily distracted him from the situation at hand.

"When is your father's birthday?" he asked, then bit his tongue. He hadn't even properly greeted her yet. "I beg your pardon, Miss Rayment." He bowed, taking his eye away from the wispy feather. "I have come to pay a call to your sister, er— and to you."

"Of course, Mr. Bolton. I received your card and came to speak to you myself. Please, come into the room here." She gestured to a door off the entry, and he preceded her through it into a small sitting room with dark furnishings and a large desk. A study?

A couch near the hearth was the only comfortable seating, and that is where she led him. "Won't you sit down?"

With his hat and gloves still in hand, as the butler hadn't returned to retrieve them, Oliver lowered himself onto the stiff cushions. Nothing about the situation made any sense. Either he ought to have been shown to an upstairs parlor or he should've been turned away.

Oliver rested his hat atop his lap, leaving enough space for her to sit, but Matilda began to pace across the rug before him, her hands clasped before her. Her movement made the feather in her hair wave with each step.

"Mr. Bolton, we have known each other a very long time. I have a great respect for your uncle, and his position, and I am genuinely happy for your change in fortune." Though she said each word kindly, there was a sternness to them that made his insides tighten.

"It sounds as though you are about to follow those pleasant sentiments with something far less amicable, Miss Rayment." He leaned back against the couch and crossed his arms, still gripping his gloves in one hand.

Her hands unclasped to run down the front of her dress, then she tucked them behind herself as she faced him. "I am afraid I must offer some caution, Mr. Bolton. As we *have* known each other for many years, I am in possession of several memories of the way you admired my sister before you left us for Lincolnshire. I confess, I watched last night to see if any of that regard remained." Her words halted, and she looked down at the carpet.

At least this conversation discomfited her as much as it did him. "What did you see, Miss Rayment?"

Matilda released her hands again and made a helpless gesture toward him. "You still hold a great deal of fondness for her, Mr. Bolton. I believe the whole room must have noticed."

"Then they noticed her attentions toward me were just as *fond*, I should think." Oliver would not allow her to make him feel guilty about spending the entirety of the evening with Beatrice. "Was there something in our conduct you personally object to, Miss Rayment?"

The woman before him took a step closer to him, her coppery eyes giving away nothing of her thoughts, but her hands were worrying themselves before her again. "No. My parents, on the other hand, are quite concerned over it. You see, there is a gentleman who is near to making an offer for Beatrice's hand. There is the fear that you, an old acquaintance, will disrupt their relationship."

"It must not be that firm of a connection if the nephew of your steward could hold sway over such an understanding." Oliver did his best to appear unconcerned, to show no fear in the face of the coming rejection. "May I ask why you, and not your father, would address me with these troublesome concerns? This seems like a conversation for the head of the family to attend, rather than the eldest daughter."

Her cheeks colored, but other than that rosy hue she appeared no less confident. "I thought to approach you as a friend, Mr. Bolton, to speak to you on these matters before things grew complicated." She abruptly came to the couch and sat down next to him, turning her body to face his. Her tone softened. "I adore my sister, Mr. Bolton, but as you may remember, Beatrice has a way about her not everyone understands."

Oliver narrowed his eyes, his reply quick and defensive. "She is a delightful young woman and has always been kind to me."

"Of course," she agreed readily, disarming him. "Beatrice has a gentle heart, but she also possesses a stubborn soul. I am afraid she can be decidedly impractical."

"Not like you," he interrupted, unable to help himself. "You have always been an impeccable example of practicality." Even as a girl, Matilda pursued interests in the running of a household rather than taking the time to enjoy entertainment or the company of others her age. When he'd come to live with his uncle, he and Matilda had both been twelve years old. She'd sought him out nearly at once to offer her condolences on the loss of his parents, with all the gravity a girl of that age could possess.

He'd both hated and appreciated the gesture for years. He never could decide if she had done it out of self-importance and some sort of curiosity regarding grief, or if she'd genuinely meant to be sympathetic.

She had nearly the same air about her today as she had at their first meeting from all those years before.

"Are you here to warn me away from her?" he asked, reluctant to allow her to guide the conversation further. "Were you appointed, as a *friend*, to tell me my attentions are unwanted?"

Matilda tipped her head to one side, her eyes shining at him. "What if I did such a thing? If I told you to leave, to refrain from seeking out my sister again, what would you do?"

"I am not merely a steward's nephew any longer, Miss Rayment. I am a gentleman of some means, though they are modest compared to your father's. I am not going to disappear back to Lincolnshire because you wish it. I am in London to create new connections and plan my future. Your sister is old enough to make up her own mind about me, or the man your family intends for her. I am not going anywhere." He tensed, prepared to stand and leave the room.

Her gentle smile stopped him. It wasn't a conniving look, or a smug one, but something about it still unsettled him.

"Bravo, Mr. Bolton. Those are honorable words, and I respect your position. I am glad to find you a man of principle. Very well. I wish you good fortune in your endeavors." She stood, her skirts brushing the edge of his shoes.

He remained sitting, looking up at her, befuddled. "You do not object to me paying a call on your sister?"

"I would never discourage someone so earnest and sincere as you have shown yourself to be," she said firmly. "Though I am afraid it will have to wait. Beatrice is not home at present. She has gone shopping with a friend. We are to go to Almack's this evening, and Beatrice is in need of a new fan." Matilda gestured to the door, her true thoughts still concealed behind intelligent eyes and a tight-lipped smile. "You may wait in the upstairs parlor, if you wish, but I must warn you that she can be about such things for the entirety of an afternoon."

He'd nearly forgotten it was Wednesday. Every member of society would be preparing for an evening at Almack's or else would spend the day pretending they didn't care to attend, because they had been unable to obtain vouchers.

"Perhaps I could facilitate an outing with my sister, if you wish."

Startled by her suggestion, it took Oliver a moment to answer. What was the woman playing at? He'd been certain her purpose in their rather strange tête-à-tête was to warn him to leave her sister alone.

"What did you have in mind?" he asked.

"Beatrice enjoys the theater. If you can secure tickets, perhaps this Friday?"

Oliver tucked his hat beneath his arm and ran his gloved hand through his hair. "You are encouraging my association with your sister, Miss Rayment?"

"As you said, you are both capable of knowing your own minds. Beatrice is nearly of age. Though I must warn you"— Matilda paused, twisting her fingers together—"Beatrice does enjoy collecting admirers." Matilda's expression seemed almost wistful, for the barest moment before she turned away to face the hearth.

Her statement didn't surprise him. Though he'd been away from the family's society for some years, Beatrice had always possessed a mischievous nature. Her flirting with him at the card party supported Matilda's words.

"Thank you, Miss Rayment. I will attend to your sister in

two days' time, for the theater." He bowed but paused midway through the motion. "Do *you* like the theater, Miss Rayment?"

She cast him a confused look over her shoulder. "I? Do I like it? Yes, of course."

"Perhaps you could attend with us," he said, though he'd much rather have a more indifferent chaperone than the elder sister attend.

"Thank you, but I—" She cut her words off, her eyebrows furrowing. "I would not wish to intrude."

"You would be most welcome. After all, we have known each other a very long time." He grinned, using her words against her.

Though she didn't laugh, he saw the gleam of humor in her eye. "Very well. I accept your invitation on behalf of myself and my sister. Thank you."

"Oh, one thing more, before I take my leave of you."

She had the grace not to appear impatient with him. "Yes, Mr. Bolton?"

He took the half step necessary to be close enough to reach out, his hand going to the little white feather above her left ear, removing it carefully from her hair. "You've lost a feather."

Matilda's lips parted in surprise, her eyes widened. "Has that been there this whole time?" she asked, the last word coming out as more of a squeak.

His lips twitched as she raised her hand to accept the feather. "Never fear, Miss Rayment. You were perfectly intimidating and stern, even with the bit of fluff." He bowed, feeling cheeky, and hastily made his exit.

He hadn't seen Beatrice, but Oliver left encouraged just the same. Robert Dunwilde kept a box at the theater. All Oliver had to do was ask to accompany his friend, and the thing would be done.

Spending a single evening in Beatrice's company had once been a dream, but if he took the opportunity to court her, who knew what his future might entail?

Chapter Four

"YOU DID *WHAT?*" LADY Granthorne asked, her voice rising dangerously. "Beatrice absolutely will *not* attend the theater with that young man, however charming he may be."

"Mother, please." Mattie stepped to the door of her mother's bedroom and closed it with haste. "Beatrice isn't going with him. She will not even know about the outing because *you* will make certain she is engaged elsewhere."

Her mother, dressed for the evening at Almack's, stood in stiff elegance beside her dressing table. "And where would that be? I cannot conjure invitations out of thin air." Her mother waved her hand about her head before rubbing at her temple.

"The Redhurst house party," Mattie said, unrepentant. "You were to leave Saturday morning. If we are clever, we can come up with an excuse for you going the evening before."

"I suppose that might work," her mother said, her brows drawing down in thought. "And their country house is only fifteen miles from London. That isn't a terrible distance, should your father need us."

Mattie clasped her gloved hands before her and considered the situation. "And we have already decided I would remain behind. So long as you return for the ball next Wednesday, you will not miss anything of importance in London. I can make our usual calls."

Her mother closed her eyes tightly. "I do worry for your father."

23

"The staff will help, and I will be here as much as possible." Mattie went to her mother's side to take up the older woman's hands, fixing her with an earnest stare. "All will be well, Mother. Once Beatrice is taken care of, we can retire to the country to help Papa."

Lady Granthorne nodded, her expression unchanging. She returned Mattie's warm clasp, and her eyes grew distant. "If only we hadn't lost David."

It took all of Mattie's strength not to flinch at the name of her little brother, who had been between Mattie and Beatrice in age. He'd been gone twenty years, and her mother rarely mentioned him now. A childhood fever had stolen David, their father's heir, and the family had never quite been the same. If David had lived to adulthood, all manner of things would be different for the family.

"Come, Mother. Let us try and be cheerful this evening. We are going to Almack's," Mattie said, whispering the last word as though it were a magic spell to cast out her mother's gloom.

By the time Mattie led the way into the sparkling ball-room, chandeliers glimmering and their light reflecting off the multitude of mirrors, Mother had regained her cheer. Beatrice followed them both with her usual grace and a roving eye that took in all the gentlemen present.

Mattie, paying careful attention to her sister, dropped back a step to link her arm through Beatrice's. "Do you see Mr. Redhurst? He asked for two dances with you this evening, did he not?"

"Hm? Oh, yes. Mr. Redhurst." Beatrice narrowed her eyes and looked around more carefully. After several moments of stretching about, Beatrice lifted a gloved hand to wave across the room at the one man who showed the most interest in her. "Here, he is coming to join us."

"Lovely." Mattie watched her sister's reaction to the man's approach, attempting to discern how much work she must do to remove Oliver Bolton from Beatrice's thoughts. Given her sister's somewhat fickle nature, she hoped it would not be an enormous undertaking.

Beatrice's bright blue eyes widened happily, and she lowered her chin almost demurely when Mr. Redhurst arrived at her side.

He was a handsome man, six years Beatrice's senior, with sandy-colored hair and eyes a few shades darker than Beatrice's. Their children would likely be beautiful, given the attractiveness of the parents.

Nothing in Beatrice's manner indicated a change of feeling for Mr. Redhurst, which eased Mattie's mind somewhat. After an exchange of polite greetings with Mattie, Mr. Redhurst swept her younger sister away for a dance.

Mattie waited patiently for Beatrice's first dance to end. Mr. Redhurst always asked Mattie to stand up with him at least once, which she counted in his favor. The man was incredibly thoughtful.

Mr. Redhurst's mother approached Mattie. "Good evening, Miss Rayment."

"Good evening, Mrs. Redhurst." Mattie curtsied to Mr. Redhurst's mother with all deference. "I am very glad to see you."

"As I am to see you." Mrs. Redhurst glanced briefly at the dancers, then back to Mattie. "You do not dance, Miss Rayment?"

"Not very often, I am afraid. Your son is always good enough to ask for at least one set. He is such a kind man." It wouldn't hurt to give a little flattery to the mother, Mattie well knew. "Beatrice often speaks of him with great regard."

"Indeed. My son speaks highly of your sister too." Mrs.

Redhurst snapped her fan open and looked about them before she leaned closer to Mattie. "Your sister is a delightful girl, and the very sort I've always hoped he might find interest in."

Hardly believing her good luck, Mattie leaned closer to the matron to speak in a conspiratorial whisper. "Beatrice knows her good fortune, my dear Mrs. Redhurst. She has spoken of your house party with great excitement. I know she wishes she might be there as soon as possible, to see your beautiful house. My father may need the carriage Saturday morning," Mattie said, improvising and hoping the falsehood was not too terrible. "Beatrice is most distressed this may delay her arrival until Sunday."

Mrs. Redhurst turned fully to Mattie, her attitude one of accommodation. "That simply will not do. We have all manner of entertainments planned. Might it be better if your mother and sister came on Friday?" She glanced again at the whirling couples changing hands and places on the dance floor.

"I believe that would do perfectly," Mattie said, holding her breath as she said the last word. Could it be so easy?

"Hm." Mrs. Redhurst raised her eyebrows. "I will speak with your mother."

"I am certain she will appreciate your generous offer, Mrs. Redhurst." Mattie took out her own fan and waved it languidly, putting on her most confident mask. "Mother is just there, across from the orchestra's perch, if you wish to speak to her now."

Mrs. Redhurst took her leave, making for Mattie's mother at once.

Now all Mattie had to worry about was breaking the news of Beatrice's absence to Oliver, who truly didn't deserve whatever painful feelings such a thing would cause. Mattie bit her bottom lip and wandered away to stand near the walls, making eye contact with herself in one of the gilded mirrors.

It's for the best. Beatrice would never be happy with Oliver, and that would make his life miserable. Who knew her sister better than Mattie? No one. And she knew enough about Oliver's good heart and hard work to want to spare him the difficulties her sister would cause in his life. Mattie would handle him gently, guiding him as well as she could from disappointment to acceptance of the situation.

On the edge of the ballroom, Mattie quietly went through her plan, assuring herself she had done the right thing.

Chapter Five

IT TOOK ALL MATTIE'S abilities to remain composed when Oliver Bolton called Friday evening. Though she'd rehearsed what she must say enough times to put even the most sophisticated actress to shame, her stomach writhed inside her. While she had little choice in what must be done, Mattie had never felt easy when telling a falsehood.

The butler showed Oliver into the parlor, where Mattie and Mrs. Clifton, her mother's old friend and the chaperone for the evening, were waiting. Mrs. Clifton, an elderly and genteel woman, had already dozed off in her seat near the fire.

Mattie stood and curled her fingers tightly, watching as Oliver's eyes darted around the room, searching for Beatrice. Finally, his eyes settled on her, suspicious and a touch disappointed.

"Good evening, Mr. Bolton." She offered the customary curtsy to his bow. "I am afraid I have rather dreadful news."

He raised a hand, forestalling her explanation, his eyes crackling with indignation. "Your sister will not accompany me to the play." He turned away, the lines of his body stiff. "You might've at least sent word and spared me the humiliation of coming to your home."

Mattie's compassion for him pricked at her heart, but she could not remove her duty to her sister. Mattie stepped closer, the silk of her evening gown swishing softly with each movement. "Mr. Bolton, please, it was not my intention to upset you. Beatrice is not here, it is true, but when she returns you may spend time with her. She did not have a choice but to go, you see, as my mother insisted upon it only this morning."

She spoke quickly over the lie, relieved he didn't study her as she spoke. It would be harder to bear up the falsehood under any scrutiny. "I thought to send round a card, but my day was taken up with helping the others pack, and then I thought it might be best to explain to you in person. They were to go to a house party tomorrow, but were unexpectedly asked to arrive a day earlier."

Mattie took the last step between them and tilted her head, trying to peer up into his expression. "I am trying to handle the matter delicately, Mr. Bolton. Will you please forgive my bumbling attempts this once?"

Oliver spared her a sideways glance, brows drawn down, before he nodded. "I suppose I must." He put a hand to his cravat and smoothed the crisp white fabric in a gesture which could ruin the elaborate cascade of folds.

Mattie raised a hand to still his gesture, but quickly pulled it back. The swift movement gained his attention, and he stared at her, eyebrows raised.

"I beg your pardon," she said, tucking the offending hand behind her back. "I am sorry for the disappointment. I wonder, Mr. Bolton, if you might still wish to attend the theater? I am dressed for it, you see. And there is Mrs. Clifton to chaperone. We might still have an enjoyable evening, though I know I am a poor substitute for Beatrice."

Those words settled heavily in Mattie's heart. Beatrice was prettier, livelier, and certainly better company than Mattie at social engagements. Most of the time, Mattie had too much on her mind to give herself up to the pleasures of society. Planning for Mr. Bolton to excuse her, the most likely thing to happen, made dressing for an evening out a less joyful affair than it otherwise might've been.

Oliver lifted his head and regarded her with a critical eye before speaking. "You would still be willing to accompany me to the theater?"

"Why, yes," she stammered, taken aback by the intensity of his stare. "It hardly seems fair to make you give up the enjoyment and make the trouble of obtaining tickets a waste of time. I understand if you do not wish for my company—"

"Not at all," he said, his words clipped. "Although I had hoped to attend with both of the Miss Rayments, I would hardly be a gentleman to retract my invitation. I have a friend with a box, and he is expecting us." Oliver hardly looked pleased as he spoke.

That he was still willing to take *her* with him, despite his disappointment in the evening, said something of his nature. She shouldn't have been surprised, yet she stood still for a moment, the prospect of going to the theater with him lifting her heart. It fell again nearly as quickly.

Truly, it almost made her feel worse about the whole ruse. Yet how could she gracefully refuse, dressed as she was?

"I will accompany you, Mr. Bolton, with the greatest pleasure. Allow me to—erm—bestir Mrs. Clifton." She hurried to rouse her chaperone, privately thinking it ridiculous her mother insisted she have one. After all, at twenty-six and with no plans for marrying, Mattie hardly thought it necessary. But even a spinster's reputation must be guarded.

It was almost insulting Matilda thought him simple enough to believe her story. Oliver may not have been a Cambridge or Oxford scholar, but he had a good head on his shoulders and sufficient instincts to know when someone lied to him. Although he suspected Matilda's motives were not entirely cruel, after their last meeting he had genuinely thought she would give him an opportunity to prove his worthiness to her sister, her family, and society as a whole.

While leaving her at home would have been the more satisfying response to her charade, he had made a fool of himself to Dunwilde and his other acquaintances by speaking of the evening with delighted anticipation. To arrive at the theater alone would be almost as terrible as not going at all.

The new world he inhabited put too much emphasis on one's social standing for him to ignore the rules of good manners.

Perhaps spending an evening with Matilda would prove educational. Observing her behavior during conversation would be enlightening. The first thing he must try to learn, of course, was whether or not Beatrice had even been aware that he had requested her company for the evening.

When they arrived at the theater, they went immediately to Dunwilde's box, where the man was sitting with a lady and the lady's mother. All rose to make their bows when Oliver presented Matilda.

"Miss Rayment, daughter of Baron Granthorne, and her companion, Mrs. Clifton."

"A pleasure, Miss Rayment," the young woman's mother said with a beaming smile. "And Mrs. Clifton. Come, you must sit next to me. We will let the young people sit at the front. Heaven knows, I have seen more than my share of plays."

Oliver showed Matilda to a chair and took his next to her. Next to him sat Robert Dunwilde and the young lady he escorted.

His friend wasted no time in leaning close to whisper. "I thought it was the younger sister you were interested in?"

Matilda stiffened in her chair and leaned forward, eyes intent upon the still-lowered curtain.

Dunwilde had never been particularly good at whispering.

"She was indisposed," Oliver answered quietly. "I am grateful Miss Rayment was still able to attend this evening."

The skeptical tilt to his friend's eyebrows said it all, and then the curtain was rising and half the room turned to the stage. The other half continued to examine members of the audience and gossip between chairs as well as between boxes.

Matilda was one of the few more interested in the stage than her neighbors. Oliver studied his opponent as covertly as possible. He knew, somehow, that he had been put in an awkward position on purpose. The lovely Matilda Rayment had never meant for him to escort her sister anywhere at all. What remained to be seen was how far she might be willing to go, what manner of tricks she might enact, to keep him distanced from Beatrice.

Appealing to the parents would do him no favors, either. The baron and baroness would most likely scoff at him for entertaining such notions as courting their younger daughter.

But if he could convince Matilda, perhaps she could persuade their parents to treat him with fairness instead of snobbery.

After all, as a landed gentleman—even if the land wasn't yet as successful as it could be—he was an appropriate choice for a suitor.

While the actors sang of love on stage, Oliver mentally prepared to do battle to win the right to court whom he wished.

Chapter Six

MATTIE SAT IN HER father's library, reading aloud while her father drew. His lucid moments, his ability to converse like himself, became rarer with each passing week. But if his hands were busy, he was often capable of maintaining greater focus on the world around him.

Though the reading wasn't exactly required, Matilda found it necessary in order to keep her mind from turning continually to the rather dishonorable lies she'd told Oliver. He'd hardly said a word all the night long, during the opera and after, though he'd been a complete gentleman.

Her voice faltered as she read, the dry text closing up her throat completely.

"Something wrong, Mattie girl?" her father asked, glancing up briefly from his sketch. "You aren't your usual lively self today."

When was the last time she'd even thought to apply the term *lively* to herself or any of her pursuits?

"No, Papa. I apologize for my distraction. Shall I continue reading?"

"You needn't. I am finished with your likeness." He handed her the folder wherein he kept his sketches, and she took it, curious despite herself. Sometimes he drew her as a child, nearly perfect representations of what she'd looked like when she was young.

Today's drawing was of her reading a book, her brow furrowed and her eyes dark with thought. She swallowed at the sight of her guilt, captured quite innocently by her father.

A knock at the door gave her leave to turn her attention away from the troubling image.

"Come in, please," she said.

A footman opened the door, and a maid came in, carrying a very large basket stuffed with every sort of flower imaginable.

Mattie rose. "Oh, dear. Beatrice would have loved these. We must endeavor to keep them fresh for her." She came to the maid, her hands outstretched to examine the blossoms.

"They aren't for your sister, Miss Rayment," the maid said, delight coloring her tone. "They're for you. There's a card."

"For me?" Mattie saw the card held by the footman and took it with murmured thanks.

Miss Matilda Rayment,

Thank you for sparing my feelings and enjoying the theater with me. I hope I might extend another invitation to you, in the name of friendship, to ride with me in the park today. Please send your acceptance to the address enclosed. If you must send your regrets, I will strive to understand. But it is good to be around familiar people in a city full of strangers.

Yours, etc.,

O. Bolton

Mattie stared at the note, the little lines and letters jumbled about in her head; when she finally made sense of them she could hardly believe it.

"Oliver Bolton has invited me to ride in the park today," she said, sparing a moment of pride that the sentence came out evenly.

"Mr. Hapsbury's nephew?" her father said, and she turned to him in shock. He sometimes forgot she was a woman of six and twenty instead of merely sixteen, but he could remember the steward's orphaned relative?

"Yes. The very same."

"Always liked that boy. Full of ambition, and a hard worker." Father chewed at the insides of his cheeks for a moment, his eyebrows drawing down. "We ought to have him to dinner if he is in town. Invite him while you are on your ride today, Mattie girl."

A direct order, issued when his thoughts were clear, must be obeyed. But—she was trying to rid the family of Oliver's intentions, not bring him more fully into the fold.

"Then you do not object to my riding with him?" she asked carefully, folding the card and running her index finger over the crease.

"Not in the least." Her father settled himself more comfortably into the couch and took up his drawing again. The maid still held the basket, and the footman still held the door. Mattie took in their expressions, noting the maid's anticipation with distress.

Really, servants ought to be more circumspect.

Mattie sighed and took in the riotous blossoms again, trying to remember when she'd last received flowers from a gentleman. It had been *years*.

"Put these in the entry, Sarah, and inform the groom I will need my horse at a quarter till five." Mattie tucked the card into the ribbon at her waist and went back to sit next to her father, picking up the book again and effectively dismissing the servants with their curious stares.

"I am glad to see a young man take notice of you," her father said, not looking up from his work. "You are a good girl, and I want you to be happy, Mattie."

Nervous laughter bubbled up inside her. "Mr. Bolton is but a friend, Papa. I am too old to be of interest to anyone. I'm content to be here with you and Mama." She looked down at the page, not really seeing it and uncertain as to where she'd left off reading.

Her father sighed and shook his head, but he said nothing more, leaving Mattie to her thoughts and suppositions of what Oliver Bolton could mean by sending her *flowers*.

Chapter Seven

OLIVER CLUTCHED MATILDA'S ACCEPTANCE in his hand with something near to triumph. Either she was oblivious to his motives or else curious to see what he could want with her. No matter the reason, she had agreed to spend more time in his presence, which meant he had greater opportunity to present his case to her.

As a youth, Miss Beatrice's tinkling laughs and witty remarks enchanted him. Now that he'd inherited, he finally had a way to enjoy the pleasure of her company, and he would not allow it to be taken from him so swiftly.

Five o'clock found him at the baron's home, with Matilda already mounted on a fine chestnut gelding, wearing a smart hazel riding habit that suited her coloring. Her cheeks were rosy and her smile easier than he had seen it so far.

"You do realize," she said after they'd greeted one another, "that Rotten Row will not afford much of an actual *ride* at this time of day? We will spend most of our time weaving in and out of carriages or standing still."

"You do not seem concerned over such a fate," he returned, not having to remind himself to be pleasant. The day was lovely, and Matilda was in a friendly mood. They took to the road, following a slow line of carriages and horsemen, most moving in the direction of Hyde Park.

"I am merely happy to be in the fresh air with good company," she stated firmly.

"A kind compliment, Miss Rayment."

She raised her eyebrows. "How do you know I meant you? I could've been talking of my horse."

For a startled moment, Oliver wasn't sure what to say, but when he saw the pink in her cheeks and her upturned lips, he started to smile. "Ah, I see. Naturally, a horse is a fine companion, especially when one intends to ride."

Matilda's shoulders noticeably relaxed, and she gave him a brighter smile. "I haven't ridden through the park in some time, Mr. Bolton. Nor has my friend Coriander."

Oliver chuckled and nudged his horse to ride alongside her. "You named your horse after a spice?"

"I name all my animals after spices. Do you not remember our kitten?"

"Basil," he said, the little black ball of fluff coming abruptly into his memory. "I rescued that loathsome creature from the eaves of a window once. How could I forget him?" He'd had to borrow a ladder from the gardener and regretted not borrowing a sturdy pair of gloves as well when the kitten unleashed its tiny, razor-like claws upon him.

Matilda had thanked him profusely, while the cat tucked in her arms glared at him, and had offered to bandage up his hands.

She seemed to be remembering the same event. "Have you any lasting scars from that encounter?"

Oliver looked down at the leather gloves he wore now, smooth and supple, the gloves of a gentleman instead of a gardener. How strange, the difference a few years could make in one's circumstances. "I think not. I healed tolerably well. What of the cat?"

"He has grown quite portly and spends his days sleeping in warm patches of sunlight and giving Cook grief," she answered, a lilt in her voice as she spoke. "He is a most abominable creature, but I do adore him."

They gave attention to the road for a time, weaving around ambling carriages, and then they were on the paths of Hyde Park. Riding abreast was less comfortable, if they wished to avoid collision with other riders or fine little vehicles with shiny wheels and tall seats. Oliver tipped his hat to every woman they passed, earning a few smiles and nods in return. Matilda made her share of greetings, calling out names when she knew them, but never stopping to speak to anyone.

When the opportunity presented itself, he urged his horse forward to her side once more. "Have you no wish to socialize today, Miss Rayment?"

She looked askance at him. "Did you have someone you wished to speak to, Mr. Bolton?"

"I am afraid my circle of acquaintances is quite small," he admitted, looking around the path. "I have seen no one I know."

She drew up her horse. "Oh. I beg your pardon. Might I introduce you to anyone? I know several of the people we've passed. I am sorry, I wasn't thinking—"

Oliver waved the apology aside without concern. "Perhaps another time." His horse slowed to a stop when the barouche in front of them halted. Oliver stood taller in the stirrups, trying to see over the crowd while his horse danced to the side.

"Have you not ridden through the park yet?" Matilda asked, and he turned to see her horse placidly bending to nibble at the grass near the path. "It is more standing still than it is moving, especially in our fine spring weather." She grinned at him from beneath the brim of her riding hat.

"I confess, I've heard that is the case, but I hoped such accounts were exaggerated."

Matilda didn't appear perturbed in the slightest. Her attention turned to the Serpentine, as they were as near its shores as one could get on Rotten Row.

"It isn't like at home," she said, her voice grown softer along with her expression. "One can have a good, brisk ride and suitable exercise without worrying if anyone notices your new hat."

"Should I have said something about your hat?" he asked, wondering where her melancholy air came from. "I am afraid the expectations of society are yet new to me."

Matilda's attention redirected to him, her eyebrows raised. "You ought not make such comments, Mr. Bolton. You are a gentleman, and you need make no excuses. In all honesty, you comport yourself as well as any lord I have come across."

The vehicle ahead of them moved, necessitating that they both continue forward, giving Oliver a moment to think on what she said. The woman barely knew him. How could she hold such an opinion of his character already?

"But you really should say something kind about a lady's riding cap. Especially when it has pheasant feathers smartly applied to the brim instead of haphazardly placed in her curls." One side of her mouth quirked upward, and Oliver had to chuckle as she tossed her head, the better to show off the headpiece.

"Forgive me, Miss Rayment. Your feathers are most becoming today." They were passing a carriage going the opposite direction, and the woman inside gave him a most peculiar look for that comment. "And very well placed."

"That is much better. Thank you." She bestowed a deep nod upon him, but as she faced forward, that wistful sort of expression came into her eyes again. "Your uncle would be proud you've adjusted to the manners of a gentleman so well. I look forward to giving him a firsthand account of your time in London."

Oliver had written to his uncle weekly since inheriting

the Lincolnshire estate, asking advice, bemoaning the run-down house and flooded fields, and finally, in the last eighteen months, sharing all that had finally gone *right* with the estate.

"I didn't expect he would tell the whole neighborhood when I wrote, but he must've for you to be knowledgeable of my work," Oliver said. "My uncle is not usually known for being talkative." He turned to share a humorous smile with Matilda, but she turned her eyes downward and fiddled with her reins as they drew to another stop. "Is something troubling you, Miss Rayment?"

"No. Not at all." Quite abruptly, she lifted her chin and fixed him with a curious look. "You haven't been in London long. Have you visited the Royal menagerie yet? Or any of the art galleries? Will you be attending services while you are in town?"

Oliver's mind puzzled over her manner, but he answered easily enough. "I have seen very little and done very little. I had hoped my friend, Mr. Dunwilde, would guide me for a time, but he's left on a shooting trip in the country. I suppose," he added with what he hoped was carelessness, lowering his gaze, "I must find my own way." Something he'd been doing a lot of the past five years.

Her tone of voice when she spoke, in a rushed manner, was perfectly sympathetic. "Oh dear, but that isn't done. You must be introduced into the correct circles, if you mean to make a place for yourself in society. Especially if you wish to court Beatrice."

The name startled Oliver out of his thoughts. Miss Beatrice. Of course. "Your sister enjoys her place in society?" he asked, moving forward again. "I imagine she is popular."

"Her company has been sought after a great deal in years past. And she did leave for that house party rather hastily." Matilda didn't look at him as she spoke, though her manner became less animated. "She is not a retiring sort of person. Beatrice enjoys being at the center of grand events."

"I cannot think how many of those I might be invited to attend," Oliver said slowly, his eyes on the horizon.

They were moving again, coming to the end of Rotten Row.

"Once people know you, they will count themselves lucky to have you at their parties and balls." Matilda cast him a genuine smile. "I have always found you to be pleasant company, after all."

He chuckled. "We did not exactly spend a great deal of time in each other's company, Miss Rayment." He could only remember a handful of their interactions, though they had lived in the same village for six years. He was forever about on his uncle's business, which was truly estate business for the baron's family, and she was being molded into a proper lady along with her younger sister.

"What about that time in the study, during that terrible storm? Do you remember?" she asked, turning her horse onto the street. "It had been raining for ages and ages. Your uncle sent you to the library for a book, I think."

For several seconds, Oliver felt certain she was mistaken in her memory, but then he began to recall such an afternoon. "I didn't know you were in the library, hiding behind the curtain."

She wrinkled her nose at him. "I wasn't *hiding*. I was sitting on the window seat."

"Behind the curtain." He narrowed his eyes at her.

"Halfway behind the curtain, perhaps," she returned, pursing her lips.

Oliver chuckled. "I know enough to refrain from contradicting a lady. Yes. I remember. You were on the window seat, and I came in looking for the book, and there was that monstrous burst of lightning—"

"And you screamed," she interrupted with barely concealed glee. "Or shrieked, more like. I didn't know *you* were there, so that frightened me, and I fell out of the window seat."

Which had made the curtains fly open—and she had hit the ground with a shockingly loud thump. He started to laugh, remembering how he'd lifted the book in his hands like a weapon only to see Matilda crawling out from under the drapes, hair in disarray and face frozen in shock. They had both stared at each other, he with raised book and she from her hands and knees on the ground.

Matilda started laughing too, covering her mouth with a gloved hand when a matron riding by sent a withering glance their direction.

"I thought you said I was good company? Nothing about that scene strikes me as evidence of that." Oliver couldn't keep the amusement from his voice, though he tried to compose himself, with poor results.

"You don't remember?" she asked, tipping her head to one side. "You dropped the book on the floor and rushed to help me to my feet." She grinned at him. "Quite the gentleman, really, considering you were as frightened as I was."

"How old were we?" he asked, furrowing his brow in thought. "Thirteen?"

"Near there, I should think. You hadn't started calling me Miss Rayment yet, but you'd been with us for a good while." She turned away, her profile lovely and expression soft. "You stayed in the library for at least a quarter of an hour, trying to soothe my nerves."

"Trying to soothe my own," he added. "It was a blow to my thirteen-year-old ego, to be so unmanned in the presence of a young lady over a crack of lightning." Missing his parents and trying to find a place for himself, Oliver hadn't possessed much confidence in those days. "I didn't want you running off to tell my uncle any tales, after all."

Matilda raised a gloved hand to her heart. "Me, sir? I would *never* do such a thing." She batted her eyes and put on an expression of innocence, making him grin. They were nearing her house. "I thought you a very nice boy. Why would I make trouble for you?"

"You wouldn't, of course. But that was before I knew the family very well. I hadn't been acquired to assist with dancing or etiquette lessons. I was only my uncle's errand boy, and I had no wish to upset him. Poor Uncle Hapsbury. He hadn't any idea what to do with me most of the time."

Indeed, Oliver could remember several instances when his uncle had looked over the rims of his spectacles in a state of befuddlement, trying to sort out whether to laugh or scold Oliver over his misadventures.

"I think he did a marvelous job with you, overall," Matilda said, her tone sincere and her eyes meeting his squarely.

"Thank you." And then, because he was starting to feel guilty over enjoying Matilda's company, he added, "I hope Miss Beatrice feels the same."

Matilda's approving look vanished, replaced by a more distant, polite expression. They were at her house again, and a servant appeared to take her horse. Matilda dismounted and turned her attention to him. "Thank you for the enjoyable afternoon, Mr. Bolton."

He dismounted as well and stepped forward, feeling an apology was in order but uncertain *what* he would be apologizing for. "Miss Rayment, I—"

The front door flung open, crashing against the wall and interrupting his words, and her father came hurrying down the steps.

"Mattie," he said, sounding breathless. A male servant followed close at his heels, eyes wide and face pale. "Mattie, I cannot find your mother, or your sister. Where have you been?" He was obviously agitated as he reached for his daughter, enfolding her in his arms upon the walk.

Matilda's face paled as she accepted the embrace, and she appeared dreadfully off balance.

Oliver handed his reins to the groom. There were few other people around, but Oliver could sense something of a scene building.

"My lord," he said, giving his attention to the baron. "I am afraid I kept your daughter out too long. We went for a ride."

"Yes, Papa. You see. Here I am." Matilda turned an apologetic eye to Oliver. "And Mother and Beatrice are well. Come inside, and I will tell you everything."

The baron looked around the street, then at Oliver, before he loosened his grip on his daughter's arms. "Won't you come inside too, young man?" he said, eyebrows drawn down in puzzlement, as though he could not remember Oliver's name.

Matilda's eyes widened, and she looked at Oliver in something of a panic. "Mr. Bolton likely has other demands on his time, Papa."

Oliver's shoulders dropped, and he looked from the horses, still standing in the grip of the young servant, around the street, where there were now several pairs of curious eyes watching their little tableau.

He lowered his voice so only Matilda and her father might hear. "I would very much like to come in, Miss Rayment, and you needn't fear. I am not wholly unaware of your circumstances, and I am a man of discretion."

Understanding lit her face. "Your uncle's letters?"

He doffed his hat. "Won't you lead the way, my lord?"

The baron's confusion cleared, and he stood straighter,

more like his old self. "Yes, of course. Come. We must go inside." He walked before them, forgetting to take his daughter's arm. Oliver moved to offer his, and they followed the baron—and the servant who had hovered at the edge of the conversation—into the townhouse.

Chapter Eight

MATTIE MADE CERTAIN HER father was comfortably settled in his favorite chair in the study, going to the trouble of giving him an extra cushion and a warm shawl around his shoulders. She tried to ignore Oliver, who stood by the window, staring out to the street, as she bustled around the room to stoke the fire, ring for refreshments, find her father a book, and then stand for a moment in uncertainty.

Mr. Hapsbury, their steward, was not a gossip. In fact, the man had been a loyal employee to her father since before Mattie's birth. But he had obviously told Oliver something of her father's ailment.

I cannot be entirely surprised, given how much he's told me of Oliver's accomplishments.

Mattie reached up to touch her hair and realized she still wore her riding cap. Grimacing, she began to undo the pins which held the lovely thing in place. Once it was removed, she laid it aside on a table.

Oliver's hands were clasped behind his back, and she couldn't see his face. It was impossible to guess what he thought of the situation, though he had acted quickly to help move everyone along to minimize what onlookers saw.

Father must've been watching at the window for her or the other ladies of the house to arrive home. His state had been one of worry and agitation. Thankfully, the agitation hadn't lasted long. Again, she questioned the wisdom of their father coming with them for the Season, though they intended to stay only so long as it took to secure Beatrice a marriage offer.

Her mother hadn't wanted to leave him on their estate, and Mattie really couldn't imagine doing so either.

Mattie said nothing as she approached Oliver. At first, before her courage built up suitably, she only gazed out the window. A carriage passed, and across the street a woman walked hand in hand with two little boys. Life continued as it always had.

"I didn't mean to intrude," Oliver said, startling her from her quiet study of the world outside the house, and outside her difficulties.

Mattie turned enough to see his cast-down expression, the frown pulling at his brow and mouth.

"I apologize if it made you uncomfortable," she answered softly. Beatrice was rarely ever near their father of late, claiming it unsettled her too much when he had one of his "fits," as she called them. Mattie knew most of society would feel similarly, and she didn't blame them. Sometimes it made her uncomfortable too. Mostly, it made her heart ache.

Oliver shook his head, still not facing her. "My uncle said your father had been forgetful of late. There is more to it than that, isn't there?"

She swallowed and lowered her eyes to the ground, trying to put her words in order before she spoke. "He is forgetful, but it is not so small a thing as mislaying spectacles or a book. He is mislaying his recent memories and living in moments from the past. Some days, he speaks as though I am still a child. Other times it is like what you saw: he becomes afraid when he cannot remember what is going on about him."

Oliver tipped his head in acknowledgement of what she said before asking, "What has the doctor said? I assume a doctor's been consulted."

"At home, yes. And Mother sought out the help of physicians here in London. None of them are hopeful of curing my father. They say it is the result of growing old, of melancholia." Mattie wrapped her arms around herself, wishing she could ward off the dread of the diagnosis. "They call it *mania mentalis.*"

"As if naming it in Latin makes it better." Oliver looked sideways at her, and his eyes swirled with compassion and concern. "I am sorry for it, Matilda," he said, her Christian name slipping from his lips, sounding quite natural. Indeed, something in his tone of voice soothed her as a gentle touch might. "Your father is a good man, honorable and kind. If there is anything I might do to assist your family, please tell me."

The sincerity with which he spoke warmed her weary heart. "No one knows," she whispered. "Outside the family and a few of the servants. If people knew, if they guessed, we would be ostracized." It was yet another reason she had to secure Beatrice's happiness with haste, in order to withdraw from London.

No one would wish to marry into a family where such diseases of the mind were present.

Oliver regarded her silently for a moment before he nodded. "I will not speak of it to anyone, Miss Rayment."

"Is he staying to dinner?" her father asked loudly, causing both her and Oliver to start. They had been speaking in near whispers.

Mattie looked from her father's inquisitive face, peering around the side of his chair, up to Oliver's almost amused expression. He didn't look disgusted or distressed. He looked, she thought, rather the same as he had on their ride. Thoughtful, kind, and handsome.

"If you would like me to stay, sir, I will most happily. A bachelor takes his meals wherever he can." He cut a glance to her long enough to offer a smile and a wink, then he strode over to her father. "Won't you tell me of your home, my lord? It has been years since I've been for a visit, and I rather miss it."

Mattie watched, attempting to remain unemotional, as Oliver settled into a chair near her father and conversed as if the scene in the road had never occurred. As if everything were *normal.* Nothing had been normal for ages.

Somehow she must dash this good man's hopes of courting Beatrice. She wished her sister might return from the house party engaged to wed, before Oliver became too attached. Sparing his feelings while diverting them from Beatrice would be challenging indeed.

Chapter Nine

OLIVER ALLOWED MATILDA'S FATHER to guide their conversation, whether the baron spoke of things long past or occurring in the present. The man's grasp on time was loose, yet his intelligence could not be questioned. While they spoke in the study, Oliver's eyes often strayed to Matilda. She remained near, though she did not participate in the conversation.

She wrote at the desk for a time, looking through what appeared to be a ledger, then took up a book and sat in a chair across the room from the gentlemen. She occasionally glanced in their direction and offered the faintest of smiles, then went back to her reading. The servant who had come out into the street, the baron's valet, came in and out of the room frequently, acting the part of a companion.

The family must've given the man additional duties when the baron's memory began to fail. No wonder Matilda had stayed behind when her mother and sister went to the house party in the country. It was obvious she stayed for her father more so than she stayed for Oliver.

This diminished his pride a touch. He'd fancied that she stayed merely to warn him away, but her duty to her father was more likely the reason for her continued presence in London.

"Mattie is a lovely girl, isn't she?" the baron said, startling Oliver from his thoughts. He realized he'd been staring at her again, while Matilda was tucked rather snuggly into the pages of her book and oblivious to the world around her.

What could he do but agree? "She is. You are very fortunate in your daughters." There. That was a good, general sort of compliment.

The baron pulled the shawl tighter around his thin shoulders. "She worries too much. Takes too much on herself." He spoke quietly, and Oliver noticed the baron's blue eyes were lucid and bright. "It isn't right for a young woman like her to worry so over her parents. She ought to have a husband and children of her own."

While Oliver had certainly been surprised to find Beatrice remained unwed, he hadn't given much thought to Matilda's situation. Now that the baron mentioned it, he found it strange no gentleman had offered for her. Matilda Rayment might not be the golden-haired beauty her sister was, but she had an allure of her own Oliver could not deny. Her dry sense of humor and the way she expressed herself with clarity and sincerity were qualities he rather liked.

And she did have striking eyes.

"Why hasn't she married?" Oliver asked, turning to face the baron again. Speaking of Matilda had naturally made his attention return to her corner of the room. "Surely there have been offers."

"There have. A few." The baron settled back into his chair and looked out the window, and Oliver wondered if that would be the end of the conversation, as it appeared the baron might lose the thread of the present again. "I think she's waiting for someone special to come along," the baron said at last.

Before Oliver could give much thought to that, the butler arrived, announcing dinner.

Matilda rose from her chair with an easy sort of grace. Most of the young women at the beginning of their time in society held themselves like statues, afraid to move in the wrong manner, but Matilda had confidence in her bearing.

"I hope you do not mind the informality of the occasion, Mr. Bolton," she said, coming nearer where he and her father sat.

"Nonsense." The baron chortled as he rose. "What young man *wants* to spend half an hour dressing like a dandy to take soup and bread? I lay odds that Oliver is happy to forgo the rituals of a formal evening."

"Oh, Papa." Matilda came forward and reached for her father's arm, but the gentleman swiftly raised it to fuss with the shawl around his shoulders.

"Ah, Oliver. Do a favor for your elder, and escort Mattie in to the table. Mattie, send Matthews to me, won't you?"

Oliver stepped in to offer Matilda his arm, noting the way her brows were drawn together in concern.

"I cannot think of a command I would be happier to obey, my lord," he said, affecting his most chivalrous grin.

Matilda narrowed her eyes at him, taking his offered arm. "Papa, I will send your valet to you at once. But no tidying your cravat. It wouldn't be fair to Mr. Bolton."

Startled, Oliver tucked his chin down in order to inspect his cravat, prepared to see the crisp white cloth wrinkled beyond repair. But the *mathematique* arrangement looked nearly as fine as it had when he left his apartments to accompany Matilda on their ride.

The woman made a sound suspiciously like a giggle, which she turned into clearing her throat. "This way, Mr. Bolton." She gestured to the hall, and he guided her to the dining room.

He helped her to a chair near the head of the table, then seated himself across from her. "How did you know about my difficulties with my cravat?"

Before answering his query, she directed a footman to send her father's valet to him. Lifting her glass rather primly,

Matilda arched an eyebrow at him. "I recall your uncle constantly telling you to look to your neckwear. I think it was a nervous habit of yours, was it not, to tug at it?"

Oliver sat back in his chair. "You remember that?" And how many times had she been in his presence to witness such a thing? "That's rather astonishing, Miss Rayment, isn't it?"

Her cheeks colored. "Where could Papa have disappeared to?" she asked, leaning to look through the doorway they'd entered. Trusting to the informality of the evening, Oliver put an elbow on the table and rested his chin in his hand.

"Miss Matilda Rayment, you are avoiding my question. Why did you take notice of the nervous habits of a servant?"

"You weren't a servant," she said, studying the tablecloth. "Your uncle holds a respected position in our employment. Besides, other than Beatrice, you were the closest person to me in age for miles and miles."

"That's true. I am—what was it? Sixty-three days older than you?" She'd wasted no time in calculating that when they'd first met, after discovering they were the same age.

The baron entered the room, and Oliver nearly felt relieved to have their private conversation cut short. He found he was far too interested in probing further into their shared past and her opinions of him.

"You haven't started without me, Mattie girl?"

"Never, Papa."

The baron took his seat at the head of the table, and the footmen moved to place platters of food upon the table.

Oliver gave his attention to Lord Granthorne. Dinner passed pleasantly, the three of them conversing on any subject the baron chose. Somehow, by the end of the evening, Oliver had agreed to accompany them both to Sunday services the next morning.

As he mounted his horse to leave, Oliver allowed himself to be pleased with the evening. He'd made a good impression on the baron, and Matilda seemed to be thawing towards him. Perhaps by the time Beatrice returned home with her mother, his company would be welcomed.

Of course, making his way through the streets of London, he realized he hadn't passed such a pleasant evening with good company in months. He didn't entertain much, as a bachelor, at Westerwind. His neighbors invited him to dine on occasion, but he had yet to feel like anything more than a dinner guest.

He couldn't think of one uncomfortable moment at the baron's table, nor could he recall any dinner companion being as intriguing as Matilda Rayment.

Chapter Ten

SOMEHOW, BETWEEN THE END of the Sunday sermon and reaching their carriage, Mattie's father had extended an invitation to Oliver for that very afternoon and coerced the young man into accepting. Really, it was almost unseemly to see Oliver three days in a row, in such intimate settings as the theater, the house, and church services.

If anyone had known, there would certainly be gossip as to what his intentions were regarding Mattie.

Mattie smiled to herself as she sat before her mirror, her maid finished tidying her hair. At least she didn't have to wonder about Oliver's motives for spending time in her company. Of course, it would be best if she stopped enjoying their conversations and showed him how wrong Beatrice was for him.

Catching her furrowed brow in the mirror, Mattie nearly groaned aloud.

She'd hardly done a thing to dissuade Oliver from her sister. Hadn't that been her plan? Wasn't it the wisest course of action?

Hopefully Beatrice would be engaged when she arrived back in London, and there would be nothing more to worry about. Except, of course, Oliver's feelings. Would he be greatly injured if Beatrice announced her betrothal? Doubtless he would take pains to avoid the family, at least for a time.

The Season would soon be over when summer's heat intruded upon London's busy streets. Oliver would then return to his home in Lincolnshire. It might be another year before she saw him again, if her family even attempted to return to London. Much depended upon her father's health.

The thought pulled her up abruptly, halting her mind the way a dam halted a winding stream. It had been good to see Oliver, once she'd become used to his grown-up self, to speak to him and be in his company. Being with him brought back memories of happier, simpler days at their estate.

He'd been a tall and lanky boy the first time she saw him, and he'd only stretched out more as he grew. She'd been jealous of him the year they turned fourteen, telling him it wasn't fair he was half a head taller than she when he was only threescore days older.

"Are you eager to tower over all the men you dance with in London?" he'd asked, his voice cracking with his sense of humor. She'd huffed at him and walked away with all the dignity a girl of that age could possess.

Mattie smiled in the mirror with the memory.

Her height, which was unremarkably average, didn't matter much anymore, as she was rarely asked to dance anyway. Unless a man was interested in Beatrice. It hadn't bothered her, as her lack of partners indicated everyone well knew her desire to remain unwed.

While Beatrice had flirted her way about London from the first moment she'd stepped foot on its cobbled road, Mattie had never been particularly interested in finding a husband. A husband would be inclined to tell her what to do, when she had a perfectly capable head on her shoulders. And she'd watched several young ladies of her acquaintance marry into less than favorable circumstances.

Oliver, a kind soul and conscientious landowner, would likely never give a wife cause to regret taking his name.

"I've never seen a man put a blush in your cheeks, miss."

Mattie started in her chair, meeting her maid's eyes in the mirror. She'd forgotten she wasn't alone, and her maid's comment took a moment to fully sink into her consciousness.

"I wasn't blushing," Mattie said, leaning forward to peer at her cheeks. "It is hot in the room." She bit her lip over the falsehood. Her windows faced east; the sun threw its heat into the opposite side of the house, leaving her room quite cool. Even if her cheeks were not.

"As you say, miss." Her maid bobbed a somewhat cheeky curtsy before withdrawing, as Mattie had thought she'd done several minutes before. The door shut quietly behind the servant, and Mattie glared at herself in the mirror.

"I *wasn't* blushing," she whispered firmly. "And certainly not over Ol—a man."

Sitting straighter, she spoke with determination. "My duty is to help Beatrice obtain a suitable match, care for Papa, and assist in running the family estate." She nodded to herself and stood from the table, ordering her thoughts.

After searching out her father, Mattie suggested they spend the afternoon in the gardens. The day was fine, for March, and fresh air would do everyone a great deal of good. When Oliver arrived to pay his call, Mattie had arranged her father comfortably on the terrace while she clipped flowers for an arrangement.

Their town garden wasn't particularly large, but it afforded enough space and greenery to make walking for a quarter of an hour quite pleasant.

Mattie had just taken her gardening gloves off and put her blooms in a pail of water when she heard steps on the terrace.

"Good afternoon, my lord," Oliver said, making his bows. "Miss Rayment."

"There's a good lad, Oliver." Having one of his better

days, the cordiality in the baron's voice was most sincere. Mattie, standing behind his bench, shared a smile with Oliver. "Tell me, have you been well since we last parted? Had any adventures?"

It was a question Mattie had heard many times in her life. Whenever she came in from play or saw her father at the end of a long day, he would ask her that very thing.

"None of which to speak, my lord. Though I wonder if your daughter might join me in a small one? The adventure of taking a turn about the garden. If you will excuse her?"

"I will, sir, if you promise to bring her back whole and take some refreshment with us." The baron chuckled and folded his hands in his lap. "And you must see to it she enjoys herself."

"I will endeavor to do my best, my lord." Oliver bowed and then held his hand out to Mattie, his eyes glimmering with humor. Indeed, he seemed *very* pleased with himself. He still wore his frock coat from attending church, but his cravat looked the worse for wear with a few more wrinkles than it should possess.

Mattie stepped around her father's bench, reaching out to take Oliver's hand. "You have agreed to a great many things, Mr. Bolton. I wonder if you can fulfill all your promises."

Her hand, ungloved, touched his, and as he curled his fingers around it, something inside her *uncurled* and grew, tiny tendrils of warmth creeping through her as if seeking the sun.

Oliver's grin revealed the dimple in his left cheek. He wasn't wearing gloves either, she realized belatedly.

"I am afraid I was in a bit of a hurry," he said, looking to their joined hands. "I forgot my gloves. I didn't wish to arrive late—"

"It—it is fine." She started to pull her hand away, but he gently tucked her arm through his.

Oliver led her down the terrace steps while her mind tried to unravel itself from whatever strange thing had taken hold of her. Noticing dimples and feeling strange sensations at a man's touch was hardly becoming, and nothing at all like her. Had she not taken his arm at the theater? Having spent several hours in his company only the day before, it was ridiculous to think any of the sensations overtaking her consciousness could be attributed to Oliver Bolton.

Perhaps she was taking ill.

"Have you had a pleasant afternoon?" Oliver asked.

Ill or not, she had a duty to perform for her family. Her mother and sister would return Wednesday.

Oliver spoke her name, and his tone suggested it wasn't for the first time. "Miss Rayment? Matilda?"

"Oh, I beg your pardon." Mattie felt the blush creep up her throat and into her cheeks. Twice in one day. "I am afraid I was thinking over the sermon."

"Ah. The weighty discussion of laying treasure up in heaven and forgoing earthly pleasures." He spoke with interest rather than amusement.

"Mm." Unprepared to actually converse on the topic, Mattie's mind didn't form an immediate answer.

"I found it most interesting. As you know, Westerwind has taken a great deal of my time these past years. There were many occasions I thought to visit my uncle and wrote to him, but he always encouraged me to remain where I was and build up my assets." Oliver's head bowed as he spoke, walking slowly on the gravel that encircled the whole of the garden. "I shouldn't have listened. He is the only family I have left, and I have lost a great deal of time in his company. That is what I thought on, when treasures in heaven were mentioned. Surely our friendships are such treasure."

The amount of thought he'd given the topic surprised her, as did the way her heart warmed to him with each word he spoke. "Your uncle would not censure you for following his advice, Oliver."

He blinked, coming out of his solemn manner, and turned to regard her with a crooked grin. "Oliver?" he said, the dimple reappearing.

Blast that dimple. She hadn't seen it since their childhood, and even then it appeared but rarely. "Forgive me," she said, drawing herself up. "But you *did* use my Christian name a moment ago. I am afraid we slipped into old habits."

"Did we, though?" he asked with an unrepentant lilt in his voice. "I almost always called you Miss Rayment after that first year. Uncle felt it was proper."

She had an answer for that, at least. "I wasn't always fond of that. It was most unfair that when we were out in company I was Miss Rayment while Miss Beatrice retained her Christian name in some measure."

"Have you any word when your mother and sister will return?" Oliver asked, his gaze lowering to the stones crunching beneath their feet. Though they walked slowly, they were nearly halfway around the garden.

Was this the real reason he'd come? To find out when her sister would return? Had he sounded hopeful when he spoke? Distracted? Disappointed?

"Wednesday, I should think. They are not very far from London, and Beatrice would be most upset if she missed a chance to attend Almack's. It distressed her a great deal when we didn't receive vouchers last Season. She carried on about it every week." Mattie tried not to wince. Laying forth her sister's shortcomings didn't sit well with her. But it must be done. "This Season, she's insisted on a different gown for each ball. The seamstress we employ is quite overworked."

Oliver raised his eyebrows at the comment but said nothing of it. He changed the subject entirely when he spoke.

"I wonder, Miss Rayment, what you are doing to stay busy while your mother and sister are gone? I cannot think you have left the house unless in my company."

Why were they talking of her when she was supposed to be finding a means to distract *him*? And why did it disappoint her when he didn't call her by her Christian name again?

"I am most content to keep my father company. When Mother and Beatrice return, we will all find amusement enough. This is quite the respite, I assure you, and I still have the occasional caller." Of course, the callers were usually looking for her mother or Beatrice. But she needn't speak of that. "Do you have any plans for your amusement?"

Oliver shrugged. "Nothing of great interest. As I am new to London, I thought I would spend tomorrow walking its streets. Have you any suggestions of sights I ought to see?"

Anything that will keep you from thinking of Beatrice.

"Piccadilly holds many interesting sights," she answered. "Book shops, a museum, and Fortnum and Mason has such delicious foods if you grow hungry on your journey through the streets."

He slowed his steps and didn't quite look at her when he spoke again. "Do you think there is a chance you might come with me? Wandering about on my own doesn't sound appealing."

"I'm not certain I would be the best guide," she said, trying to demure though the idea of walking through her favorite shops pulled at her. It had *nothing* to do with being in Oliver's company, of course. "And I would need to secure a chaperone of some sort."

"Chaperone? Surely a maid would do. We will be on the paths, in open air, most of the time." He paused, turning to face her; his tone turned almost cajoling as he spoke. "Do come with me, Miss Rayment. I find you are very good company. I would endeavor to make certain you enjoy yourself."

His sincerity touched her, and guilt crept into her heart. Oliver was nothing but kind. If only Beatrice could be happy with his modest circumstances. But Mattie knew her sister, knew what she would expect of her future, and she knew they were running out of time. At twenty-two, Beatrice was growing out of the age when men would be dazzled by her. She needed to be married, to be cared for, before their father worsened.

Before we are all in the country, caring for him and hiding from the gossips.

Going with Oliver on another outing, especially one where she might point to all of Beatrice's favorite expensive shops, might help her endeavor. Arrangements would have to be made to attend to her father, to keep him from agitation. If they went earlier in the day, which was usually the best time for her father's mind and clarity, there might not be any difficulties.

"I would enjoy the outing, Mr. Bolton. Would ten o'clock be an acceptable time for you to begin our expedition?"

"More than acceptable," he answered, the dimple appearing again and a triumphant gleam appearing in his eyes.

Oh dear.

They returned to the terrace, where her father appeared to have been dozing until they came near. He rubbed at his eyes and smiled, a very tired smile, up at the two of them. "Back so soon? And tell me, were there adventures?"

"Perhaps the start of one," Oliver answered before Mattie could respond, settling into the chair near her father as though intending to stay for a long time.

That warmth she'd felt earlier made itself known again, wrapping around her heart in an alarmingly familiar manner.

Mattie swallowed and took a step back. "I will see about some lemonade," she said, her voice sounding hoarse to her ears. She spun on her heel and hurried into the house, failing to outrun the stirring of an emotion she had long denied herself. She certainly wasn't about to fall in love with Oliver. Not when she was attempting to keep him from her sister.

Not even when it would be so easy to turn her admiration for him into something more.

Chapter Eleven

OLIVER SAT IN HIS rented rooms, his valet seeing to his clothing for the next day and tutting over the state of the cravats. It had gone against his nature, to have another man wait on him hand and foot, and one older than him too. But Thompson excelled in his position.

"Will that be all, Mr. Bolton?" the servant asked, arms full of cravats in need of ironing.

"It will. Thank you, Thompson."

"Sir." The valet bowed and exited the bedchamber, leaving Oliver alone before the low-burning fire in his hearth. The days grew warm enough to enjoy the outdoors, when the wind wasn't biting, but the nights were still cold. The fire was certainly appreciated that night.

He'd finally done it. He'd broken through Matilda Rayment's carefully constructed, oh-so-practical shell.

Oliver couldn't think of a time in his life when he'd ever seen Matilda flustered, apart from when her father came out into the street the day of their ride. But seeing her that evening, first stumbling over her words in the garden and then looking at him with something akin to shock when he'd done nothing more than invite her on another outing, showed he had made progress.

Then she'd grown quiet after the refreshments were served, watching him almost covertly from beneath her eyelashes. But he'd seen it. He'd seen the curious light in her eyes, the hesitancy. His determination to be nothing but affable was working. Matilda didn't know what to make of him, and he hoped her desire to see him vanish had begun to crumble.

The best part of his plan he hadn't even anticipated: he found he enjoyed Matilda's company. She had a quick wit, and her rare laughter was enchanting. He saw glimpses of the child she'd been when they'd first met, and the tiniest hints of the young woman she was when he left to claim his unexpected inheritance.

Oliver made his way to his bed, removing his dressing gown and climbing between the sheets. He tucked his hands behind his head, thinking through his plans for Piccadilly. It would be diverting to squire Matilda about town, allowing her to tell him of her favorite shops and books, her favorite things to see and do.

Yes, he could only look forward to the next day with a grin of self-satisfaction. They would enjoy each other's company, and—and of course, he would eventually be nearby when Beatrice returned.

Oliver had thought it would be an honor, a boyhood dream fulfilled, to call on Beatrice in a formal manner, to escort her around town. Beatrice's beauty was beyond compare; having a woman such as her on his arm would elevate him in the eyes of society and give him the opportunity to come to know her as an equal. She'd hardly bothered to notice him years before.

Not like Matilda. From the first moment they'd met, she'd spoken to him with gravity and even her practical compassion.

But it didn't matter what Matilda thought. His goal was to gain Beatrice's attention, and he would not be satisfied until he did. The sooner the young woman, with her winning smile and lively blue eyes, came back from the country, the better.

He drifted off to sleep, trying to enumerate Beatrice's finer qualities, but all he could think on was the flash of surprise and the charming blush in Matilda's cheeks when he'd called her by her Christian name.

Sleep had not come easily to Mattie. After spending long minutes of the night trying not to think of Oliver, she decided to invest time planning how best to turn his thoughts away from Beatrice and the family as a whole. Her efforts were wasted, as every conversation she made in her thoughts trailed away into admiring his laugh, thinking of how kind he was to her father, and trying to recall every detail of the letters he'd written to his uncle.

She'd never read the letters personally, of course, but Mr. Hapsbury had delighted in telling her all of his nephew's doings. As her father's ability to remember present concerns dwindled, Mattie took on the responsibilities of the household. Mr. Hapsbury had been understanding of her situation and often used the advice he gave Oliver to guide Mattie as well.

"I don't care that you're a young lady," he'd told her when they'd been bent over account books for what seemed like years. "This responsibility could fall to any person, regardless of sex. There are many who would take advantage of you, but if you know how to handle these matters yourself, you can demand fair treatment."

Neither of them knew, of course, how long Mattie would have to take on her father's responsibilities. At first, she'd hoped the doctor could help him and her time in the steward's office would be short. But the weeks bled into months. Soon Mattie found she enjoyed managing things. Her heart grew to love the challenge of numbers, the responsibilities of caring for her family and their tenants, and meeting with the steward every week enlivened her thoughts.

"I would give it up in an instant for you, Papa," she whispered into the darkness of her bedchamber, fighting back the sting of tears.

If her brother had lived to adulthood, it would fall to *him* to see to all these matters. And he, as heir, would ensure his mother and sisters never went wanting. But a second cousin of twice Mattie's years would receive the title, estate, and everything but the girls' dowries and their mother's portion.

Which is why Beatrice must marry Mr. Redhurst. He can provide her the style of living to which she is accustomed.

Mattie pulled the blankets over her head, attempting to smother the uncharitable thought.

I only want what is best for Beatrice. Mattie rolled over and willed herself to sleep.

Chapter Twelve

DONNING A LOVELY BONNET with sprigs of tiny white flowers, Mattie fought the desire to tuck a feather into its brim as well. Jesting with Oliver over her continued use of feathers in her head-dressing would not serve any purpose other than to increase the familiarity between them. Today she must be civil, polite, but haughty. She must speak of all of Beatrice's favorite, and most expensive, activities. Mattie took stock of herself one last time in her mirror, lifting her chin and setting her shoulders into a straight line.

In the reflection of her mirror, a face appeared over her shoulder, startling her enough that she gave a little leap. Then, inexplicably, her heart thudded against her chest almost painfully.

Beatrice had returned and apparently entered Mattie's room without so much as a knock.

"Matilda, *there* you are. I heard you were going out, and as I just came in, I wanted to see what you are about and if it cannot be put off." She practically floated to Mattie's bed, where she perched with dainty grace. "We had the jolliest time in the country, but I am rather relieved to be back in town."

How had the room turned cold with such speed? Mattie bit her lip and studied her sister silently. Did Beatrice appear as an engaged woman? Her manner was the same as it had always been: playfully superior to the world around her.

"I am going to Piccadilly," Mattie said, her voice soft.

Beatrice lounged back onto the bed, staring up at the

canopy. "I always wondered why you had this room done in green. Pink, or a nice pale blue, would be so much more the thing."

"Beatrice," Mattie said, coming nearer the bed, approaching her delicate sister the way one might approach a lion. "Did anything of note happen while you were away? Did you spend much time with Mr. Redhurst?"

Beatrice's hands clenched at her side, and she grew very still. "Mr. Redhurst," she said slowly, "is engaged."

Hope blossomed in Mattie's heart, yet she held her breath as she asked, "Are you engaged to him?"

Her sister pushed herself back to a sitting position, eyes narrowed, and made a sound of disgust. "No, I am not. The fortunate miss is some childhood friend of his. A *merchant's* daughter."

The blooming excitement withered away to dust. "He is betrothed to someone else?"

"Is that not what I said?"

"Beatrice, I—I am sorry about—"

"Do not be concerned. There are other men in the world besides Mr. Redhurst." Beatrice sniffed disdainfully. "What is it you are about? Going to Piccadilly? To do what? Bring more books to Father that he's read and forgotten?" The blonde-haired beauty stood and stretched. "Just give him one from the shelves downstairs and pretend it is new. He won't know the difference."

Had Beatrice come across the room and slapped her, Mattie couldn't have been more shocked or hurt. "Beatrice, what is wrong with you? How could you speak that way?" Her sister's disappointment surely colored her words.

For a moment, regret appeared in Beatrice's countenance, but then she shrugged it away. "All Mother did in the carriage ride home was weep about Father and about me. She seemed to think Mr. Redhurst and I would come to an understanding during the house party. Obviously he was not as enamored of me as you both believe."

"He seemed to care a great deal about you, to devote so much attention to you," Mattie said, but Beatrice waved away her protest impatiently.

"It is of no consequence. He is to wed another. It is done. Really, Matilda, you are more disappointed about it than I am."

A maid appeared at the door.

"Mr. Bolton's here, miss." Making her joyfully innocent pronouncement, the maid disappeared before Mattie could give any instruction.

"Mr. Bolton?" Beatrice's voice rose with interest. "What is he doing here? He cannot know I've returned to town already."

Mattie closed her eyes and willed her heart to stop racing. How had everything turned so wrong so *swiftly*?

When she answered her sister, Mattie managed to sound indifferent. "Mr. Bolton has come to escort me to the shops. He's never been to Piccadilly."

"Oh? Go and speak to him, Matilda." Beatrice hurried to the door, her mood obviously brighter than it had been mere moments before. "I will change and be down in a quarter of an hour. I'll accompany you." She disappeared into the hall, her lovely pink dress showing her slim figure off perfectly.

"Why change?" Mattie muttered, a strange melancholy taking hold. "You're beautiful in everything. And *ruining* everything."

There wasn't time for a conference with her mother to determine what must be done next, nor comfort the baroness in regards to their failed plan. Nor was there any opportunity for her to slip away with Oliver—Beatrice would find a way to join them or tell Oliver she had been purposefully left behind.

Whatever plans Mattie had made—and they had been the frailest of plans—were dashed to ruin.

Mattie's steps were unhurried as she entered the hall and went to the stairs.

Beatrice would flirt, simper, bat her eyes, and giggle delightfully for hours. And Oliver? He would do as so many other gentlemen had done. He would bask in her sister's glow, and Mattie would shadow them both, nothing more than a chaperone.

There would be no smiles from Oliver for Mattie, no teasing comments, no childhood remembrances. No gentle words or kind looks. Beatrice would be on his arm, not Mattie. Beatrice would receive his every word and gesture.

Mattie froze midway down the staircase and gripped the rail tightly, frightened she might fall without its support.

In truth, Mattie realized, she was not so much concerned with Beatrice's behavior as she was with what it would mean regarding Oliver. She didn't want to see Oliver fawn over Beatrice, didn't want to witness the sight of his dimple appearing when Beatrice laughed, and she most certainly did *not* want to watch him fall in love with her sister.

Because I love him.

The realization brought the briefest beam of happiness into her heart before it was swallowed in pain and grief.

Mattie sank down on the steps, not caring if anyone saw, and wrapped her arm through the spindles of the banister.

It couldn't be love. The thought was firm and commanding. *When has there been time for me to fall in love? Surely it takes a great deal of knowing a person—*

She'd known Oliver since they were twelve years old. He touched many of her childhood memories with his presence. And she'd always admired his kindness, his thoughtful words, the respect he showed others whether above or below him in society.

Having planned out her whole life years ago, leaving no room for love, confronting it now gave her a shock.

Examining her heart carefully, she dared not move from her spot.

How did she know it was love she felt and not something petty, like jealousy?

Because all she had to do was think on walking about the garden on Oliver's arm, and she blushed. Thinking of his smile made *her* smile. Planning to remove him from her family's sphere gave her pain from the first moment she knew it must be done. And she admired him, greatly, for his work to turn an impoverished estate into something better, for his letters to his uncle, and for his kindness toward her father.

"I hadn't realized you now greeted callers from the stairs."

Mattie peered down to the ground floor, between the rails, into Oliver's gleaming eyes. His smile was wide enough to make the dimple appear, and his countenance shone with cheerfulness.

Mattie's heart faltered, and she raised a hand to her lips to keep from blurting the truth to him.

His expression changed from happy anticipation to concern. He came to the foot of the staircase and made as if to come upstairs, but he hesitated. "Matilda? Is something wrong?"

The use of her Christian name undid her, and she parted her lips to speak—

"Oh, Mr. Bolton! Wonderful. I mean to join you today," Beatrice's voice sang from overhead. "But I neglected to ask Matilda if we are in an open or closed carriage. I cannot choose a bonnet until I know."

Oliver's eyes had risen the instant her sister began speaking, but they dropped again to Mattie, their depths full of confusion.

"I've borrowed an open carriage, from a friend," he said, looking at Mattie though he answered Beatrice's question.

"Lovely. I shall wear my tallest bonnet, and we will be seen by everyone near and far." Beatrice's laugh made the air sparkle, and then her steps receded. Mattie hadn't looked up at her beautiful sister even once. She knew well enough the way Beatrice would tilt her head to one side, the pose she would affect, and how she would purse her lips, waiting for Oliver to answer her question. It was always the same with Beatrice.

Mattie used the seconds granted her to compose herself, so she could offer at least a tight-lipped smile to Oliver when she stood.

"Good morning, Mr. Bolton," she said, trying to take pride in her even tone. "As you can see, my mother and Beatrice have returned." She took the steps down slowly, deliberately. His nearness would not have the slightest effect on her. It could not.

His eyebrows pulled downward. "Miss Rayment," he said, formal once more. "You appeared to be in some distress a moment ago. Are you recovered?"

Mattie couldn't imagine ever recovering from the pain in her breast.

"I am quite well, thank you. If you will excuse me, I need to inform my maid we will not need her services." She started to walk around him, calling forth every lesson on deportment she could remember to keep moving without stumbling.

A strong, warm hand closed gently around her arm, halting Mattie in her steps. Looking up into Oliver's concerned eyes, Mattie's heart gave a hard twist.

Why? Why must this happen now?

"You are troubled." It wasn't a question, not the way he spoke it and certainly not with the way he stared intently at her, as though trying to see into her very soul. "We needn't go today," he added, his voice softening. "Is it your father—"

"No," she said, cutting him off as quickly as she could. Discussing Beatrice with Oliver was the very last thing she wished to do. "No, Papa is well. Beatrice is too." She gently tugged her arm away from him. "I didn't sleep well last night. I am a little fatigued." It wasn't a complete lie, but it was the best excuse she could summon at the moment. "The spring air will cure me, I'm certain." Mattie forced her lips upward in a smile.

"Miss Rayment—"

"Excuse me." She turned and walked away, measuring each step while the click of her heels against the ground echoed in the hall.

Chapter Thirteen

THE PLEASANT MORNING OLIVER expected to spend in Matilda's company took on a decidedly different shape with Beatrice present. For one thing, he'd meant for Matilda to sit with him at the front of his borrowed phaeton, instructing him on the best shops in London. Instead, she sat quietly behind him, and Beatrice beside, the younger woman offering her raptures over the fashions of the day and speaking of people he'd never met.

Elation at obtaining Beatrice's undivided attention ought to have filled him the moment she airily presumed to take the seat next to his. Instead, he found himself trying to look over his shoulder in a way that would afford him a glimpse of Matilda.

Matilda might've had perfect posture, but the downcast expression she wore tore at his heart. With her head turned to one side, he could only view her profile.

Beatrice noticed his distraction and glanced over her shoulder at her sister, her brows pulling together.

"Oh, Matilda," she said, and Oliver kept himself facing fully forward, relieved Beatrice might finally offer some consolation to whatever had upset her sister. "Are you ill? You must stop sulking. Do liven up a bit, or else we will have to take you home. I have no wish to be seen about town with such a miserable-looking sister."

He nearly pulled the horse up in that moment, so shocked was he by the unfeeling words. Never, in all his time at the Granthorne estate, had he seen the sisters regard each other with anything other than kindness.

"Are you unwell, Miss Rayment?" he asked over his shoulder, trying to gentle Beatrice's admonishments. "We can stop for refreshment, if you wish?"

"I am well. Please, do not trouble yourself. I'm only thinking." He heard the forced lightness of her voice.

Whatever it was she thought on, it must've been of a gloomy and fretful nature.

Beatrice made a humming sound, then filled the rest of their drive with her conversation and a few pointed compliments to his driving, suit of clothes, and the like.

This is ridiculous. I wanted Beatrice's notice, now I have it, and I'm fretting over Matilda. Enough. Oliver took himself in hand and determined to enjoy every minute of their exploration.

Before long, he had managed to join in Beatrice's chatter, asking her questions about how she'd spent the Season thus far and other such pleasantries. The conversation never went deeper than the very sort of thing one could discuss in a quarter-of-an-hour morning call, but it remained amiable.

Upon their arrival in front of the bookseller's, Oliver found a boy willing to look after his horses before helping Beatrice down from her seat. Then he extended the same courtesy to Matilda, offering her a gallant bow and smile.

She looked down at him, her expression placid but unsmiling, and took his hand.

There's no reason she can't enjoy herself. Even if she is off balance with Beatrice's presence.

Before Matilda could withdraw it, Oliver tucked her hand into the crook of his right arm and secured it to him by covering it with his hand. "You promised to be my guide, Miss Rayment. You cannot do that if you walk behind us."

Matilda's eyes widened and flew up to meet his. That had been precisely what she'd intended, to follow them about all day as a chaperone. It wouldn't do.

Miss Beatrice slipped her lace-gloved hand onto his other arm. "We will both guide you, Mr. Bolton," she said in her high, airy way.

Matilda focused her gaze on the street and stepped a little away from him, though her hand remained on his arm.

The ensuing hour spent walking in and out of shops, peering through windows, and nodding to passersby proved to be one of the strangest in Oliver's memory. On his left arm, he had the young lady he'd admired in his youth, knowing he would never be in a position to do more than look on in wonder as she lived a life he dreamed of. And here she batted her eyes at him, paid coy compliments, and flirted most sweetly. It ought to have been rewarding.

Yet on his other arm, quiet and withdrawn, was a woman whom he'd never taken special notice of until the previous week. But that wasn't right either. He possessed memories full of Matilda Rayment's practical advice, kind smiles, and serious eyes looking across a room at him.

While he'd stared after Beatrice, thinking her a fairylike creature, he'd hardly noticed she never once glanced at him. But Matilda had been there from the start, expressing her condolences over his loss.

They had just stepped into a little green area, to partake of a basket of crackers and jellies purchased, when Oliver's thoughts finally burst out upon his tongue.

"Miss Beatrice," he said in so abrupt a manner that the young lady stopped walking. "Do you remember when you had to learn the minuet, and your dancing master insisted your sister and I join you to practice?"

After her lovely blue eyes blinked at him twice, the young

woman shook her head. "I am afraid not, but I suppose I must now thank you for those services. You must've been quite the accomplished dancer, because I haven't had even a moment of trouble with those steps since my come-out." Beatrice's eyes strayed from him to glance about the lawn. "Oh, there is a bench. How perfect." She released his arm and went toward it.

Oliver watched her, thoroughly befuddled. It had been one of his favorite memories, dancing with the sisters, even though it had also been somewhat embarrassing. He could hardly hold it against Beatrice if she did not remember it the same way.

"You trod on her gown," Matilda said, voice gentle and soft. "It wasn't one she liked, so she didn't mind."

He turned his attention to her, aware of her steady presence at his side.

"You remember?" he asked, searching her eyes.

Matilda nodded, and the smallest of smiles turned her lips upward. "Did you ever learn the minuet, Mr. Bolton? Or do you still require your partners to whisper the steps to you?" There was nothing unkind in her words. She spoke with the air of one sharing a jest or secret, then she released his arm and went ahead of him, joining her sister in arranging the impromptu picnic.

It struck him, like a bolt from heaven, that while Beatrice might've been the sister he hoped to impress, it was Matilda who had been the one worth befriending. Matilda, the thoughtful sister, who observed the world around her while her sister flitted about with no more care than a butterfly.

Oliver knew Beatrice to be a charming person, and she had it in her to be kind. Matilda *had* been trying to keep Oliver from spending time in Beatrice's company. But perhaps not for the reasons he had suspected.

Beatrice called his name and waved, bringing him back

into the moment. Matilda sat on the bench beside her sister, staring silently at him, waiting.

Somehow, Oliver had tangled himself into an affair of the heart.

He walked across the grass, fixing a stiff smile on his face. *Unraveling this mess I've made might prove difficult.*

Chapter Fourteen

"I CANNOT UNDERSTAND WHAT went wrong," Mattie's mother said with a note of despair, taking her turn at sitting on Mattie's bed. "Mr. Redhurst seemed enamored of her. Then we arrived at the house party, and the other young woman was there. And your sister acts as though it doesn't affect her in the slightest."

"Perhaps she wasn't as invested in the match as we hoped," Mattie said as the maid put the finishing touches to her hair in preparation for dinner. The Pomona-green evening gown Mattie wore was one of her favorites, due to the way it called forth a similar shade in her eyes. For a fleeting moment she wondered if Oliver would notice—but she wistfully put that thought aside.

The baroness was silent for a moment before speaking again, with some uncertainty. "But you believe having Mr. Bolton at our dinner table tonight will help in some way?"

Mattie had made the suggestion the moment they returned from their outing with Oliver. Watching Beatrice flirt for more than an hour had given her a great deal of time to feel wounded, and to understand something she hadn't considered before. If Beatrice did not get what she wanted, she only went after it until she achieved her object or was denied so thoroughly—usually by their father—that she dared not try for it again.

Papa wasn't able to help them with situations such as this.

Not in his current state. Vexation of any kind usually ended in his confusion.

The maid tucked small matching feathers into Mattie's hair in an artful manner.

"I think it will," Mattie said, not meeting her mother's eyes in the mirror. Instead she pretended to study her gloves. What she didn't say, what she couldn't say, was that if Oliver could love Beatrice, they might find happiness together. If her sister could love Oliver, surely that love would be more important than social status and income.

Oliver might find the encouragement to put his suit firmly before the family. Though the idea gave her some measure of hurt, Mattie could do nothing to stop it. At least, that's what she told herself, refusing to examine her feelings any further. What right did she have to feel anything beyond friendship for Oliver Bolton?

The maid curtsied and departed, leaving Mattie and her mother alone.

Her mother sighed and then spoke as though she had seen into Mattie's thoughts. "Perhaps we were wrong to encourage a match with Mr. Redhurst. Though Mr. Bolton is not of the position in society Beatrice may have wanted, he is familiar with the family and with her. If she loved him, they might do well together."

The words sent a chill into Mattie's heart, which jerked painfully in response. Somehow she kept her voice steady as she responded. "I confess, I had similar thoughts."

Mother stood and came to stand near her eldest daughter, resting her hand on Mattie's shoulder, almost as though she needed the support. Finally, Mattie looked up, meeting her mother's deep-brown eyes. The tears brimming there startled Mattie.

"Matilda," her mother said, her voice trembling. "I only

want to be sure Beatrice is happy. And that *you* are happy. Your place in society doesn't matter so much as whether or not you find joy in your life. I hope you know—that you can understand—that is all your father and I have ever wanted for both of you."

Her own eyes growing full with unwanted tears, Mattie covered her mother's hand with hers and forced a lighter expression on her face. "You know I am content, Mother. I always have been." Did her mother hear the way her voice broke? Did she suspect there was more to it than the emotion of the moment?

Bending down, the baroness pressed a kiss to Mattie's forehead, then rose and stood with the perfect posture many a young lady struggled to obtain. "Come. It is nearly time to go in to dinner, and I am certain our guest will have arrived."

Mattie rose from her chair, reaching up to run a finger along a feather in her hair, then followed her mother from the room.

Beatrice's laughter floated up from the first floor, where the dining room and parlor were located. Mattie and her mother exchanged a look, both realizing what it meant.

"Whatever will we do with our girl?" her mother asked, weariness in her tone. She descended the steps with her arm linked through Mattie's.

They entered the parlor, and Mattie's eyes found Oliver quite on accident. He stood at the window, eyes on the street below, his shoulder against the casement. Candlelight made his dark hair glow, and his folded arms made his dinner jacket pull rather attractively across his shoulders. She realized the colors they'd worn were rather complimentary and blushed as though she'd somehow contrived to make it so.

In that moment, he turned in her direction, as though sensing her study. Their eyes met and he immediately pushed away from the wall, standing straight, and one of his hands raised to tug at his cravat. Mattie couldn't help but smile at that familiar habit. Oliver's hand froze and he tucked it behind his back and he shrugged, as though to say, *I cannot help it.*

"Lady Granthorne, Miss Rayment. Good evening." He made his bow.

"Mother," Beatrice said, her voice ringing merrily through the room. "You ought to hear what Mr. Bolton and Matilda have been up to. I am sorry I missed all the entertainment." Beatrice giggled again, covering the dainty sound with a slender hand.

Mattie turned her attention to Oliver, her heart aching. "Oh, we didn't do a great deal. Nothing of true importance."

Oliver didn't say anything. Rather, his eyes were still trained on her, even when Beatrice began speaking of their engagements.

"They went to the theater, a ride in the park, he's come to dinner, and even church. I think, had I known you would be here so often, I would've stayed in town rather than run off to the country."

His eyes didn't waver, though Mattie forced herself to turn away. The notion that he watched her almost lifted her spirits, but then, he'd been worried earlier in the day about her change in mood.

He is only concerned I am unwell, because he is kind. Thankfully, she could put a smile upon her face that felt almost natural.

The door opened, and her father entered. She glimpsed his valet in the hall and nodded her thanks to the man. Likely her father had lost track of time.

"Oh, good evening." The baron bowed to their guest. Then he turned to his wife and went to her, reaching out. Mattie's mother took his hand, and Mattie saw the love shining in her mother's eyes, touched with a gentle sorrow most would not even see. The baron bowed over his wife's hand and laid a kiss upon her knuckles.

"As always, my dear, you are most lovely." The genuine affection in her father's voice and manner warmed Mattie's heart.

Oliver came away from his window to stand near her. He leaned her way and spoke quietly. "They are now as I always remember them."

The simple statement, given without any sort of contrived tone or gesture, endeared him further to her.

"I am told dinner is ready," the baron said to the room at large, and Mattie forced her eyes away from Oliver's. "Shall we go in?" He offered his arm to his wife, and a momentary panic took hold of Mattie. She saw her mother hesitate but take her husband's arm.

Mattie must go in after her parents, and Oliver would be forced to escort her instead of Beatrice. She felt she ought to apologize or make it clear she did not mind—

"Miss Rayment?" Oliver held his hand out to her, and he hadn't hesitated even a second to do so. It was as though he never intended to take Beatrice to the table.

"Oh, yes. Thank you," Mattie stammered, hastily giving him her hand and trying not to make anything of the gesture. Oliver was kind. He didn't want to cause anyone discomfort. That was all it could mean.

Chapter Fifteen

BEATRICE PROVED TO BE the most talkative person at the table during dinner. Oliver noticed she spoke with animation and spirit, directing most of her conversation to him. No one could call her anything other than gracious. But he missed Matilda's conversation. Her dry and humorous observations, her delightful smile, had filled much of the last several days. The memories stirred by their time together had begun to emerge as long-forgotten treasures from a chest.

When he'd come to the neighborhood, it had been Matilda who took him about to meet the tenants, and she who had remembered to speak kind words to him on the anniversary of his parents' deaths.

The ladies departed for the parlor without Matilda saying more than a handful of words at dinner, though he'd attempted to draw her out.

"My lord," Oliver said once they were gone, his heart finally taking hold of him. "Might I have a word, before rejoining the ladies?"

Lord Grandthorne, on the verge of standing to do just that, lowered himself back into his chair. "You have something to say, young man?" he asked, fixing Oliver with a mock-stern expression. "Here, at the table? It isn't a traditional location for a gentleman to declare himself."

Oliver had to smile, noting the same dry wit in the baron as in the daughter. "I assure you, that is not my intention tonight, my lord."

"But it may be in future?" the baron asked, proving that his mind retained some of its sharpness even if he grew forgetful.

An anxious sort of excitement shot through Oliver's stomach at the thought. "Perhaps, my lord. But there are things I must see to first, and other conversations I must have. I wonder, my lord, if you would excuse me for this evening?"

The baron's eyebrows raised at the unexpected request. "You are leaving? Now?"

Oliver couldn't help but grin. "With your permission. I have come to understand your daughters are particular in the company they seek. I should like to prove I am capable of joining that society."

"I doubt such things are as important as you seem to think to Mattie," the baron said, surprising Oliver with the sudden brightening of his expression. "They say I forget many things, but I began to think I'd lost more than memory when my wife declared you were a suitor for my younger daughter."

"Please, my lord. Say nothing yet." Oliver could not be sure how things would work out, if Matilda even *liked* him in a manner more than what she'd shown. From the beginning of their interaction in London, he'd known she disapproved of him for Beatrice. Would she think him beneath herself as well? After all, she'd declared she had no interest in marrying.

"You have my promise." The baron reached out to clasp Oliver on the shoulder. "But do not be long about your business, Oliver. She's waited long enough."

"Thank you, my lord. I will go as quickly as I can without misstep." Oliver bowed. "Good evening." And he hurried out of the room and to the ground floor, where a footman helped him find his coat and hat.

There were things he must do, and swiftly, if he wished to present his suit to the lady of his heart's choice.

Chapter Sixteen

WEDNESDAY EVENING ARRIVED WITHOUT Oliver making an appearance. Matilda lingered over her toilette, her thoughts distracted, long after the maid had finished arranging her hair. She held a feather in her hand, left on the little table from two nights before. She twirled it between her fingers, watching it twist in her grasp.

Oliver had sent a note Tuesday morning, begging her mother's forgiveness, along with a basket of delicious fruits to atone for the sin of leaving a dinner party too early.

Mattie shook her head, remembering how easily Beatrice had taken the loss of a suitor with barely a shrug of regret. She didn't seem to think on the loss of Mr. Redhurst with any ill humor, either.

Mattie finally stood and went to her window, looking down into the street. Horses and carriages moved along the cobbled road, filled with men and women in fine evening dress with little to vex them.

She ought to take a page from her sister's book. It was best to continue holding her head aloft, smiling serenely, and letting no one guess at her own sentiments. Despite her desire to remain at home, she hadn't even suggested the ladies of the house forgo their evening at Almack's. Really, it would've been odd had she suggested such a thing after all the work she went to in order to procure their vouchers. She'd sent gifts and notes to each of the six patronesses, along with gentle promises of good behavior for herself and her sister, in order to make certain they were permitted to ascend to the ballroom.

Tonight she wore her favorite gown. Not because she cared what people saw, but because she needed the bravery the emerald creation lent her. In this gown she could stand in the presence of the royal family and be equal to the moment. *And yet I feel so lost.*

"A feather for you, miss?" her maid asked, spotting the thing in Mattie's hand.

Mattie shook her head and laid the feather down on her table again. Taking up her fan, Mattie left the room and went down to join her sister and mother. Almack's waited for no one.

In the entryway, her family stood, Father complimenting her mother and admonishing her not to dance with any dashing young men. Beatrice stood aside, eyes turned away from the scene. How was it that a sight which brought Mattie comfort served to do the very opposite to Beatrice?

After the goodbyes were said, the ladies entered their carriage and were away for an evening of dancing.

They arrived at the address on King's Street behind a lengthy queue of carriages, their bobbing lamps moving like fairies in the night. Despite her desire to be practical, Mattie still felt the magic of evenings when the splendor of the *ton* glittered all about them.

Ladies in pale gowns and glittering jewels filled the walkway, and gentlemen in black coats and tall hats guided them down the paths.

Mattie, her mother, and her sister joined the throngs. They presented their vouchers and were permitted entry into the upper rooms, where the bright light of candles reflecting off dozens of large mirrors made the room the brightest in London.

Beatrice opened her fan to hold it near her mouth, covering her words from all but Mattie. "I do hope someone asks me to dance. I cannot abide being without a partner for long. I do love dancing."

"As do I," Mattie murmured. Without the kind Mr. Redhurst giving attention to her sister, Mattie likely wouldn't be dancing. She'd become too much of a fixture for anyone to take notice of her anymore, whether or not she wore her favorite gown.

"Miss Beatrice," a voice said from behind, startling both sisters. They turned, a young gentleman of their acquaintance standing there. He bowed, despite the crush of people around them. "Might I claim your first dance?" He stepped closer and held his hand out to her, his eyes barely flicking to Mattie.

"Mr. Whitby," Beatrice said, batting her eyelashes. "Yes, of course." Beatrice's perfectly pink lips quirked upward, and she put her hand in his.

Letting out a puff of exasperation, Mattie watched them leave for the dance floor. She opened her fan, more for something to do than any need to cool herself, and paused when she realized she'd picked up the wrong accessory. This was not her white lattice fan, but the one made with feathers. She hadn't noticed in her haste to leave her room that evening. It didn't even match her gown.

Mattie turned to find her mother and was startled to see they had been separated by the crowd. Moving carefully through the throngs, attempting to be graceful when in reality she was dodging between elbows and skirts, Mattie had nearly arrived at her mother's side when a hand caught her elbow, stopping her.

Preparing a sharp retort at being handled, Mattie faced the person who had dared to grasp her—

Oliver. *Here?*

He grinned. "Miss Rayment."

She realized her mouth hung open and snapped it shut, then cast her eyes about to see if anyone else was watching.

"You said you didn't have vouchers," she said, her voice squeaking at the very last word. Why had he come? Was he here to see Beatrice? Had he sneaked inside?

"When I said that, it was true." The good humor in his voice and the warmth of his hand still upon her arm nearly gave her leave to relax. But his nearness, the dimple in his cheek, and the way he gave her his full attention in the crowded ballroom made her rather unsteady.

Mattie stepped closer to him, telling herself it was only to make easier conversation. While his proximity unnerved her, she sought to be closer. For at least a moment.

"You haven't come to visit or sent word," she said, voice lowered. Then she bit her lip. She sounded like her sister berating a suitor.

His eyes sparkled down at her. "I thought you were trying to be rid of me?"

Her cheeks warmed, and she looked down at his waistcoat. Of course he knew that. "I did a very poor job of achieving it, seeing you as often as I did." Mattie glanced toward the whirling couples in the center of the room. "Beatrice is dancing now, and the next set, but if you ask her after—" Oliver stepped closer.

"I haven't come to dance with Beatrice." He said the words gently, giving each one a weight of significance Mattie could not ignore. She raised her eyes, keeping her head lowered.

"If you have come for the refreshment, I must warn you, it is vastly disappointing."

His eyes widened, and a laugh escaped him, earning them a few glances. "Then it is a good thing I haven't any intention of seeking out the food."

The hand at her arm moved down to her wrist, then his fingers entwined with hers. "Will you dance with me, Miss Rayment?" He lowered his voice, his eyes alight with an emotion she could not put a name to. "Matilda?"

"I—yes. Yes." She stumbled over the simple acceptance, her body swaying toward him. Mattie didn't understand what was going on, or how Oliver had gained admittance to Almack's, or why he no longer sought out Beatrice. But her heart was aglow with hope that somehow it had to do with *her*.

Oliver led her onto the floor. The dance wasn't complicated; it was a reel, necessitating that they change partners several times. But he never took his eyes off her, and Mattie could not remove hers from him either. The skipping ladies, the clapping gentlemen, all became muted. The world around them was nothing more than a landscape, and Oliver and Mattie were the subjects of a masterpiece she did not quite understand.

She took a moment in the dance to ask, her curiosity overcoming her, "When did you get vouchers to Almack's? And how?"

"I spent two days going from one patroness to another," he answered when he took her hands, as the dance called for it. "Begging them to let me in so I could prove my worth to a certain lady."

Her heartbeat almost doubled the rhythm of the dance. His worth had nothing to do with his fortune, or his ability to enter the upper rooms of society. It had everything to do with his kindness, his smile, and the care he showed everything he touched.

At the end of the dance, Oliver took her from the floor and out of the room. The scandal of being seen leaving with a gentleman hardly made an impression on her. Mattie found she cared only for what Oliver wished to say. In a moment they stood behind a corner of the hall, people still near and servants walking to and fro.

"Oliver," she said the moment they paused, delighting in speaking his Christian name once more. "Almack's doesn't mean a thing to me. I needed admittance for Beatrice. All the trouble you went through to be here—thank you."

Oliver's deep-green eyes studied her, as though committing every detail of her expression to memory. "I know you do not think me a suitable match for your sister," he said, his tone most serious. "But I must ask if it might be possible, someday when I have made more of my estate and myself, if I might be a suitable match for *you*."

Mattie's breath caught. "Me?" she asked, the word coming out as a whisper.

His brows drew together, and his expression turned more earnest. "*You*, Matilda. In the time I spent in your company, I've realized how much I've always enjoyed being near you. You are intelligent, practical, and graceful. And you are honest, kind, and direct." Then his lips twitched upward. "And I rather adore your sense of humor."

Oliver wanted *her*. But of all the things he'd said, he hadn't mentioned the one most important to her in that moment.

"But is that all, Oliver? Is there any other reason—?"

"I suppose there is one," he admitted, and as he leaned closer her heart raced. "I think I'm falling in love with you."

Mattie grasped his hands tightly in her own, wanting nothing more than to throw her arms around him, to dance or sing in her delight. "Oh, Oliver."

Oliver grinned and leaned down, as if he would kiss her in that very moment.

Someone cleared her throat from very near, causing Mattie to jump and look over her shoulder. Beatrice stood only a few feet away, one hand on her hip and eyebrows raised.

"Perhaps you ought to escort my sister home, Mr. Bolton, to look in on our father." Beatrice's lips slowly turned upward. "Before she's accused of being a flirt." She waved them down the hall. "I will make your excuses for you."

Despite the heat in her cheeks, Mattie smiled her thanks at her sister, and Oliver drew her with him to the steps.

"I hope your father is well," he said loudly as they asked for his carriage to be brought around. "It is my pleasure to escort you home."

Mattie refrained from giggling at his dramatics, as there were few enough people about to even notice what they were up to. The moment they were inside Oliver's hired carriage, him sitting across from her and reaching for her hand, she finally laughed.

"It will still cause rumors, you know," she said, though she didn't much care in the moment. "People will talk."

"And so they always will. But, darling, you still haven't answered me. Would you consider a courtship, Mattie? A real one."

The cherished nickname bestowed on her by her father sounded so natural coming from his lips. She found she never wanted him to call her anything else, ever again.

"I have considered it," she said softly, grateful for the little light from the carriage lamps. "And I will say *yes*, Oliver."

His hands tightened around hers, and he bent to kiss her gloved fingers.

Her practical side began to assert itself, warring with her rather giddy emotions. "But—what about my parents, Oliver? My father . . ." She swallowed, hoping her parents would not disapprove of her courtship. "You will ask my father for his blessing?"

Oliver moved to sit beside her and gently put his arm around her shoulders. "My darling, I already have. The moment your carriage left for Almack's I spoke to him."

Mattie laughed. "He likes you a great deal."

"Thank goodness for that."

Mattie leaned against his shoulder and felt his kiss upon her brow. Warmth spread from her heart throughout her body. She tilted her head back to look at him through the shadows. He was so near, and he bent still closer. Mattie tilted her chin back and met his lips with hers, the soft caress of his kiss making all coherent thought leave her for several long moments. When they parted, her lips tingled, and she laid her head upon his shoulder.

A courtship with Oliver would certainly be an adventure.

Sally Britton is sixth generation Texan, received her BA in English from Brigham Young University, and reads voraciously. She started her writing journey at the tender age of fourteen on an electric typewriter, and she's never looked back.

Sally lives in Arizona with her husband, four children, and their dog. She loves researching, hiking, and eating too much chocolate.

Visit Sally online: AuthorSallyBritton.com

My Unfair Lady

Elizabeth Johns

Chapter One

"WHAT SHALL WE PLAY for this time?" Sutherland asked as he arranged the billiard balls.

"Bragging rights?" Deverell suggested, knowing it would fly past the ears of his friends.

"No one will play seriously for such paltry terms," Sutherland's brother, Lord Edward, scoffed, leaning against the edge of the oak table. Their normal wagers did tend to be outrageous, Deverell mused, such as the time he had dared Sutherland to dress the statue of King Henry in a lady's corset, or when Lord Edward had dyed the Serpentine red, or . . .

"The Season is about to begin." Sutherland interrupted his reflections with a gleam in his hazel eyes, which Deverell knew meant trouble.

"What has that to do with anything?" Tindal asked. "None of us have darkened the door of any *ton* events since we were too green to know better."

"Nor are we welcomed at most of them," Lord Edward said dryly. With a flourish, he tossed back the amber liquid in his glass.

No doubt they were all recalling the time he had put a live bird in Mrs. Drummond-Burrell's coiffure, Deverell conjectured, observing his friends' wry grins.

"What do you have in mind?" he asked lazily from his position in a leather chair. As usual, he was feeling bored. Perhaps he was growing too old for these games.

"What is the worst punishment you can think of?" Sutherland asked with a grin.

"Almack's!" All three of them groaned simultaneously.

"Since Edward's and my sister is making her comeout, I think the loser should have to join me at some of these tedious events," Sutherland suggested.

Deverell and the other men groaned.

"I have just remembered, my mater needed me home for dinner," Tindal said, making for the door. "Some bosom beau of hers is bringing his fubsy-faced daughter."

"Get back here, Tindal. You ain't a coward!" Sutherland snapped.

Tindal hung his head like a whipped puppy and sat back down.

"Exactly. The loser has to attend Almack's and dance with five wallflowers."

"That's not fair! Deverell always wins. That means the odds are not even fifty-fifty, since you and Edward have to go anyway," Tindal protested.

"I do not have to dance with wallflowers merely by being present."

"True," Tindal conceded. "Very well. Let's hope Deverell has an off night."

Sutherland scoffed. "One more thing."

The three of them leered at him for such an ungentlemanly act as adding conditions.

"One of the dances has to be with my sister."

Tindal shrugged as if it was no matter, but Deverell looked up. "That should be no chore. Caro is hardly an antidote."

"Is it truly as hard as all that to procure a voucher?" Lord Edward asked. "There is someone I had thought to bring to London for a Season."

"Birth and fortune play little part in who the patronesses select, I hear," Sutherland said.

"Pure whimsy," Dev agreed. "Whoever is *à la mode* gets the nod."

"If I were Deverell, they would be throwing them at my feet," Lord Edward teased without heat.

"I did not know you had a ward." Sutherland frowned. "I think I should know such things about my own brother."

"She is not a ward, per se. She is the sister of one of my lieutenants from my unit and left orphaned. I promised him I would look after her when he was dying. I thought to bring her to London for a Season before she must find a position."

"What do you know of her family?"

Lord Edward shrugged. "Her brother was a decent chap from rural Yorkshire. His father was a vicar though the girl has some little dowry left by an aunt."

Dev could not think a small dowry enough to account for a poorly bred country miss, but he held his tongue.

"Perhaps Mother would sponsor her, since she has to take Caro," Sutherland offered.

"That is unnaturally kind of you to offer your mother's assistance," Deverell said coolly.

"Perhaps we should allow you to take her on as your project," Sutherland taunted in return.

"We know nothing of her."

"Precisely. However, your charms are legendary as a beau. Do you doubt your ability to make a gently bred vicar's daughter a success? It is not as though she were a Cockney-speaking ragamuffin from Seven Dials," Sutherland argued.

Close enough, he thought to himself.

"People would accept her anyway, if he told them to," Tindal agreed.

Dev cast his gaze heavenward. It would perhaps alleviate

the boredom that had fallen over him since returning from the war. Managing estates was tedious at best. However, this was a person's life they were considering, and he could not agree without the lady's consent. "How would the girl feel about such an arrangement?" he asked, still lounging in the armchair. Not for a monkey would he show his hesitancy to his fellows.

"I do not know many girls who would forgo the chance of a London Season," Sutherland countered.

They all looked at Dev, who waited for them to see reason.

"You could be saving her the ill fortune of becoming a governess or companion," Lord Edward said.

"Well?" Sutherland asked. "Will you accept? Save this lady from her fate?"

"Just how do you think I, a confirmed bachelor, could take an orphaned vicar's daughter into my home and bring her out?" He shook his head. "That is as good as tying a noose around my neck."

"He has a point," Tindal said.

"She could stay with my mother and sister, but you will guide her . . . make her the belle of the *ton*. All you need do is give her the proper attention and then you won't be necessary any more."

"Define proper attention."

Sutherland narrowed his gaze in thought as he twirled his cue. "I have it!" He slammed his palm down on the billiards table. "Vouchers and a dance at Almack's, since that is the rest of the wager. It should be simple enough for you to make her sufficiently presentable."

"Very well." Dev shrugged. "But only if I lose."

"If you lose, you owe me a monkey, and we all go to watch."

All four agreed. Dev could see the others did so begrudgingly by their expressions. He never lost at billiards once he touched the cue.

"Deverell goes last," Tindal said, interrupting his thoughts.

He shrugged. It made no difference to him. He watched as Lord Edward took the first shot and sent a red ball flying into the corner pocket. His mind strayed from the game, deliberating the small matter of squiring a young girl about London. All he had to do was obtain vouchers to Almack's. How hard could that be?

It was idle curiosity, for he had no intention of setting up his nursery in the next decade. He would, however, bestir himself to help this poor girl. *Assumptions, Dev?* What if she was a prudish church miss who wanted nothing to do with a London beau?

He frowned, uncertain whether his reputation would help or hinder her. He knew he was much sought after, but not necessarily for reasons a virtuous miss would think desirable.

"Are you going to take your turn this century, Dev?" Lord Edward asked. Dev started a little, not realizing he had drifted so far away from his surroundings.

Taking his cue, he slowly lined it up with his cue ball. He hit it and deftly pocketed the red ball across the table, followed by it ricocheting off the side cushion and also pocketing both remaining cue balls, neatly winning the game. He sat back down with no little satisfaction as his friends still stared at the table.

"Impossible!" Lord Edward groaned.

"Best two out of three?" Tindal asked weakly.

"I have nowhere else to be," he drawled. "But only for different stakes. I quite fancy seeing you prancing through a quadrille."

Tindal cued off first for the next game. Sutherland refilled everyone's glasses and watched as Tindal had a rare run of luck. When he pocketed the winning shot, he looked up in disbelief and smiled the most childish grin of delight. Lord Edward chuckled.

"That had nothing to do with me," Deverell pointed out.

"I know. Isn't it grand?"

"It all comes down to this last game," Sutherland said as he positioned the balls again. "Who will be the lucky devil who goes to Almack's with me?"

Tindal flexed his fingers, cracking his knuckles, and danced around as though he were about to go a few rounds in the ring with Gentlemen Jackson.

Deverell shook his head and smiled. "You may go first again, Tindal. I will not have it said I took advantage."

Tindal looked at him suspiciously. Even Sutherland raised an eyebrow.

"Luck never holds. If your skill is that good, then I will gladly accept defeat."

"Very well," Tindal said with a burst of confidence, holding his head higher.

Deverell had never seen him play so well before and did not think his friend could freeze him out two games in a row. He was wrong. Tindal cleared the table.

"You have improved greatly since we last played," Deverell murmured.

Sutherland slapped him on the back. "Better polish your dancing slippers, my friend."

"Not quite; I have not lost to you. Tindal and Lord Edward are off the hook, but this is not over yet."

"Fair enough," Sutherland agreed good-naturedly. "Shall we play billiards again or something else?"

"I want to know what the forfeit is if Sutherland loses," Lord Edward put in.

"Perhaps he should have to dance with five ladies of my choice," Dev said lazily, looking at his fingernails. "I will even let you choose which sport."

"I am not sure it matters. You usually beat me at everything."

"You could have luck tonight, like Tindal did."

"Devil take it, I am going to have to go now, just to watch!" Tindal declared, looking very put out. "I don't even own knee breeches or dancing pumps."

"When one suffers, we all suffer, my friend."

"But will I be allowed through the door?"

"I will tell Aunt Emily to put us all on the list. How can she refuse four eligible lords?" Sutherland drawled, his eyes crinkling at the corners with what Dev considered to be unnecessary enjoyment.

Rua Postlethwaite had cursed the fates when her brother was killed at Waterloo. She had cursed her luck when her parents died from the influenza last winter. She was not quite certain what to curse when she read the letter from a complete stranger.

"One would hardly know you for a vicar's daughter, Rua," her friend Jane remarked as she heard the muttered oaths, which were decidedly not fit for a fine lady.

"I beg your pardon, Jane. It is this letter."

"Are you going to enlighten me?" Jane placed another stitch in the stocking she was darning. "Have they found someone to replace your father?"

"No, I am not being evicted yet." Rua began to pace about the parlour, a frown creasing her face. Feeling its ache, she recalled her mother's strictures on ruining her looks and was forced to swallow fitfully.

"Well?" Jane put her darning down and looked irritated.

"I have been invited to London!" She threw up her hands in exasperation and had to ignore another maternal criticism.

"Oh, how lovely! I always dreamed of a London Season!" Jane exclaimed. "I did not realize you had any connections in Town."

"Nor did I. It seems a Captain Lord Edward Parker was with Ewan in the Greys. He says it would be his honour to invite me to stay in London for the Season and be brought out with his sister, Lady Caroline. He says it is just what Ewan would have wished."

"How splendid for you," her friend said, a wistful look in her eye.

"Splendid? This is a disaster!" Rua exclaimed. "I cannot indebt myself to some . . . some"—she flipped over the letter to examine the franking—"son of a marquess who feels obliged to honour some deathbed promise made to Ewan. I will be a laughing-stock! You have heard the way Lady Trewlaney and Mrs. Merriweather speak of the 'upstarts' and 'country bumpkins' when they return from Town. Who am I to them? I shall be no better than a poor relation or an object of charity. The fact is, I have no money and possess no Town bronze, and I rather prefer it that way."

Her friend stared at her. Jane was unaccustomed to seeing Rua in such a case, yet she was still clearly unconvinced. "But Rua, this could secure your future! You could meet a fine gentleman and not be obliged to marry ol' man Everett."

"I will find a position first." Rua scowled, heedless of the consequences. Possessed of a modest dowry of a mere thousand pounds and living off the per cents, she had no more than twenty-five pounds per annum to live on. Since such a sum was barely enough for necessities, she would certainly have to marry or find a position. Two of her brothers yet lived, but neither could afford to take her in, even though the one who was not a soldier had offered. Somehow, joining his small vicarage household, with four children and a domineering wife, did not appeal to her one little bit.

"Your time is running out. The new vicar will be arriving soon to take his place and house. Perhaps this is a gift from God."

"Like my red hair and unruly tongue," Rua muttered. She could not but be reminded of those defects every day since she was named for her fiery hair.

"Your manners are as fine as a duchess when you so choose."

Rua scoffed, unconvinced.

"It was what your mother always hoped for you," Jane added softly, twisting the knife in so very deep. She stood up and gathered together her belongings. "I must return for dinner with Richard. Do sleep on this before making a hasty decision."

"Ha! It seems they could not countenance my refusal. A carriage will arrive one week hence to take me there."

"See. It is meant to be." Jane kissed her cheek and winked mischievously before hurrying down the tulip and daffodil-lined path to the white fence which enclosed the vicarage garden.

Rua spent several hours vacillating between sending a polite letter of regret and wondering what London would be like. While she was no traditional miss, she did have a great sense of adventure (having grown up with three brothers) and could not help wondering what it would be like to dress in finery and dance the night away. Not that she had any finery beyond her mama's pearl earrings, or had ever danced anywhere more exciting than the York Assembly Rooms.

First, she fretted over what she would wear if she went to

Town. "It does no good to have a Season if one looks shabby at best," she murmured to herself, fingering her worn kerseymere which had seen four winters. The sad truth was she had none any better that had not been dyed black. She had two gowns fine enough for local assemblies, a green silk and a lavender muslin. "They are still not fine enough for London," she muttered again, recalling images in the *Lady's Magazine* Jane shared with her when she had a copy. Her mother's possessions had been long packed in trunks, but Rua went to the attic and began to rummage through anything that might be of use. If Rua's dresses were out of fashion, then her mother's hoops and powdered wigs would have her laughed back to Yorkshire. There was a fine sable muff and a cream-coloured scarf of Norwich silk which had been a wedding gift from her father. Rua had packed it away, feeling sentimental, but now saw the necessity and usefulness of the item.

Making her way back down the stairs with these few finds, she did not see any way not to look as provincial as she was. Sitting at her father's old desk, in his study, she pulled out a sheet of paper on which to write her regrets. After she had penned a very pretty note declining the great condescension they had shown her, she sanded and sealed the letter to be posted the next day. Overcome by despair, she went to bed knowing she had made the right decision, yet in deep melancholy nonetheless.

Unfortunately, it did not take long for word to spread of what the small village considered a windfall for the poor, orphaned vicar's daughter. There was no more generous girl than Rua Postlethwaite, but she was so often in a scrape, the matrons nodded tolerantly. It was the fiery red hair, in addition to being a man of the cloth's daughter, which caused the trouble, Rua's detractors avowed, acknowledging with pursed lips that these factors were often cited to excuse her occasional lapses. A sojourn in London could be the very thing to curb her ill-conceived starts. Therefore, while Rua was deciding she was not fit for London, the village of Bagsby was deciding how to make it happen.

The next morning, before Rua had finished her coffee, Jane was at her door to deliver some news.

"Mrs. Merriweather has condescended to hold a tea party in your honour, so we can see what needs to be done!" Jane was so excited she looked as though she would burst.

Rua eyed her over her cup, trying to think of a tactful way to let her friend down. In fact, Rua needed several more cups before tact came naturally to her.

"I am not going to London," she blurted out.

"Nonsense!" Jane was not to be deterred.

"I know you think I have made my decision in haste, but I assure you, it is not possible. I have already written my regrets."

"No!" Jane hurried from the room to find the letter before it was posted. She returned after a few minutes, holding the missive high. "At least come to the tea party and see what may be done."

Rua considered her friend with distaste. "My reduced circumstances are common knowledge; however, speaking of them before the ladies of the village is not my preferred pastime."

"Everyone only wants to help." Jane looked shattered, and Rua felt enormous guilt.

"Oh, very well." She conceded defeat. "I shall come, but it won't make a hap'orth of difference. I have nothing but pearl earrings, a muff, and a shawl to recommend me."

With a giddy smile, Jane clapped her hands. "Two o'clock this afternoon!" She left on the words and took the letter with her.

Thus it was with great reluctance that Rua arrived at Mrs. Merriweather's Georgian manor house that afternoon, precisely at two. The drawing room was full; every lady with any claim to gentility was present, and Rua felt her cheeks blush with embarrassment.

Jane ran over to greet her and whispered into her ear. "They mean well, dearest. Allow them to do this for you."

Rua tried to remember that as she sat demurely on the edge of a chair while being discussed as though not there. It would perhaps have been preferable not to be.

Mrs. Merriweather presented her with some of the former's outmoded gowns to be refashioned. Lady Trewlaney also felt the need to instruct Rua on *ton* etiquette, as though she had never been taught to be a lady.

"You must not prattle on about the country or all your relations. No one cares and will think you very gauche. Come to think of it, you should not prattle at all. You must develop a sense of *ennui*, my dear. Do not act shocked as though you are a green girl first come to the big city."

Rua *was* a green country girl on her first visit to the city. She was beginning to wonder if she would like London at all if she had to behave as though she had swallowed a tack or was suffering from indigestion.

"Never dance more than twice with the same gentleman," Mrs. Merriweather said, though it was much the same in Yorkshire.

"No galloping in Hyde Park or riding astride . . ." The lady looked pointedly at Rua, who might have had a habit of doing such a thing when riding with her brothers. To be fair, she had not done it since being out of the schoolroom.

"You must be chaperoned everywhere you go in Town. It is not at all like here where you can gad about on your own." She sent a quelling glance as though she did not approve of more than just Rua walking around alone. "St. James's, for instance; you must not go there even with someone."

"Whyever not?" Jane asked.

"It is where all of the gentlemen's clubs are, of course! She would be labelled as fast—or worse. Only a certain type of female ventures there!"

"Which reminds me, for goodness' sake, do not mention a gentleman's *chères amies,*" she whispered loudly to Rua, though the latter was quite certain everyone in the room was all ears.

Although she knew very well it was the polite term for mistress, Rua maintained an innocent expression despite her distaste for such evils—driven by her conviction they destroyed families. She had three older brothers, after all, and had overheard lurid tales . . . Nonetheless, there were some scandalous behaviours occurring in Town, which Rua was glad to know about beforehand.

"Most of the gentlemen have them, of course, but you must never mention it. There are also those of a certain sophistication who engage in flirtations—and you must take care to avoid such a thing, especially with those above your touch."

"That will be almost everyone," Rua muttered.

Lady Trewlaney nodded. "The most exclusive part of the Season is Almack's, but you must gain the favour of the leaders of the *ton* to gain admittance. I would not set my hopes as high as that, my dear, for the patronesses are known to be contrary. Why, sometimes they give vouchers to a husband and not a wife if they think he married beneath him!"

This fact garnered gasps from many of the older ladies who had not enjoyed the advantage of a London Season.

"I, personally, believe it all comes down to fashion and fancy," she added. "If you should be given a voucher, do not waltz without the permission of the patronesses. 'Twould be fatal!"

This drew more gasps from the ladies of the village where the waltz was still thought scandalous.

"Then we must do our best to see our Rua gives no one cause to look down their noses at Yorkshire," Jane pronounced.

Rua was less and less comfortable with the notion of her representing anything, fearing she would be sent straight back before she stepped across the threshold of the Sutherland residence. Nevertheless, the ladies had a purpose, and it would be badly done of her to refuse their kindness.

Mrs. Winters contributed two very fine lengths of silk she had found in a trunk from her days in India. The widows of the parish had banded together to purchase her a new pair of gloves. Jane gifted Rua the high-crowned bonnet she had been coveting for some time, while even ol' man Everett decided to be generous and gave her a fifty-pound note! Rua was quite overcome with emotion but could hardly refuse the opportunity with the entire village supporting her.

Thus, when the carriage arrived, seven days after the shocking letter from Lord Edward, Rua felt as though she would not embarrass herself completely.

She had never been to a city larger than York, and she was intimidated by the prospect of going to such a grand place, though her pride would never allow her to admit such a thing.

When the striking carriage with a crest, pulled by four matched bays, arrived in front of the small cottage-like vicarage, Rua tried to remember Lady Trewlaney's reminders about how to comport herself as a London lady. Therefore, she waited until the footman—in smart green livery—had closed the door and the carriage had lurched forward before emitting a scream of excitement into her muff.

It was a full hour into the journey before she had stopped exploring every inch of the luxurious conveyance and all its wonders. Who knew there would be compartments with travelling games, a writing desk, and oil lamps? Never had her father's small income, while respectable, allowed for more than a plain carriage of the useful sort.

It was therefore some time before she could settle enough even to attempt to read the new book Jane had gifted her for the journey. She was going to London!

Chapter Two

SEVERAL WEEKS HAD PASSED since Deverell had accepted the wager to bring Lord Edward's project into fashion, and it had quite slipped his mind. Therefore, when he was sparring at Gentleman Jackson's Saloon, he barely dodged what would have been a painful right hook when Sutherland mentioned the girl had arrived in Town. Rarely one to lose his composure, he quickly recovered, but his mind would not allow him further enjoyment of his sport that day. He quickly disengaged and began to ponder his next course of action. Frequently bored, with few people to match his wit, he started viewing this as a potential source of amusement for the next few months. As he and Sutherland dressed, he became annoyed that his friend had said nothing more.

"Well, am I to know naught of the girl?"

"Oh, yes, we have not made plans, have we?"

"I believe the wager only stated I was to bring her into fashion," Dev reminded him. "How did Lady Sutherland receive the news of her new protégé?"

Sutherland shrugged. "Mama takes everything with aplomb. I only caught a glimpse of the girl, mind you, but my mother said she had absolutely nothing to recommend her."

Dev's brows lifted slightly, but Sutherland continued. "Personally, I felt as though she had rather too much to recommend her, if you know what I mean."

"Please spell it out for me."

Sutherland favoured him with a roguish smirk. "She looks as if she belongs in Covent Garden."

"The devil!" he said, surprised into a brief lapse of control.

"Quite," Sutherland agreed.

Dev still was not certain it would not be amusing to thrust such a one amongst the High Sticklers, but he needed to see what kind of challenge he faced.

"When is your mother holding her next at-home?"

Sutherland cast a sideways grin in his direction. "Are you certain you wish to throw yourself to the wolves?"

"Where else am I to gain an introduction?"

"I will have to discover if Mama is ready for her to be seen yet."

"As bad as that? Perhaps I should call when you are home. I am certain you can contrive for us to meet."

"It might be better to come when Mama is out. She was beside herself with obtaining a proper wardrobe for the girl at the busiest time of year. If she thought you were coming, she might have one of her nervous fits."

"Why don't you send word when you find a time which would be convenient? I have not seen Caro in years, so it would not be inappropriate to greet an old friend."

"I will send word as soon as Mama leaves the house for any length of time, then."

The men shook hands and parted company at the door to Bond Street. Dev took longer than usual reaching his front step, so deep in thought was he about the possibilities. He was imagining all sorts of interesting options and how the *ton* would receive the girl. As the door swung open, he felt a rare smile break out on his face and thought his butler might have a heart seizure at the uncommon sight.

Dev's curiosity was not to suffer a long wait. He received

a note within the hour that Sutherland's mother was making morning calls but Caro and Miss Postlethwaite were remaining at home until the latter's wardrobe was ready.

Dev made a sound resembling laughter at the thought of the personage which would meet his eyes.

"Burroughs!"

"Yes, my lord?"

"My curricle, at once!"

"Yes, my lord."

When Lord Deverell arrived not half an hour later at the Sutherland town house, no one of his acquaintance could have guessed the rare anticipation he held in meeting the source of his entertainment for the next few months. He was dressed in his usual understated, impeccable fashion, with fitted pantaloons, gleaming Hessians, a dark-blue, superfine coat and a crisp white neckcloth.

After a brief exchange of civilities, Lord Sutherland sent for Lady Caroline and Miss Postlethwaite to join them.

"I have to admit, I am looking forward to this more than I ought," Sutherland confided. "Of those I have seen, the rest of the new crop is as tedious as you might expect, but I think you will have your hands full with her, Dev. I am going to enjoy every minute of this. It is a pity Edward had to return to his regiment and miss all the fun."

"What will his hands be full of, brother?" Lady Caro asked as she made her entrance into the room. A vision in a bright jonquil muslin, she caused the men to swallow their mischief. "Lord Deverell!" she then exclaimed, keeping the gentlemen from answering.

"Lady Caroline. You are a sight to behold." He took the hand she held out to him and kissed the air above it.

"Fustian! It has been years, though," she said, a rosy bloom rising in her cheeks.

Lady Caroline was pleasant enough to look at, with fine

dark hair and eyes and a willowy figure. Dev said all that was proper, but he confessed to himself that his thoughts were more intrigued by the shock of red hair and buxom figure of the girl standing behind Lady Caroline. Her drab blue kerseymere dress looked as shabby as he had anticipated, yet there was nothing shabby about the woman wearing it. Her hair was an unusual shade of red—not carrot, not copper— and was enhanced by an expressive pair of violet eyes, a creamy complexion with her cheeks flushed becomingly and a perfectly moulded set of lips.

"Lord Deverell, may I introduce our guest, Miss Postlethwaite from Yorkshire. Her brother served with Edward in the Greys."

He made a polite bow, lowering his lids over his own dark eyes so as to reveal nothing of his thoughts.

She curtsied, and her eyes flashed more fire than her hair could ever hope to. He was more than pleased with the prospect before him, especially as the girl seemed annoyed by him.

"How are you enjoying London so far, Miss Postlethwaite?"

"It is quite different from Yorkshire, my lord," she said, her voice carrying a slight burr.

Dev's ears perked up. Had he imagined it? He glanced from Sutherland to Caro, and they also looked a little uncomfortable.

"It is, quite. Is it your first visit here?"

"I have nay been past York before, my lord."

"Then you shall have to allow me to show you some of the sights here while you are in Town."

Sutherland covered his laughter with a cough, and Dev could tell Caroline turned away quickly to hide her astonishment. Deverell never escorted any female about.

"Oh, that wahn't be necessary, my lord. I don't mind a bit

of adventure on my own."

"Oh!" Caroline exclaimed. "You cannot wander about in the city without a chaperone, Miss Postlethwaite."

"I don't see why not. I went everywhere alone in Bagsby. I can nay imagine anyone would notice me in this 'ere big city."

"Dear me," he heard Caroline whisper.

"Ever since I was a little girl, I have just longed to see Vauxhall, Astley's and the Tower!" She clapped her hands in childish excitement.

"Then we shall see to it, Miss Postlethwaite. However, I must agree with Lady Caro. It is not at all the thing for a pretty young lady to gad about alone here. London is not only more dangerous than York, it can do irreparable damage to a lady's standing in Society."

Dev could have sworn the lady's eyes narrowed when he called her pretty. She would give him a run for his money if she did not know how to flirt a little, but he was not about to make a cake of himself, even to win this wager.

"Ay, and I remember Ewan jabbered of watchin' prime articles and eatin' oranges in the pit."

"I am certain you will enjoy it more from a box, Miss Postlethwaite," Sutherland said with an impressively straight face.

Dev felt a muscle quirking at the edge of his lips but quickly repressed it and composed his features into impassivity. This Season was looking more promising by the moment. Either this girl was very clever or was as unsophisticated as a new calf.

Either way, she presented a challenge. He hoped it was the latter, for it would be much more entertaining.

118

"Miss Postlethwaite!" Lady Caroline exclaimed after Lord Deverell had left. "You must not offend him! He is the leader of fashionable Society. One word of approval from him and you will be assured of success. He showed great kindness in offering to show you around Town."

Was it kindness or condescension? Rua frowned as she recalled the tall, dark man, with black, arching brows over hooded lids, who had gazed at her with ruthless and brutal scrutiny.

"Indeed. Deverell is one of the most fashionable beaux in London Society. Many ladies would swoon, break an ankle or surrender a fortune for a chance to be seen in his company," Sutherland added dryly. He was lounging in a chair, his legs crossed casually, with a look of amusement shaping his face that Rua did not quite trust.

Mrs. Merriweather had warned her about the games sophisticated gentleman played to amuse themselves, including shamelessly flirting and raising the expectations of young girls who did not know better.

"I did not mean to offend him."

"It is not important. Dev is not easily offended. He rarely gives thought to eligible misses. He did not earn the nickname 'Dark Devil' simply because of his dark good looks and attire," Sutherland assured her before also taking his leave.

Nothing he could have said could have infuriated her more. "Lord Deverell thinks himself above such company, does he?"

"No, I do not think it is that so much as he truly does not care, which of course only makes everyone seek his approval all the more."

Rua thought London ways were quite backward.

"Miss Postlethwaite, if I may be so bold?" Caro interrupted her mental tirade against Deverell.

"Of course you may, but please call me Rua."

"Very well, Rua." She hesitated. "Do you realize you spoke with an accent to Lord Deverell?"

"Accent? Whatever do you mean?" Rua attempted to control a blush. Why did the devil have to come out in her tongue? She had overheard the quip from Lord Sutherland as they were descending the stairs and had suspected it had to do with her, and hence she had given them a country bumpkin!

"Perhaps I am mistaken, but it seems you spoke differently just now."

"I apologize if I embarrassed you, my lady. I will try not to let it happen again."

"Oh, please do not worry yourself over it. I am sorry I said anything." The girl looked so tender-hearted and contrite, Rua had to admit her sins.

"Lady Caroline, it is I who must beg your pardon. May I confess something to you?"

"Of course, but you must call me Caro. Let us remove to my sitting room, where we may speak in private."

As they climbed the marble staircase, crowned by a domed ceiling painted with Greek gods sitting upon cottony clouds, Rua was still feeling overwhelmed by the luxury surrounding her. They entered a beautiful sitting room done in pinks and greens, with finely papered walls covered in tiny birds, which alone must have cost more than her father's annual salary. Her gown was most definitely not in fashion, and her tongue had run amok.

Lady Sutherland had said all that was welcoming and proper when Rua arrived, but had struggled to hide her astonishment at her old gowns and was quite taken aback when she discovered her mother had been cast off after marrying beneath her. "I hope they do not snub you in public!" she had responded with a frown. Not yet twenty-four hours had passed since her arrival, and Rua fully felt her lack of sophistication!

"I hardly know you, but since your family has decided to take me into their home for a few months, I may as well take you into my confidence."

"Of course. I wish you to feel completely comfortable."

"I have a suspicion your brother and his friend are cutting a sham."

"They are always up to something," Caro said in complete agreement. She kicked off her slippers and tucked her feet up under her in a relaxed manner Rua was certain her mama would not approve of.

"I do not really have an accent, but I believe they were speaking of me when we walked into the room, and I decided to bamboozle them."

Caro's nose wrinkled adorably. "Oh, that is too bad of you!" She laughed. "Do they truly speak such strange words in Yorkshire?"

"Yes, and much more!" Rua assured her.

"Perhaps you may be right. How may we find out?"

"I do not wish to do anything to offend you or your mother or spoil your Season in any way."

Caroline's eyes twinkled. "I think my family's reputation is safe enough. Did you have something in mind, or are you worried your presence will taint the Sutherland name?"

"Not my presence precisely, but my behaviour."

"Your behaviour is lovely; you have nothing to be concerned about. Some of the old tabbies will look down their noses at anyone who does not meet their exacting standards of dress and decorum, but there is no reason to think your Season will be a failure."

"I cannot help but suspect there is something suspicious going on. If there is, I want to give them a taste of their own medicine. That is why I wished to take you into my confidence."

"You may very well be correct, although I do not see why

you think they were speaking of you, from the little we overheard."

"Is it your brother's habit to invite you to meet his old friends?" Rua asked.

"Not usually, no," Caro answered carefully.

"And if Lord Deverell is such a leader of the *beau monde*, why would he invite me to see the sights upon the occasion of our first meeting? Especially when he is so clearly a Pink of the Ton and I a dowdy country miss?"

"I think you undervalue yourself; you are hardly dowdy, even in that dress. Perhaps he sees your potential, in spite of the clothing?"

Rua shook her head. "I have been a vicar's daughter too long. No fine gentleman would have any interest in one such as me."

"He has been the most sought-after bachelor and has made it clear he has no intention of being caught. Perhaps he thinks to set you up as his flirt for the Season? Mama warned me that he has a new one every year."

"I have no delusions about Lord Deverell," Rua said in reassuring tones, "although I would not be averse to a reasonable match. However, I cannot resist toying with this toplofty gentleman just a little."

Caro looked concerned. "How much do you intend to toy with him? I am not certain I would go too far. He could ruin all your chances with one word!"

"Oh, I will not let it go as far as that, I assure you. My main desire is to see if my estimation is correct. I grew up with three older brothers, after all."

"And I with two." Caro smiled. "Very well, then. I will help you as best I may. What do you have in mind?"

"Does your mother have any old gowns in the attics?"

Chapter Three

DEV WAS VERY PLEASED with himself after he had left Sutherland. The girl was too delicious. Would Society accept her, was the question. If she behaved prettily—minded her tongue—and obtained a new wardrobe, then perhaps it could be done. He could, of course, call in any number of favours from the Almack's patronesses to win his wager quickly, but where was the sport in that?

In all probability, they would think he had set her up as his latest flirt and pity the poor girl. He frowned. Hopefully, she would not develop a *tendre* for him, but she seemed to have more pluck than most of the young débutantes. He would tread carefully.

Wasting no time, he arranged an evening at Astley's Amphitheatre, thinking that would be the best place to further his acquaintance with Miss Postlethwaite, without the critical eyes of the *ton* upon her.

A box was procured for the next evening, and an invitation sent for Sutherland, Lady Caroline and Miss Postlethwaite to join him. He also invited Lord Tindal so it would not yet look as though he were singling anyone out.

Dev dressed in his usual understated fashion, this time in solid black, the only relief being his gleaming white neckcloth with a ruby pin. The red he chose in honour of Miss Postlethwaite's hair. Would she notice? He wondered at the absurdity and why he bothered.

Arriving precisely at the appointed time, he alighted

from his elegant chaise and four, which, singular to its owner, was also understated and lacking any embellishment. He did not like announcing his presence with tawdry ostentation.

Upon arrival at the Sutherland town house, he was promptly shown into the drawing room, where he was greeted by Sutherland and Tindal. In these opulent surroundings he expected to wait for the grand arrival of the two ladies while enjoying a customary glass of spirits. Counter to his supposition, however, within a few moments the footman hurriedly opened the door to a flushed Miss Postlethwaite, who was wearing the most outdated creation Dev could have imagined. Attired in an apricot confection, complete with modest hoops and ruffles, she only wanted her hair to be powdered to fit into the past century. To his considerable surprise, it was a struggle to keep his face schooled to its famed stoic indifference.

"I am so 'appy you are 'ere! I 'ave been waitin' on tenter'ooks all day." She clapped her hands together as though she were a very young girl escaped from her nurse and spoke in the most atrocious Yorkshire burr he had ever heard. He did not think even his head groom at Winfield could do any better. Indeed, she barely remembered to bob a curtsy at the end of that distinguished speech.

"I say, this ain't a costume party, is it?" Tindal asked too loudly into the shocked silence which followed.

Sutherland choked on his drink. Meanwhile, Lady Caroline entered the room with proper decorum save for a slight look of exasperation, although the way she clutched her reticule indicated she was somewhat harassed. Her demeanour highlighted the difference between the two ladies' behaviour and dress, since she was wearing a tasteful pink gown in the latest mode of high waist and narrow skirt.

Dev cast a glance at Tindal, who was staring openly at the guest with a mixture of admiration and astonishment.

"Are you going to introduce me?" he asked Sutherland once he had apparently recovered the use of his tongue.

"Do forgive my lack of manners. Lord Tindal, this is Miss Postlethwaite, our guest from Yorkshire."

"Well, now that the niceties are out of the way, shall we depart to the entertainment?" Dev suggested.

"I rather think we have it aplenty right here," Tindal retorted, flicking a glance at the guest.

With a finger, Miss Postlethwaite was twirling one of her curls, the rest of which had been tied up with a large bow appropriate for a girl still in the schoolroom.

"Miss Postlethwaite! We discussed your speech," Lady Caro remonstrated in a loud whisper.

The girl straightened immediately and looked repentant. "Please forgive me. I forget myself when I am fuddled," she said in very proper accents.

Dev gallantly proffered his arm to escort Lady Caroline to the carriage while Lord Sutherland escorted Miss Postlethwaite.

Tindal followed in his own curricle, as he had other plans after Astley's. Dev was not certain even the four of them would fit into the carriage with Miss Postlethwaite's hoops.

During the journey, she looked out of the carriage window, completely ignoring the company, her eyes wide with wonder as the equipage drove through the streets and crossed Westminster Bridge, the occasional "Ooh" and "Ah" escaping her lips.

Dev stepped out of the chaise first, wanting to hand her down and see her reaction to the theatre. He was not disappointed.

"Eee bah gum!" She stood there, mouth gaping, her eyes wide as she surveyed the majestic theatre with the wonder of a five-year-old child.

"I beg your pardon?" he asked, trying to interpret her exclamation.

She covered her mouth and shook her head. "I must remember to speak properly. I was taught to do so, you know."

He could not prevent a faintly sardonic curl forming on his lips, but refrained from comment and led her on to his box while she continued to look around her with amazement. While their presence drew a few curious stares, Miss Postlethwaite's behaviour was all that a young lady's should be . . . until the show began.

He had obtained one of the best boxes, with seats on the front row. Once the show began, she squealed with delight and began to bounce in her seat. It did not appear anyone else noticed, as their eyes were equally entranced with the juggling clowns, rope-walkers and tumblers displaying their talents before them, but Dev could not take his eyes from the performance next to him. He was not surprised at her running commentary on the scantily clad acrobats or her delight in the pig who could tell time and allowed a monkey to ride on his back.

Yet when Mr. Ducrow, the famous equestrian, began his act, 'The Flying Wardrobe,' Dev was wholly unprepared for Miss Postlethwaite's reaction. Ducrow began speeding around the ring on horseback, pretending to be drunk and deliberately falling off the horse as part of the act. The crowd laughed and roared, but he noticed Miss Postlethwaite had stiffened and had a look of abhorrence on her face. Before he realized what she was about, she stood up and began to shout at the man.

"Stop! You will harm yourself!" she shouted between cupped hands, to the laughter of those in the neighbouring boxes. When the horse played dead, she proceeded to shout, "You numbskull, you have killed him!"

Lady Caro groaned and put a restraining hand on Miss Postlethwaite's arm. "It is all a part of the act, Miss Postlethwaite. Do, please, sit down."

"Oh! I beg your pardon. I was reet flummoxed!" Sitting down, she looked appropriately chastened, behaved through the rest of the act, and even laughed at herself in a becoming manner when it ended. Dev was almost growing bored again. Then, the rider stood atop his beast and she proudly announced, "I can stand on an 'orse's back, too!" At this, she gathered up her skirts and made as though to climb over the barrier with the obvious intention of joining in. Groaning softly and praying no one who mattered was there to witness this spectacle, Dev bestirred himself to intervene by putting a restraining arm out to prevent the atrocity.

"I am certain you do so most handsomely, Miss Postlethwaite, but they frown upon the audience joining in."

"That is very unsportin' of them!" A very pretty pout adorned her face, and he would have sworn there was a twinkle in her eye, but she sat back down and offered no more shocking entertainment that evening.

The ladies only just succeeded in reaching Caro's chambers before bursting into laughter. Rua was holding her sides from the ache.

"I think that was the most fun I have had in my whole life!" Lady Caro had tears streaming down her face. "It was too bad of you to deprive me of the look on their faces when they first saw you! I do not know how you kept your composure."

"It was a very close thing, but I could not be fashionably late on our first outing! Now do help me get out of this horrid gown!"

Caro complied by loosening the laces. "They will be disappointed to see your new gowns from Madame Therese. I imagine they are, even now, wagering on what you will wear next!"

"Quite possibly," Rua agreed. "I do have one of Mrs. Merriweather's old gowns which I have not remade yet. It is not meant for hoops but far more suited to a grandmother." She laughed.

"How long do you mean to continue with this charade?"

"Oh, I would dearly love to have them admit to their scheme first. I am more convinced than ever that is what this is about! Did you remark the glances of the gentlemen throughout the night?"

"They were too composed, I think. It would be grand to see Deverell blush," Caro admitted.

"He is as cool as ice."

"He still seemed to find you charming. I saw his eyes follow you when you were not looking," Caro said as her maid arrived to help her out of her gown.

"We shall see. I think it is all a game, but I will admit to having fun. Thank you for humouring me!"

"No harm has been done yet. We will not always be so fortunate as not to have Mama's eye on us," Caro warned.

"When do you think we have another excursion?"

"Mama was waiting for your new gowns to arrive. We cannot let her hear you speak in that shocking way."

"I want to be sure I will not embarrass your dear mother. I must consider how to go on."

The next day, however, Lord Deverell called during Lady Sutherland's at-home, surprising every grand dame present. Every conversation ceased, and every head turned at his appearance, so wholly uncharacteristic as it was. Having not yet received any of her new gowns, Rua affably agreed to stay abovestairs and read a book. She did not think her refurbished dresses were so terribly shabby, but she bowed to the more knowing Lady Sutherland, who was all graciousness.

Therefore, when Lady Caroline gently knocked and entered the sitting room where Rua was comfortably ensconced in *Pride and Prejudice*, she was quite unprepared to be called forth to the den of matrons.

"Is it over already?" Rua asked, barely looking up from the pages of the book. Mr. Darcy had just commented on Miss Eliza Bennet's fine eyes.

"You must make haste. You will not believe it, but Lord Deverell has called and specifically asked if you were at home!"

"Whyever would he do such a foolish thing?" Rua asked, not hiding her irritation.

"He must be playing a very deep game. He has never before attended one of Mama's at-homes. She is torn between exultation and fear of your reception!"

"The poor dear!" Rua stood and straightened her simple Pomona-green muslin. "Will I embarrass you dreadfully?"

"You are just what they will expect of a country miss new to Town. If your manners are pretty, there will be nothing for them to remark upon."

Caro tucked a stray tendril of hair back into Rua's simple knot, and they made their way downstairs. It felt much like the tea at Mrs. Merriweather's, Rua reflected, though she smiled as demurely as she was capable of at the several faces surveying her with critical eyes.

Caroline proceeded to introduce her to eight different ladies. Some of their names she was familiar with, having been warned about them by Lady Sutherland. Rua curtsied and said as little as possible.

"Postlethwaite, you say? What kind of name is that?" one

of the ladies asked as she raised a lorgnette and looked at Rua through it.

"Yorkshire, my lady."

"That does not explain the unfortunate red hair. Who was your mother, gal?"

"Mary Campbell before her marriage, my lady." Rua deliberately left off the 'Lady' in front of her mother's name since she had done so after her marriage.

"Campbell, eh? One of Argyll's daughters? I remember her. She could have had any one of her suitors and she chose the poor curate."

"Yes, my lady. They were very h-happy." She drew out the *h* on purpose to show Deverell she did know how to speak like a lady.

The lady pursed her lips but seemed to give a nod of approval. The rest of the room appeared to release their collective breath all at once.

Lady Jersey scarcely said a word, which was apparently a rare feat, for her nickname was 'Silence' in mockery of her chatty nature; yet her abstinence spoke volumes when added to the rude appraisal of Rua's gown.

"The poor girl is an orphan. Her brother was in Edward's regiment and fell at Waterloo. He wanted her to have a proper Season," she heard Lady Sutherland explain to those near her.

Lady Cowper was the kindest of the patronesses, and Lady Caroline had mentioned she was a relation. "My condolences on the loss of your brother, my dear," she said kindly, and Rua thought perhaps not all of the patronesses were as high in the instep as she had been warned.

"Thank you, my lady."

"If I may intrude?" Lord Deverell asked. "I would like to steal Miss Postlethwaite and Lady Caroline for a drive."

"What a lovely idea!" Lady Sutherland exclaimed, a little

too eagerly. Caroline inclined her head, and Rua followed her out of the drawing room into the entrance hall, where the butler handed them both a pelisse as though he had been expecting such a request.

Rua could not say she was not delighted to escape the drawing room, and being a country girl at heart, she welcomed any entertainment out of doors. She could overhear the ladies speaking about her as if she were already long gone, though they had not waited for the door to close to speak of her.

"I wonder what he must be about? Is she some sort of relation or his latest flirt?"

"She must be a relation. He would not bother with a country provincial like her."

Putting on her best smile as though she had not heard, she tied her bonnet beneath her chin.

"It will be slightly crowded in my phaeton, ladies, but if you do not mind, then I am sure I do not." Lord Deverell looked dashing, Rua had to admit, in his buff pantaloons and Hessians, topped with a dark blue coat and high-crowned beaver hat.

"Phaeton?" Caro asked as they stepped outside to view the offensive vehicle which stood about five feet high. "I am afraid I must decline the honour, Lord Deverell. I cannot abide the height. I will see if my brother will take me." She curtsied and left Rua standing on the pavement feeling abandoned.

"Traitor," Rua muttered as Lord Deverell promptly assisted her into the high seat, and she at once wished herself otherwise. Seconds later, Lord Deverell was sitting right beside her, and it was nothing like being seated in close proximity to one of her brothers. They never caused her to feel self-conscious. They never caused her stomach to flutter or her cheeks to flush.

"That is a bang-up pair of greys you have there, my lord!" She could not resist a mite of impish fun as he sent the matched horses on their way with a slight flick of his wrist and proceeded to negotiate the traffic very handsomely.

"Do you appreciate horseflesh, Miss Postlethwaite?"

"I have brothers, two of whom were in the cavalry, Lord Deverell. I was put in the saddle before I could walk."

"Do you see your remaining brothers often?"

This was beginning to feel like an inquisition. "Unfortunately, no." Should she play the silly country girl or try to draw from him his proposed scheme? She was unusually conflicted. However, his eyes were keen, and she knew she could not play him for a fool for very long. "May I ask, sir, why you are payin' me such marked attention? Clearly, I am not in your usual style, and I 'ave no prospects."

"Frank speaking," he said with an appreciative gleam. "My usual style was becoming a bore."

They had arrived at the entrance to the park, and having negotiated the vehicle through the crowded gates, he steered the horses away from the people and towards the reservoir where they could speak more freely.

"You handled Countess Lieven well."

"Like a 'orse?" she quipped without thinking. "I did not know she needed to be 'andled," she added with an innocent air.

"Some of the patronesses can be particular. You mentioned your mother's family. Are you unacquainted with them?"

"They would 'ave nowt to do with my parents after their marriage, so I 'ave never met any of them."

"*Nothing* and *have*. Remember your aitches, Miss Postlethwaite," he corrected with a swift glance, revealing a gleam in his eye and a slight quirk of his lips, before he returned his gaze to the horses. "Tell me more about life in Yorkshire," he suggested.

"Have you ever been there, my lord?" she asked, emphasizing the pronunciation of the aitch.

"I have only journeyed through the county, I fear, though I would have stopped had I known of its delights."

She suspected he was quizzing her, so she emphatically ignored his flirtatious remark. Enjoying the cloudless afternoon, the tangy breeze from the Serpentine and the full-leafed birches, maples and willows, she was quite content to remain in the park. However, they had tooled back towards the crowds of fashionables, some in their landaus or atop fine mounts, some on foot, but all in their Sunday best, as they said in Bagsby, and Rua noticed they were beginning to draw some curious stares. Quite impervious to this scrutiny and the fact that this was to be the *on dit* of the Season, Rua continued to watch the show about her with almost equal fascination to that she had shown at Astley's.

"Who is that?" Rua asked as they passed a dandy tricked out in a garish costume of bright yellow pantaloons and an equally bright tangerine coat embroidered with flowers and fruits. He pranced along in high-heeled pumps, pulling a toy poodle behind him.

"A mere Tulip peacocking about. No one worth your notice," he drawled. She rather agreed, though it was hard not to notice.

They passed Sutherland and Lady Caroline travelling in the other direction, and Rua took one more opportunity to be gauche. She feared this game would soon be done. Sutherland was dashing in his own right, not unlike Deverell in many ways, and yet, strangely, Sutherland had little effect on her insides.

"Hallo! Lady Caro!" she called with a wild wave of her arm. Caro gave a brief lift of her hand and Sutherland tipped his hat, but Rua could see them trying not to laugh and felt satisfied with her efforts.

"You remembered your aitches! Well done!" Deverell congratulated her with a faint, contemptuous smile. "Has anyone ever told you how enchanting your eyes are?"

Unmoved by his attempts to offer blandishments, she reminded herself to guard her sensibilities and pronounced blithely: "All anyone speaks on these days is a pair of fine eyes."

Dev did not want the drive to end, but knew he must remove them from the park before Miss Postlethwaite did something unforgivably outlandish beneath the gaze of the *haut ton*. His credit would only gain her so much leeway.

"Would you like to stop at Gunter's for an ice?"

"Would that be proper without a chaperone?" she asked, as though she suddenly had a thought for appearances.

Dev could have sworn he saw a slight twitch of her lips, but if so, she quickly repressed them back into order.

"I assure you, Miss Postlethwaite, that there will be no question of impropriety about procuring an ice. In fact, you will not have to leave the conveyance to do so." That there would be plenty of talk otherwise, he had little doubt.

Dev had already left the park and driven to Berkley Square, pulling his phaeton into the line before Gunter's. It was a warm spring day, so there were all sorts of persons to be found there, seeking the cool pleasure of an ice: nurses with their charges, more dandies prancing in their latest costumes, and mamas showing off their silly daughters. It was almost more crowded than the park. He looked sideways, expecting to see Miss Postlethwaite taking it all in, but instead she was pulling faces at a young child whose nurse was more interested in a handsome footman.

The little boy rubbed one shoe up the back of his other stocking and pretended to hide behind his nursemaid's skirts.

"Peek-a-boo!" he cried, giggling, springing into view again.

Miss Postlethwaite opened and closed her mouth in imitation of a fish, and he giggled some more, which caught his nurse's attention. Giving his hand an admonitory tug, she bobbed a curtsy at the occupants of the carriage.

"Thomas, do not importune the lady. Make your bow, please."

"May I serve you, my lord?" As Thomas obliged, a waiter from the confectioners appeared beside the carriage, ready to fetch their desserts and thus claiming their notice.

"What is your pleasure, Miss Postlethwaite?" Dev enquired, glad to have averted another scene.

She looked around to see what others were partaking of and frowned. "I have never had such a thing, sir."

"There are flavours to suit almost any fancy. From sour to sweet or creamy to sorbet—like frozen juice."

"What is your favourite?"

"I prefer the Parmesan or Gruyère, but most ladies seem to prefer the lighter bergamot or muscadine."

"Surprise me, sir, for I have no notion of how any of them should taste."

Dev nodded to the waiter, and he rushed back across the street, dodging traffic, to fulfil their order.

When the waiter returned with their desserts in fine porcelain dishes with tiny spoons, she looked at Dev, and he nodded his encouragement. She piled as much of the purple ice as she could on the little spoon, and it was all he could do not to roar with laughter.

When she at last took a bite, she closed her eyes with undisguised pleasure and groaned with delight. "Ohhhh."

"You approve, I take it?"

"Approve? I do believe this is what Heaven will taste of.

Is this the muscadine? It tastes a little like the elder wine our cook makes."

"I cannot say I have ever considered that Heaven will have a taste."

"Oh, I think so," she said emphatically. "One of God's greatest gifts to us is our senses. I should like to think of Heaven with ices," she said as she took obvious pleasure in another indelicate bite.

"I should like to think of it graced by red-headed beauties with violet eyes," he commented with his usual air of indifference, while watching her from beneath hooded lids.

"What nonsense you speak, sir!" she declared, though her eyes were twinkling.

Dev had used some of his best lines on the chit, and she was reprimanding him! "A word of advice, Miss Postleth-waite: you must play the game a little."

"I thought we *were* playin' a game! Forgive me, 'ave I bruised your feelings by not returnin' your compliment?" she asked, eyes dancing with merriment. She was laughing at him!

"Served my just *desserts*," he retorted and shoved his own spoon, full of ice, into his mouth. Miss Postlethwaite gurgled with laughter, which was the most pleasant sound he could recall. Perhaps Heaven would sound like her laughter.

It was at that moment that an unfortunate visitor chose to walk up to the phaeton.

"Deverell." The newcomer inclined his head but watched Miss Postlethwaite with undisguised appreciation.

"Campbell." Dev returned the greeting, though he kept his voice cool. He felt the lady tense and sit up straighter. An awkward pause ensued, and Dev realized they were wholly unknown to one another. From his demeanour, Campbell clearly expected him to rectify that oversight, committed by the man's own family. Dev was in half a mind to drive on when the lady cleared her throat.

"Mr. Archibald Campbell, may I introduce you to your cousin, Miss Postlethwaite?" he conceded at last, not troubling to hide his reluctance.

"So it is true," the man said, brows lifted—half in curiosity, half in admiration—as he walked around the equipage to greet her properly. Dev watched as the well-dressed man with dark blond hair and blue eyes smiled and bowed over her hand, feeling a strange urge to box Campbell's ears. Dev could not blame the poor fellow for his reaction, but this was hardly the place for a family reunion. "Charmed, dear cousin. I dearly hope you will allow your family to become suitably acquainted."

"She is staying with Lady Sutherland, if you should like to rectify the situation in a proper fashion, Campbell," Dev hinted, if not subtly.

The man's eyes narrowed momentarily before he stood up tall and looked back at Dev.

"Perhaps I may have a word?"

Dev grumbled but handed his reins to his tiger.

"We will only be a moment, cousin," Campbell reassured Miss Postlethwaite. As soon as they were out of earshot, Campbell wasted no time venting his misgivings. "What are you about, Dev? There are bets all over the books about you and my cousin, and none of them reputable. As a male relative, I must look out for her best interests."

"Doing it too brown, methinks, Archie," Dev replied severely. "Since I made the introduction, I hardly think it is your place to suddenly claim kinship when she is a grown woman."

Campbell glared. "Are your intentions toward her honourable?"

As much as Dev was inclined to teach this impudent pup about duty, he did not wish to further jeopardize Miss Postlethwaite's reputation by duelling over her. Their conversation was already attracting notice. Those who did not know of her connections to the lofty House of Argyll before today would do so by the morrow. He saw Willoughby Greaves, the most notorious gossip, slipping away through the crowd, and sighed inwardly.

"I mean her no harm," he temporized. "My word as a gentleman." He willed his dark brown eyes to betray no emotion.

Campbell released the visible tension in his face and shoulders and backed away a step. "Very well. My grandmother was taking a pet that you meant to set her up as your mistress."

Dev looked over to where he had left the young lady, but she was no longer in the phaeton. He flicked his gaze back and forth, searching for her in the crowded square.

"You insult me, sir, I think," he said. At that moment, he caught sight of the person he sought. Skirts held indecorously above her shapely calves, she was chasing a ball across the lawn in the centre of the square. He heard high-pitched laughter, and turning slightly, saw the little boy, Thomas, whom she had been making faces at earlier. As Dev watched, mesmerized, she threw the ball to her new friend, whereupon he kicked it again and the game continued.

"I forget there are still such innocents in the country," Campbell mused as they watched her with mutual fascination, completely heedless of what others thought of her behaviour. She was not doing anything vulgar, yet she was hardly comporting herself as a young woman of twenty years ought while in London, amongst the *beau monde*. "I beg your pardon."

"Perhaps I should ask what your family means to do by your cousin, having ignored her for twenty years."

"I did not know of her existence until yesterday!" Campbell stammered. "I had met her brother before, by chance, but he did not mention he had a sister. We received word her parents had died last year, and Grandmama was quite distraught about it! She dispatched me to find the girl as soon as Lady Cowper sent word."

"Then you may reassure the Dowager Duchess that she will come to no harm from me. I hope she will be recognized. Lady Sutherland has taken her in—a stranger!"

Campbell looked properly abashed, so Dev ceased his attack.

"I must not keep her waiting. Your servant!" He clicked his heels, nodded and strode briskly across the lawn to fetch Miss Postlethwaite from her playmate.

Word of Lord Deverell's attentions to the new, unknown country girl spread like fire on old timber. Rua was not comfortable with the attention, for she knew it to be false and she quite feared she was in over her head, playing the proper lady for one audience and the ignorant, innocent country lass for the other.

Having had no word from the other branch of her family her whole life, she thought very little of her meeting with her cousin, other than he seemed to think highly of himself. She deemed anyone who could ignore relations due to reduced circumstances unworthy of her affection or attention, so she quite put the meeting out of her mind.

However, her life soon took on a new whirl: she was suddenly receiving invitations, flowers and callers to whom she had never been introduced. She suspected it was to gawk at Deverell's latest curiosity.

A few gowns arrived from Madame Therese, and that arresting event was enough to draw Lady Sutherland's attention. While Caro and Rua were admiring the new creations from the seamstress, Lady Sutherland joined them, caution and concern written all over her face.

She sat quietly, and Rua waited, knowing she had something to say.

"These gowns are quite lovely. It was so kind of your friend to give you those silks."

"Yes indeed," Rua agreed. "I am certain I have never owned anything so fine." She fingered the exquisite cream fabric and its sheer golden overdress with something akin to awe.

"I did not expect them for at least another week, with this being the busiest time for a modiste," Lady Sutherland said slowly.

"I must credit your good name for that," Rua said frankly.

"Perhaps, but I suspect it has as much to do with Lord Deverell's attentions to you."

Rua and Caro both stopped and looked at the lady. She continued cautiously, "It is a credit to be noticed by one such as he, but I feel I would be doing you a disservice if I did not warn you against losing your heart. He is a renowned flirt, but he never has marriage in mind."

"My heart is in no danger, I assure you, ma'am! I know I am nothing more than a diversion to him." She must keep reminding both herself and her heart.

The good lady's face relaxed; she was clearly not enjoying the burden of speaking of anything so delicate. However, she frowned again. "What I do not understand, is why he has singled out you, a young country nobody, to play with this Season. Never before has he bothered with anyone eligible!"

Rua overlooked the slight—which the lady did not even realize she had given—and said amiably: "I do believe I am the object of some sort of wager, ma'am. You can rest assured that I am fully aware he has no true interest in one such as I! Nonetheless, it would be foolish of me to refuse the advantage he has given me by bringing me into fashion. Perhaps someone who can overlook my status as a poor vicar's daughter will take notice."

"Oh, indeed! You are such a good girl, is she not, Caro?" the lady said, quite missing the sarcasm, and evidently satisfied she would have to bestir herself no further.

"Yes, Mama," Caro agreed cautiously.

Lady Sutherland stood up, having discharged her duty without any unpleasantness, and seemed quite pleased. "I almost forgot! Emily sent over vouchers to Almack's for both of you."

Caro and Rua looked at each other, exchanging sceptical expressions.

"We have Lord Deverell to thank for that as well, I surmise. I was not expecting such a singular honour!" Rua tried to hide the cynicism she felt.

"Not at all! Emily had already agreed before he arrived. It certainly did not hurt your estimation with the other patronesses, it is true, but she is on good terms with your Campbell relations as well as myself and was happy to oblige."

Once Lady Sutherland had left them, Caro and Rua stared at each other for a moment before bursting out laughing. "You must forgive Mama," Caro said.

"No offence taken. I was well informed of my social status before I left Yorkshire. But what do we do now?"

"Well, I did find out from my brother that your suspicions were correct. I overheard him speaking with my mother, and he was upset when he saw the vouchers!"

"And you only now thought to tell me?" An involuntary grin, doubtless full of mischief, spread across her face. "Do not keep me waiting!"

"They did have a wager to see if Deverell could procure vouchers to Almack's for you, but he did not, and so I wonder how this will affect their game?"

"Is that all? I am glad I was able to oblige their expectations!" Rua said, amused, before losing herself deep in thought for a moment as she contemplated. The devilment was still in her, and she could not back away from good sport. "Besides losing the wager, I would dearly love to repay his kind offices," she remarked wryly.

"How? You could refuse to dance with him, I suppose, but that might be disastrous to your reputation, and you could dance with no one else all evening!"

"That is to suppose he will ask me. Very likely he will not attend, now that he has lost."

"Oh, but that was part of the wager, too. They have to dance with five wallflowers, including myself."

"You are hardly a wallflower!" Rua objected.

"No, but I think my brother wished to see me become a success, which happens when much sought-after gentlemen pay marked attention to one."

"I suppose that is a brother's distorted way of being helpful. I could see mine thinking some such rot. How bored they must be to come up with such ridiculous notions!"

"I think we should make it impossible for them to dance with us," Caro suggested. She seemed to be taking an equal enjoyment in the mischief as Rua was.

"How may we do that? It is not easy to refuse a gentleman which is the only way I can see to do as you said."

"Why, by being so dashing that we will not be available. Word has already spread, and you will not lack for partners."

Rua shook her head.

"I cannot wait to waltz! I was finally approved to do so," Caro said dreamily, beginning to perform some of the steps around the room.

"They allow the waltz here?"

"Yes, for some time now. But you may not dance it until one of the patronesses gives you permission."

"These patronesses seem to have all the power in Society."

"Along with some of the fashionable gentlemen, like Lord Deverell and formerly Beau Brummell, yes. It is ridiculous, but it is the way things are done. People come in and out of fashion at their whim, it seems."

"No fewer than three people have now seen fit to warn me not to waltz! The dance was thought scandalous in Bagsby, so I have not had the opportunity."

"You do not know how to waltz?" Caro asked, eyes wide with astonishment.

Rua shook her head again. "I know, I am devilish underbred," she added.

Caro's face lit up. "Perhaps that is how you may refuse Lord Deverell! I have never seen him bother with any other dance. If you do not know how to waltz and you have not been given permission, then you may refuse him."

"I should still like to know how to perform it, all the same," Rua replied, feeling the wicked gleam of naughtiness even if she could not see it.

"Perhaps Mama would play the pianoforte, and I can teach you."

"Would you do so, please? I will still be able to refuse Lord Deverell in good conscience because I will not have been given permission."

"True enough! Let us go and find Mama, then, and see if she will oblige us."

The ladies hurried down the hallway to Lady Sutherland's chambers.

"You are familiar with the other dances, are you not?" Caro asked suddenly, her brow puckered with the afterthought.

"Of course I am! What do you take me for, a provincial?"

Chapter Four

"IT LOOKS LIKE YOU owe me a monkey," Sutherland said with a smug gleam in his eyes as he sat down in the chair next to Dev, who had just settled back comfortably with a glass of cognac in Sutherland's study.

"Pray tell," Dev said, feeling bored. "The Season has only just begun. How can I have already lost the wager?"

"Because my aunt Emily sent vouchers to Miss Postlethwaite on her own accord, by Jove! Had it from my mother's mouth just this morning!"

Dev paused before speaking, ignoring the little sensation of regret he felt within. "Surely this does not mean I lose because someone beat the fox to the chicken?"

Sutherland frowned. "Perhaps not. Deuce take it, this quite ruins the wager!"

"I would not go that far. I am more amused this Season than I ever remember being before."

"Ah! That is the way the wind blows, eh? You had better beware or you will end up leg-shackled!"

"I have no intention of ending up in any such case, you may rest assured," he said imperturbably. "I have already danced attendance on her rather enough, I would say."

Sutherland looked sceptical. "I suppose you may see if you can waltz with her this week at Almack's since the vouchers are moot. I should be surprised if they allow her to do so when she is new in Town. I must say I rather like her pluck. Might dance with her myself," he answered.

144

Dev scowled at his friend's words. He rather liked Miss Postlethwaite's pluck as well and had already intended to claim one of her dances, regardless of the consequences. For some disturbing reason he could not lay a finger on, he felt invested in her future. He sat up straight.

"What precisely did you tell your mother?"

Sutherland looked guilty. "As little as possible, but she knows about the vouchers and the dances with wallflowers."

"You betrayed all?"

"I tried to prevaricate." He held his hands up. "You know how it is when a mother is determined to discover something."

"Was she angry?"

"She gave me a look that made me feel as though I was back in short coats, but then she relented. How could she be angry when I secured five dances for my sister?"

"Will she tell your sister and Miss Postlethwaite?"

"Oh, I asked her to keep her own counsel. I am not certain Caro would appreciate knowing I had arranged her partners for her."

"No, the effort would be quite unappreciated," Dev agreed, wondering how much of his suspicions to disclose to his friend.

"She will take it as her due, of course, and never know her brothers conspired to help. I must say, I cannot wait to see how Miss Postlethwaite takes."

"I suspect we have grossly underestimated the young country lass. I suspect she is playing us for the fools that we are."

"Why would you suspect such?" Sutherland seemed taken aback.

"Because, my friend, she occasionally forgets to play her part. If she fails to make a good match, she has a future on the stage!"

"If that is the case, I think I like her the more for it! She is a game one if she would risk her reputation to dress up in that old garb merely to thwart our wager!"

Dev paused to consider. "Indeed. She must have overheard us speaking that first day."

"Well, what do we do now if the game is up?"

"I suspect we should be *en garde.*"

"You think they mean to try to roast us?"

"Of a surety."

"But how? What could they possibly do to us?"

"They are no fools . . . best not to underestimate them. If they have been on to us from the beginning, I suspect they will do something unexpected—something clever. I do not think either of them to be spiteful." That circumstance, in itself, was refreshingly novel and unlike most ladies of his acquaintance, he reflected in some surprise.

"Should we change tack?"

"Not yet. I rather want to see what they have planned."

"What should we tell Tindal?"

"Nothing, I think. We shall go to Almack's and dance as we had intended. Perhaps I am mistaken."

"You never cease to astonish me, Dev."

"I rather surprise myself at times," he conceded.

Sutherland frowned. "What do you mean to do after Almack's? You have paid marked attention to the girl, and it has not gone unnoticed by the tabbies."

"I do not think I will need to do anything. If my suspicions are correct then she will have no need of me." The thought chafed somewhat. Dev rose to take his leave, and as he was being handed his hat and greatcoat, he overheard music coming from the drawing room. "A waltz, I do believe," he remarked.

"Mother is playing the pianoforte so Caro can teach Miss Postlethwaite the dance."

Dev knew he should continue out of the door and not look back. Curiosity got the better of him, however. He held a finger to his lips, and Sutherland nodded. They walked to the ballroom but could not, of course, open the door and gawk.

"Psst. This way." Sutherland motioned for Dev to follow him, and they went through a maze of servants' corridors and doors until they were on the other side of the house and hidden behind a screen where the musicians normally sat to play for parties.

"If you were a good brother you would offer to dance with them," Dev chided in a whisper.

"Why do I think you mean for me to partner my sister and not the lovely Miss Postlethwaite?" Sutherland retorted.

"Your sister does lead rather well," Dev reflected as he watched the pair with a gleam of amusement.

"I think I agree with you and thus will not be goaded into furthering your chances of getting Miss Postlethwaite to dance a waltz with you at Almack's. What is to stop you from asking her now, if you partner her?"

"Nothing at all, my friend. You have found me out."

Sutherland's gaze turned mischievous. "We may rescue them if you will partner Caro."

They watched Lady Caroline teaching Miss Postlethwaite the steps to the waltz, and Dev had to admit to himself that the young lady from Yorkshire was quite charming. She was an elegant dancer, and it piqued him a little to know that she had played him for a mutton-head. He had meant her no real harm, after all. She was a worthy opponent, and he was shocked to discover he looked forward to the next round.

"One, two, three; one, two, three . . ." Rua was counting

to herself, trying to mind her steps to this new, elegant dance. Caro had been a very patient teacher.

"Rua, do you see what I see?"

"All I can see is your neck; a very graceful neck it is too, but if I look elsewhere, I will be ruining your slippers."

"Then, I beg you, do not look, but I see Gareth and Deverell spying on us from the musicians' gallery."

"Why ever would they do that?"

"Do you think they suspect us of retaliation? I am sure they do not know I overheard my brother telling Mama."

"More than likely, they want to see whether or not I will embarrass them if they offer to partner me," Rua retorted.

"Shall I call them out of hiding?" Caro asked.

"I suppose this ruins my plan to say I cannot waltz." Rua pouted.

"Unfortunately, I do think they have seen enough to surmise you are quite competent. Why did they not simply walk in through the ballroom doors if they wanted to watch?"

"They mean mischief. Yet should we let them know we see them? It is quite beneath the dignity of a grown man to do such a thing." Her lips began to quiver, and she could not contain her mirth. She burst out laughing and missed several steps.

"What is it, my dears?" Lady Sutherland noticed the mishap and stopped playing.

"We were trying to decide what was so interesting in the musician's gallery? Good afternoon, Lord Deverell. Gareth."

"Oh, how lovely! Now you may both have partners," Lady Sutherland exclaimed, not seeming to realize the oddity of their positions.

"Walters had asked me to look at something up here. I am afraid we must be going—to an appointment, you must know. Good afternoon, ladies." Sutherland bowed and tried to make a hasty exit, but his mother was not to be deterred.

"Come down here. I do not wish to strain my neck or my voice in order to speak to you. There is no reason you cannot assist Miss Postlethwaite with the waltz to ensure she is ready for her first Town ball."

By the time the men had descended to join them, neither gentleman looked the least bit repentant at being caught red-handed, and the devil had taken over Rua's tongue again.

"Actually, my lady, I am feeling a little shy. I do not think I am yet ready to dance with anyone else. My upbringing was rather strict, I admit, and perhaps I will grow accustomed to the dance once I see others perform it."

Lady Sutherland seemed to be bereft of speech, and Lord Deverell flicked a piece of imaginary lint from his coat.

"Perhaps you could show her one time since she has never seen it performed," the lady finally suggested.

"An excellent idea, to be sure," Sutherland agreed. "Dev, would you care to partner Caro?"

"I think I would prefer to watch first, myself, if Lady Caroline does not mind. Perhaps I can convince Miss Postlethwaite to overcome her reservations and join us."

"You are too kind, my lord," she demurred, and went to sit in one of the chairs lining the dance floor. She did not miss the scathing look of reproach Lord Sutherland cast his friend and could not but wonder what it meant.

Lady Sutherland began to play a waltz, and the brother and sister performed it beautifully, twirling around the floor in perfect harmony. Rua could not imagine any of her brothers doing such a dance, but reflected sadly she had spent very little time with them at formal parties.

"Have you never been to a dance?" Lord Deverell asked her.

"A few simple country ones, my lord, that is all. I am but a vicar's daughter and was brought up with strict notions of propriety. 'One must set the example for one's flock,' my father always used to say."

"The waltz being the pathway to Hell, I assume? How tedious!"

"You delight in mocking me!" she rejoined.

"You make it so delightful, how can I resist? Then you refuse to dance, and I find it quite irresistible not to make it my new purpose to persuade you to do so."

"When I have most emphatically stated that I do not wish to? How ungentlemanly!"

"What can be your objection? Watch Sutherland and Lady Caroline. If brother and sister may perform it, how can it be scandalous?"

She took a few moments to watch the dance and quite had to bite her tongue to keep from accepting his offer. She wanted nothing more than to float about the ballroom in the arms of a dashing partner, but she was also a fierce competitor. Searching for objections, she was finding little to cavil at.

"His hand is on her waist!" she exclaimed in mock astonishment.

Deverell's face lit up, and he made a sound resembling a laugh. It quite transformed him.

"Yes, but they are standing a proper distance apart," he finally countered.

Before Rua could find anything else to object to, Lord Deverell had taken her hand and was pulling her to her feet.

"My lord!" she reprimanded.

"There are only a few measures left. It will not harm you," he said as he placed that scandalous hand on her waist and began to twirl her about the room. She said nothing, for she was minding her steps and trying to think of her next move. The warmth of his hand and his musky, masculine scent were driving her to distraction. Curse him for always being one step ahead!

"What I would not give to know what is going through your mind," he said. "You dance quite well, but it is customary to exchange a few niceties with one's partner."

"Even when one has nothing nice to say?"

"Even then," he agreed jovially.

She dared to look up for a moment, ready to issue a scathing set-down, only to catch his eyes laughing at her.

It was really too much to be borne! What clever trick could she ever play on him when he was up to every rig? Rua was certain even her father, rest his soul, would agree Deverell needed to be brought to heel . . . yet how?

"I do not think I have ever been so properly snubbed," he mused as though it pleased him.

"I beg your pardon? I was not attending."

"Precisely! If I cannot charm you even in this dance, I am utterly unmanned!"

"Is that what Londoners consider charming?" Rua was fighting to keep a straight face, and had to think of her dear departed parents in order to do so.

He released her from the dance and bowed. "I beg you will forgive the impertinence to your person!"

Rua was wondering if she had indeed gone too far this time, except he did not look in the least offended.

"Will you allow me a chance to make it up to you?" he asked, surprising her instead.

Now what was he about? "There is nothing to forgive, my lord. I beg you will forgive my old-fashioned ways."

"Perhaps the Tower? A museum? Vauxhall Gardens?" he suggested.

Her mind was awhirl with possibilities. "Well, now, I was a-wantin' to see a play, my lord."

"*Taming of the Shrew*, perhaps?"

"I believe that to be *Much Ado About Nothing*!" she retorted.

151

Chapter Five

IT WAS SEVERAL DAYS before Dev again saw the intriguing country miss who had begun to occupy more of his thoughts than was natural. He had purposefully avoided going to places where he might come across her, so concerned was he at the effect she was having on him. Never before had he been susceptible to the baser emotion which he considered infatuation to be, so he had spent the past few days trying to ascertain precisely what it was about this unlikely woman which was capturing and maintaining his interest.

Having already determined that when the stakes were a person's welfare, wagering was no longer amusing, he wasted no more energy on something he could not undo. However, the manner in which he would resolve the dilemma wherein he found himself entangled was constantly occupying his thoughts. His friends would be shocked to know how far his contemplations had taken him, and would have lost exorbitant sums had *that* been the subject of a wager.

Exercise was his preferred remedy for maudlin thoughts, which rarely afflicted one with such an indifferent nature as he, so he took himself for a ride early that morning, certain not to encounter the cause of his discomfort.

Whilst putting his splendid black gelding through his paces, he was already feeling much more the thing when he heard hooves approaching at a gallop from behind him on Rotten Row.

"What the devil?" he muttered, but then had to keep his

152

own horse under control as Sampson took exception and endeavoured to further his own wish to run. "Most likely some tomfool young buck," Dev exclaimed angrily. Then he saw a flash of red hair and a violet form as a chestnut flew past him. He urged his own horse forward at once as recognition dawned, feeling it his duty to rescue the lady from her folly. Instead of pulling up when he approached, she turned and laughed.

"Race you to the gate!" she called.

Arguing was fruitless, so Dev enjoyed himself as he appreciated her riding with as fine a seat he had ever seen atop a horse. His Sampson quickly caught up and surpassed her winded mount, yet he only beat her by one length.

When she reined in and turned towards him, he saw her hair had come loose from its pins and her cheeks were becomingly flushed. He could not recall thinking anyone more beautiful than she in her smartly cut velvet riding habit, which made her eyes sparkle like amethysts.

"You are determined to ruin your character before your Season begins!" Dev chastised. Her eyes immediately widened with astonishment, and for a moment, she looked repentant before those glorious eyes then flashed with anger. "How dare you reprimand me!"

"Clearly, there is no one else to do so. Does Lady Sutherland approve of the style of your morning ride? Have you no groom to attend you?"

"Give me some credit, I beg of you. I bid the groom wait for me at the gate."

This ridiculous explanation caused a slight, involuntary lift of his brows, but he did not scold further. "Then allow me to return you to him."

Although it was clear she wanted to object, for her jaw was clenched and her eyes were shooting daggers at him, she did not. She inclined her head without speaking as she turned her horse. They proceeded at a more considered pace, slowing to a walk before they reached the groom who stopped leading his horse about when he saw them approach.

"I assume I have committed another social solecism?" she asked.

"Indeed. It is considered fast to be seen galloping in the park."

"Fast was precisely what I wished to achieve!"

He had to suppress a smile. She was an original, but if she did not take care she would be ruined. To his surprise, that thought troubled him. "Hopefully, no one other than nurse-maids with their charges noticed your escapade."

"I'll be taken all-a-mort, my lord, if you have any interest in my reputation other than your own amusement."

A group of cavalry men approached before he could reply, and—at least to him—it was obvious by her expression she bit back whatever stinging peal she was about to ring over his head. He wished them to the devil.

"David? David!" She waved heartily when she recognized one of the navy-coated soldiers.

"Rua? What are you doing in London?"

"I would ask the same of you!"

"We arrived just three days ago, from the Continent."

By the time he had finished speaking, she had slipped down from her horse and handed the reins to the groom, with whom Dev would have a word later. Although, to be fair, he could easily imagine how it had come about that he was left behind.

The soldier thus addressed had also dismounted and was greeting Miss Postlethwaite with more affection than Dev cared for. To his further annoyance, he noted that David was the masculine counterpoint to her feminine beauty, with his golden locks and blue eyes.

The young man quickly made introductions to his fellow

soldiers, but they were much younger than Dev. He recognized some names and coolly inclined his head to the four jovial young men.

She, in turn, introduced him, and upon discovering that this was her younger brother, Dev wholly understood the glare he received. His reputation preceded him.

The brother excused them and pulled her off to one side, but Dev's ears were keen and he was able to overhear.

"What are you doing out here unchaperoned? It ain't the thing, sis. And with Lord Deverell, too! He is not known for his honourable intentions toward the fairer sex, if you catch my meaning."

"Perfectly, David," she snapped. "I am staying at Sutherland House. If you will call on me, I shall explain how I come to be in London. I will be attending Almack's Assembly Rooms tonight, if you should care to dance."

The young soldier whistled. "High and mighty company you are keeping here, Rua. Be careful. I cannot keep my horses waiting, but I will call on you soon." He brushed a kiss on his sister's cheek and cast a warning glare at Dev, who smiled insouciantly and inclined his head at the insolent young pup.

While Miss Postlethwaite watched her brother and his friends ride away, Dev dismounted and sent the groom back to his waiting place near the gate with a small wave of his hand.

"May I assist you to remount?" he offered gallantly.

"No, thank you. The groom is well able."

"Yes, but I am here. Do you know, Miss Postlethwaite, many gentlemen would take an affront at their chivalry being refused thus."

"Fustian! You are not so puddin'-'earted!" She smiled impishly as she waved to the groom and placed a boot in the stirrup.

"No, indeed!"

"And we need not pretend you are making advances to me, so you may save your tender emotions for your *chères amies!*"

He could not repress a bark of laughter. "Just so!"

The park was beginning to fill with gentlemen out for their morning rides, so Dev took it upon himself to boost Miss Postlethwaite into the saddle, regardless of her preference for the groom.

A satisfying "Oh!" escaped her lips, and he mounted his own gelding with the intent of escorting her back to Sutherland House.

"You insufferable, odious man!"

"So I have been told."

"Do you always ignore others' wishes?"

"Not always."

Nevertheless, she had fallen in line beside him, and as they crossed Piccadilly, she began to survey her surroundings.

"Where are we going, my lord? I am almost certain this is not the way to Sutherland House."

Dev wanted to remove Miss Postlethwaite from the prying eyes of the *ton* and was not yet ready to end his tête-à-tête with her. It had, however, slipped his mind that there were milking cows in the neighbouring park, and her interest was fixed there before he could draw her attention away.

"Well, I will be sparrow-blasted!" she exclaimed. "Who would have thought to see such a thing in the middle of a fashionable park!"

"People must have their milk, even in the city," he said imperturbably.

"Yes, of course, yet it seems such a strange thing to come upon! Oh, look! It is my friend from Gunter's!"

Dev frowned, trying to quickly recall of whom she might be speaking. Could it be Campbell?

Miss Postlethwaite had dismounted, without a thought for his accompanying her, and was leading her chestnut towards a little boy who was watching the milk cows with great interest.

"Good morning to you!" she said. The little boy turned and greeted his new friend with the enthusiasm any boy in short coats might at the sight of such a fine horse. His attention was at once diverted from the cows to the horse.

"Ooh, may I ride her? Do say yes, I am a capital rider. Papa says so!" he begged, much to the dismay of his nurse.

"That big 'orse, Master Thomas? Certainly not! If you was to fall, I should lose my place!"

"Oh, do allow him to," pleaded Miss Postlethwaite. "She is a very gentle mare."

Clearly the maid was unaccustomed to country manners and a boy's thirst for adventure, Dev observed, watching the whole scene with amusement.

He could almost see the farce unfold before it happened. The boy was placed atop the horse and Miss Postlethwaite began to lead him around, to squeals of delight. Alerted by the sounds, one of the cows ambled towards them and mooed dolefully. The mare stopped, ears pricked forward and every muscle taut. She snorted loudly, and several of the cows ambled closer to get a better look at this odd beast. Young Thomas screamed; the cows bellowed, and the horse took fright. She began to stamp and sidle about. Miss Postlethwaite spoke soothingly and remained in control . . . until one of the cows decided to charge. The mare reared, then set off at a spanking pace across the park. Miss Postlethwaite made a valiant attempt to keep hold of the reins, but being hampered by skirts, she had little chance. Even as Dev urged Sampson forward to rescue Miss Postlethwaite, she lost her footing, fell and was dragged. The boy screamed, the mare quickened stride, and with a gnawing sensation in the pit of his stomach, Dev drove Sampson faster.

The slight frame of the girl pitched and rolled, lurching from one bruising thud to the next. Dev winced and yelled to her to release the reins. Fool woman, she could be trampled! Anger combined with a fear foreign to his stony heart clutched at him, and a cold sweat prickled his brow. Drawing near at last, he was thankful when she had the sense to follow his instruction. The mare checked; urging Sampson up on her other side, Dev plucked the boy from the back of the chestnut in a deft manoeuvre. Having settled Thomas in front of him, Dev circled Sampson around and rode back to discover whether the lady had come to any serious harm. She had been helped her to her feet by a growing crowd of spectators from all walks of life and was herself trying to comfort the nurse, who had gone into hysterics. The relief Dev felt was overwhelming. At one and the same time he wanted to strangle her and yet embrace her.

Dev restored the boy to the nurse and made quick work of dispensing the crowd—milkmaids, Cyprians, artists, loiterers, and a pie seller—back to its own business by the simple expedient of threatening to call the constable. Then he walked Sampson over to where Miss Postlethwaite stood, covered in grass stains and mud, a quizzical expression on her face.

"That did not go quite as planned!" she remarked.

Dev bit back the thundering scold that was on the tip of his tongue, and instead began to laugh. She joined him, and the best he could do was shake his head.

"Come, let us find your chestnut."

The mare, who happened to be munching on lush grass a short distance away, behaved as though nothing had occurred to upset her. Dev once more assisted Miss Postlethwaite into the saddle.

"Allow me to escort you to Sutherland House. I think that is enough excitement for one day!"

"Oh no, my lord, tonight is my début at Almack's!"

Rua would love to be able to capture the image on Lord Deverell's face. It made the whole sordid adventure worthwhile. He had been remarkably stoic throughout. She could only imagine what a picture she must present at the moment and prayed she could sneak into the house, her adventure undiscovered. Having been gone far longer than she had planned, she hoped fortune would smile on her a little longer. Knowing she could have been seriously hurt that morning, she decided no wager was worth repeating such folly.

The groom took the horse, and Rua hoped Lord Deverell would be so kind as to leave. No such luck was to be had; he insisted on accompanying her to the entrance.

The butler opened the door and did not so much as blink at her appearance.

"My lord, Miss Postlethwaite. You have visitors in the drawing room."

At this hour? She had not even breakfasted. "Of course. I will go and make myself presentable. Thank you for your assistance this morning, Lord Deverell."

"Deverell? What's this?" a loud voice demanded from the upper hall. Rua looked up to see an old lady with whom she was totally unfamiliar.

"Your Grace." Lord Deverell bowed to the woman. "May I present to you your granddaughter, Miss Postlethwaite?"

"Come up here, girl, and let me get a better look at you."

"I will take my leave of you now, Miss Postlethwaite."

She shot him a look of betrayal, not stopping to wonder

why she would feel so. As he left, she felt oddly alone in the world. Hesitantly, she climbed the stairs to greet her grandmother. Part of her was curious, and the other part was filled with reluctance.

"What happened to you?" The old lady made no bones about her critical survey of what Rua could only suppose resembled a disaster. "I trust this is not your normal appearance?"

"I fell from my horse, your Grace," Rua pronounced with a deep curtsy, showing as much dignity as she was able. "Will you allow me a few minutes to rectify my toilet?"

"It is of no consequence now. You look just like her, you know," the old lady said, taking a seat on the white brocade sofa in the saloon, "except for the red hair."

"It is an unfortunate occurrence," Rua agreed. She remained standing, not wishing to soil Lady Sutherland's immaculate upholstery and not certain she was ready to welcome this woman to her bosom. Quietly she waited to see what her grandmother wanted.

An awkward silence fell. Rua was determined not to grovel. She was quite content to wait until the lady said what she wished or had had her inspection.

"You are as stubborn as your mother, I can see."

"A family trait, then," Rua noted dryly.

The lady, in whom Rua could see a notable resemblance to her mother, glared.

"Humph! I came to see if you might wish to stay with me at Argyll House for the rest of the Season. I am not as spry as I used to be, but I believe I could chaperone you on occasion."

"I am quite content here with Lady Sutherland, your Grace. Do not feel obligated to me."

"I am to pay for the slight to your father, am I?"

"With all due respect, ma'am, I would call it more than a slight."

160

"When you grow older, you will realize how much folly you committed when you were young. I regret what happened and that I never had the opportunity to apologize nor say my farewells."

"My mother held no grudge," Rua said, softening, though she could not understand why she was comforting the old lady.

"No, she would not have done. She was far better than all of us," the Duchess said, looking distant, as if she viewed another world.

Suddenly, the stern matron did not look so formidable; instead, she looked miserable. Rua tried to swallow her pride, for she knew her parents would wish her to mend this breach.

"You are as much a stranger to me as Lady Sutherland," Rua explained.

"Will you spend some time with me while you are here? Perhaps I can see you suitably situated. I think your mother would wish it of me."

"I have no notion, but I would like to know you better."

The lady gave a slight smile. "I heard you have vouchers for Almack's. Your uncle would like to escort you there. There has been some rumour of hoydenish behaviour, I gather, but that will set it all to rights, I assure you."

"How kind of him."

The Duchess eyed her with suspicion, as though suspecting her of an impertinence, and then smiled.

"I suppose you have something suitable to wear?"

"Yes, your Grace. Lady Sutherland has been most kind in that regard."

The Duchess opened her reticule, took out a handsome velvet pouch and handed it to Rua. "These were your mother's. I think she would have liked you to have them."

Opening the pouch, she pulled out a string of pearls.

They would go beautifully with her cream evening gown and the earrings. "Thank you," she was barely able to mutter as she fought to hold back tears.

The grand lady nodded, as though she were uncomfortable with praise. "Now, about Lord Deverell . . ."

"Do not fear. You have no cause for concern in that regard!" Rua held up a hand.

"Well, if you should manage to hook him, I could not say as I would be disappointed," she finished, eyes twinkling, before standing to leave.

"I am afraid you will be disappointed, then. He has no thoughts of marriage, I assure you!"

"Humph!" She appeared unconvinced, but refrained from further comment on Lord Deverell. "You will come to me tomorrow?"

"Yes, I will."

Rua remained standing with her face turned away, her eyes on the prospect outside as she fingered her mother's pearls for some time after her grandmother had left and wondered what it might mean for her future. She laughed aloud at the thought of Lord Deverell offering marriage to her.

"Nothing could be more unlikely, Grandmother," she muttered into the silence.

She realized then she was coming to like the man and was going to be sad when the approaching night, and the wager, was over. For even though she had been the object of that distasteful game, she could not bring herself to despise him for it.

Chapter Six

DEV AND TINDAL ARRIVED at the hallowed Assembly Rooms at a quarter before eleven, the latter determined to pay his debt and be done with the matter as soon as possible. It was like the town sinner being forced into the sacred walls of a church, Dev mused, as he noticed the shock cross the faces of the matchmaking mamas in the crowd. The two of them were excellent catches, but their reputations were such those mamas warned their innocent daughters away. In truth, some of the reputation had been earned, but Dev wished he might have enjoyed half the fun he was credited with. Trying not to scowl, he scanned the crowd of near-infant girls decked out to look like fluffy clouds. Whyever did they think this fashion was attractive to men?

"I cannot do it, my friend," Tindal said, beginning to back towards the door.

Dev grabbed his arm and held him still. A dance ended, and a hush fell over the crowd as they noticed the intruders standing by the steps.

Sutherland made his way over to greet them. "Chicken-hearted?"

"Chicken everything," Tindal replied.

"Well, you had better come and greet my aunt Emily. She sent me over here to fetch you."

"I imagine she did," Dev muttered, but allowed himself to be led away from the best view of the curious.

"I think the wager might not have been needed,"

Sutherland said as they made their way through the throng. "Neither Caro nor Miss Postlethwaite has lacked for partners. Even Argyll has put in an appearance, escorting his niece and dancing with her."

"Are you calling the wager off?" Tindal asked, looking acutely uncomfortable in knee breeches and dancing slippers.

"Of course not."

Tindal cursed in protest, to the disapproving glares of several mamas within hearing. Tindal then began making frantic noises in his throat, as though simply by being present he was somehow becoming contaminated.

"Control yourself, Tindal. You can leave any time you wish."

"Hide me. My aunt Louisa is here and will expect me to do the pretty with all four of my cousins!" he croaked.

Dev shook his head and Sutherland pressed close to help conceal him from view.

"I suspect it is too late, my friend."

"Ah, here they are. Mama, you remember Deverell and Tindal?"

"How could I forget?" she said with a radiant smile.

"Lady Sutherland." Dev and Tindal bowed gracefully.

Dev took the opportunity to search for the notable redhead who was the sole purpose of his attendance. He finally found her, performing a quadrille with a dashing soldier in regimentals. She was enchanting. A gown of cream silk with shimmers of gold floated about her when she danced. Combined with her red hair, she looked like an angel. Dev noticed he was being watched and tried to divert his gaze— and his blatant admiration—away from the latest dashing beauty.

Arriving as late as they had, he was certain Miss Postlethwaite would not have many sets left, but since he was unconcerned by the nicety of finding other partners, he decided to remain next to Lady Sutherland and Lady Cowper. He might have need of one of the patronesses.

Caro also did not lack for partners, he noticed, so he was perfectly content to charm the dowagers and matrons while he watched Tindal do the pretty by some astonished wallflowers or, perhaps, his cousins.

Almack's was as tedious as ever: dry cake and bland beverages, stiff-rumped sticklers of Society and all the rigid rules of propriety being observed under hawkish gazes. However, this time Dev was not bored. He was quite certain the two young ladies had some trickery in mind, but he had forced himself to arrive as late as possible in order to put at least a partial spoke in that wheel. It had quite exercised his restraint, but he had to keep his head. Never before had he seriously considered anyone for the title of his countess. He was not certain he would enjoy the wedded state, but no one had ever intrigued him as Miss Postlethwaite did. The House of Argyll having recognized her put any thoughts of unsuitability to rest, despite her ridiculous efforts to convince him she was the worst sort of vulgarian. A laugh escaped his lips.

"Did you say something, Deverell?" Lady Cowper asked, giving him a knowing look.

"I beg your pardon. My mind was quite elsewhere."

"Yes, that much was obvious. Are you going to ask her to dance?"

"You know I only waltz, my lady. I dare not ask for such a favour."

"Indeed? I thought there was nothing you would not dare." She pursed her lips. "I urge you to reconsider. The consequences, you know. I would think, after bringing her into fashion, you would be weary of her. She has been so popular tonight, I do not know if she has any other dances left unclaimed. I will oblige you, if you are certain it is what you wish to do. I rather like the girl." She cast him a glance of warning.

He inclined his head and moved away from the ladies. Lady Cowper was right; it would draw more unwanted attention towards Miss Postlethwaite, and unless he was ready to make that commitment tonight he needed to further consider the consequences, irrespective of the wager. He could not care less about that at this point.

He moved to where Miss Postlethwaite would be led at the end of the quadrille, but he was one of many hopeful solicitors for her hand. He checked in disgust and backed away. There were certain lengths he would not go to, and making himself ridiculous over a female was one of them.

"I think Lady Caro is avoiding me, and I cannot even get near Miss Postlethwaite!" Tindal exclaimed from next to Dev. Sutherland had come up beside him as well and was looking greatly amused.

"I am dashed if I will pay you a monkey when I cannot get near the ladies!" Tindal said, affronted.

"A wager is a wager," Sutherland quipped.

"The whole intent behind it was so your sister would not lack for partners!" he argued.

"*Au contraire.* Equally as much of my intent was to be amused by seeing you make a cake of yourself!"

"I shall remember that next time!" he retorted.

"Yes, do!"

"Now, where did Caro go? She was just here." Tindal looked around with frustration.

Dev had no notion where Caro might be, but he looked up and spotted Miss Postlethwaite's retreating back. Following at a leisurely pace, the strains of a waltz falling upon his ears, he noted with interest that she appeared to be in a great hurry.

Where could she go without her bevy of suitors following, but to the retirement room? Yet she did not go there but towards the refreshments. After selecting a glass of orgeat, she lingered near some potted trees.

Was she hiding from her brother and his friends? Dev was too curious to withdraw. Being over six feet tall, he concealed himself as best he could behind groups of people, and zigzagged his way towards her hiding place until it was too late to retreat. He was behind her and waited for her to turn and notice him. It was perhaps ungentlemanly of him, but her withdrawal wanted explanation.

"Oh!" she cried, jumping slightly.

"Miss Postlethwaite." He bowed. "I did not mean to startle you. I was trying to determine if it was you before I spoke to a stranger."

"Lord Deverell," she said somewhat breathlessly before falling into a curtsy.

He reached down and clasped her wrist to help her up; then he slid his hand into hers and brushed a kiss over her glove.

"Sir? I—" A small wrinkle formed between her eyebrows, and he felt the sudden urge to brush it away, but he remembered where he was just in time and restrained himself.

"I came here to dance with you."

She frowned fully, and those violet eyes sparked with a fire he felt to his toes. It started an interesting sensation within his breast that, at this moment, he did not care to investigate.

"I am afraid I must decline. I know Sutherland forced you into coming here. You have my permission to leave." She placed a hand on her hip in defiance, and he had to force his gaze back to her face. A few freckles dusted the bridge of her nose, but otherwise there was little resemblance to the hoyden of the past few weeks.

"Please."

Her lips thinned, and he could see the indecision on her face.

"There are any number of young ladies desperate for a partner," she argued.

"Do not make me beg, Rua." He leaned forward and whispered next to her ear, "I do not intend to accept a rebuff from you."

Apparently he had said the wrong thing, for she stiffened her spine, pulled her hand from his and walked away.

Rua could not pretend any more! Much though she had tried to guard her heart, she could feel it breaking. She knew she was unsophisticated, but she could not play these wretched games and remain unaffected. Something about the way he had looked at her and whispered in her ear had caused her accustomed resilience to snap.

Though she searched wildly for some niche where she could recover her composure, everywhere she turned was crowded. Forcing a few smiles, she continued to fight tears and tried to control her speed as she sought a refuge. How could she have been so stupid? Finding herself back in the ballroom, she stopped and attempted to remain unnoticed behind a group of onlookers who were chatting amongst themselves.

"Miss Postlethwaite." Rua looked up to find Lady Cowper smiling kindly at her. Rua curtsied and did her best to appear unmoved.

"May I present to you a partner for this dance?" The lady

stood back to reveal Lord Deverell, and Rua was trapped. Like a fox at bay she was well and truly caught. She could not refuse in front of all eyes at a ball, and he knew it.

"Thank you, my lady," she replied graciously, and took the hand Deverell held out to her.

A mixture of humility and anger—mostly at herself—kept her from speaking. There could not be a full dance left, she told herself, forcing her gaze anywhere but into his eyes, for she would then certainly come undone.

The floor was crowded with twirling couples who looked magical beneath the glittering candles, which bounced light from the gilt mirrors about the room. In another situation, she would have been in ecstasy.

"I am sorry, Rua," he said after a full turn about the ballroom. "I did not mean it to go so far."

She shook her head. "Please do not do this. Not here. Not now."

"I must."

"You must what? Complete my humiliation in front of the *ton*?"

"Is that what I am to you? An embarrassment?"

"Of course not! I thought I could play your game, but I . . ." She choked on her words and looked away.

"You . . . ?" he prompted. His hand on her waist tightened.

"Never mind. I do not wish to play anymore or be anyone's object of sport."

He did not reply. She at once began to brood on the injustice of it all, but then checked her thoughts. He was partly to blame, yes, yet she had thrown herself whole-heartedly into the game and could not now cry foul. It was she who had broken the rules by allowing her feelings to overcome her good sense and then falling for the rogue.

Around them, couples circled, but she scarcely saw them. Forcing her lips upward into a neutral line, even if she were unable to smile, she made an effort to savour these last moments in his arms. She closed her eyes and allowed herself to be lost in the strength of his arms and the gentleness of his touch, for he was an excellent dancer and she had no fear he would lead her amiss. Pretending, for these few moments, that things were different, she absorbed his musky scent, the way she fitted perfectly within his embrace and the euphoric feeling of being in the arms of the one you love. Never could she have anticipated such a sensation.

As the music drew to a close, and reality once again encroached, she could not help but satisfy her last question.

"What do you win?"

"I beg your pardon?"

"What is the prize for the wager you have won?"

He stopped, still holding her in his arms. "I fear I have lost more than I ever hoped to gain."

"I do not begin to understand you," she replied, stepping back from his arms.

"Can you not?" The expression in his eyes gave her pause and caused her insides to churn.

Although most of the couples had left the dance floor, those remaining were beginning to stare. Rua barely registered the odd looks and titters; she was too intent on the gentleman before her. Yet had she but known, the shocked members of Society, so unused to Deverell's unflappability, were marvelling at what strange start had come over him.

Footsteps broke the trance-like gaze in which she was locked, and her brother appeared beside her.

"Rua, people are staring," he said quietly through a smile, bowing to Deverell as though nothing was out of the ordinary. Rua could only be grateful her brother did not say something foolish.

"I beg your pardon. We were having a fascinating discussion," Deverell explained.

"Perhaps you may continue the discussion in private?" Her brother took her arm to escort her away. The dancers took their places behind them for the next *contredanse,* and the music resumed.

"I will call on you tomorrow, Miss Postlethwaite," Lord Deverell said when they reached the edge of the ballroom. Rua could not meet his gaze, and suddenly wished the evening to come to a swift close. Convinced he had said the last for the benefit of those nearby, she did not put any great hopes into receiving his lordship again.

Later, Rua gave up trying to sleep, finding the effort fruitless. Her thoughts were travelling in circles around Lord Deverell's behaviour. She must put him out of her mind— nothing would come of it, and she must put the whole experience behind her. She rose, splashed her face with cold water, and began packing in order to remove to her grandmother's house. Much though she would like to return to the country and pretend none of this had happened, she was still practical enough to know that time was running out and she must secure her own future. She did wish at least to know her mother's family a little, though she doubted they would ever be close.

Rua answered a soft knock on her door to find a sleepy Caro standing there in her dressing gown.

"What are you doing awake at this hour?"

"I heard you moving about and wanted to discover what had happened. You were already abed by the time I reached my room last night." She frowned when she saw Rua's trunks part filled, and her belongings scattered about. "So you are truly leaving?"

"I am only removing to Argyll House for a time. I will not be so far away."

"It is not the same as having you in my own house! I will miss you, Rua."

"And I, you. I will ever be grateful for your kindness to me."

"And I will always remember this Season fondly, for the great adventures you brought to me!"

Rua laughed, and then tears began falling down her face.

"Whatever is the matter, my dear? Have you been crying?" Caro came over and placed an arm around her. It was too much for Rua's raw emotions to bear. Unable to contain her anguish any longer, she sobbed upon her friend's shoulder.

"I am the stupidest girl alive!"

"Whatever do you mean? You were the belle of the ball last night. Every gentleman wanted to dance with you, and the attention from Deverell was much remarked upon."

The mention of that name caused Rua to lose her composure again.

"Oh, dear girl. Have you lost your heart to him?"

All Rua could do was nod as Caro's comforting arms cuddled her close.

"There is naught to be done about it, however. I shall recover in time."

Another knock on the door interrupted their discourse.

Rua looked up. "I did not expect everyone to be about so early!"

"It is already noon!" Caro exclaimed. She opened the door to one of the footmen.

"Begging your pardon, my lady, but Miss Postlethwaite has a visitor."

"Very likely it is my brother," she responded. "He was overly concerned last night. He is to escort me to our grandmother's house."

She sat at the dressing table and put her hair up in a plain knot before rising again and smoothing out the wrinkles of her new lavender poplin dress.

"Will I do, all things considered?" she asked with a self-deprecating laugh. Her eyes were red and swollen and held no sparkle. She knew this pain would eventually ease, but it would be impossible to feign her normal gaiety and carelessness.

"You only look a trifle peaked. You still take the shine out of any other lady!" Caro assured her.

"You are too good, Caro!" Rua kissed her friend's cheek.

"You will say goodbye?"

"Of course!"

Rua was glad to have her brother back, at least for a short time. That would be as good a distraction as anything, and he would not tolerate her blue devils. The footman opened the door to the small saloon, and when Lord Deverell turned to look at her, she could not have been more astonished.

"My lord?"

"Why the surprise, my dear? I told you I would call." He came to her and, taking her ungloved hand, kissed it, sending a shiver coursing through her entire body.

My dear? "So you did, but I was not so foolish as to set any store by it."

"I suppose I deserve that." He released her hand and walked towards the window with his hands behind his back. It took a great deal of fortitude not to beg him to return to her. She had no notion of why he was here. He had already apologized for the wager, and meeting like this could only cause more pain. She was a sorry case, indeed. Her throat began to burn with unshed tears, and she looked down in an effort to hide her emotions from him.

As she studied the patterns of blue, gold and red on the Persian carpet, his polished Hessians came into view.

"Rua." His index finger gently lifted her chin, forcing her gaze to his.

With difficulty, she looked into his handsome face … and the look of tender affection she saw there set off a small spark of hope within her.

"I think, by now, you may guess at what I mean to say. I have apologized for my behaviour towards you with regard to the ridiculous wager, though I cannot be sorry for it, since it brought me you."

Her brow must have wrinkled, for he lifted one finger to smooth it. She closed her eyes from the sheer pleasure of his touch.

"Do go on," she encouraged, which elicited a chuckle from deep within his chest.

"My dearest girl—my love. Will you put me out of my misery and tell me you will marry me?"

A gasp of shock escaped her. "Are you—can you be sincere?"

"I have never been more so in my life!"

"But how can this be? Forgive me; I be fair betwattled!"

"As am I! But it has become clear to me over the past few weeks that your presence was essential to my future happiness."

"I am not fit to be a countess!" she protested.

"Where, pray tell, is there a *rôle résumé*? The only requirement is for you to say yes. Well, and for you to remain just as you are. I have never been so diverted in all my life!"

"I never imagined to be rewarded for coming Yorkshire over you!" When he raised his brows, she added quickly, "For trying to bamboozle you."

"My dear girl!"

Suddenly, Rua found herself locked in a passionate embrace, leaving her little doubt that her feelings were reciprocated. Could he really intend marriage?

"I still cannot believe it," she said shyly, daring to look up into his twinkling eyes. "You are not trying to bamboozle me again?"

"It would be my greatest pleasure to convince you further," he replied, with that devilish grin which had always made her insides lurch with anticipation. Their lips met again, expressing mutual love and admiration, and it was thus that they were found by both families of Sutherland and Argyll, some half an hour later.

Their embrace was interrupted by the door opening.

"That's my girl!" the Duchess of Argyll approved with a cackle of laughter.

A throat cleared, and her brother's voice said, "May I be the first to offer my felicitations?"

Too embarrassed to reply, Rua promptly hid her face against her betrothed's shoulder.

"I knew if anyone could tempt you, Deverell, it would be this baggage. It was just the same with Argyll and me," the Duchess remarked fondly.

"And did you employ such unfair tactics to reel him in?" he asked.

"To be sure! All is fair in love and wagers!"

National bestselling author **Elizabeth Johns** was first an avid reader, though she was a reluctant convert. It was Jane Austen's clever wit and unique turn of phrase that hooked Johns when she was "forced" to read *Pride and Prejudice* for a school assignment. She began writing when she ran out of her favorite author's books and decided to try her hand at crafting a Regency romance novel. Her journey into publishing began with the release of *Surrender the Past*, book one of the Loring-Abbott Series. Johns makes no pretensions to Austen's wit but hopes readers will perhaps laugh and find some enjoyment in her writing.

Johns attributes much of her inspiration to her mother, a retired English teacher. During their last summer together, Johns would sit on the porch swing and read her stories to her mother, who encouraged her to continue writing. Busy with multiple careers, including a professional job in the medical field, author and mother of small children, Johns squeezes in time for reading whenever possible.

Visit Elizabeth online: ElizabethJohnsAuthor.com

Six Wishes

Sarah M. Eden

Chapter One

Lindsworth, Sussex, 1816

FELICITY AND ANGELINA BANBURY shared a bond even stronger than most sisters. They had been inseparable from the time Felicity was born, almost precisely one year after Angelina. Neither could remember a time when the other was not in her life. They'd shared a nursery, a governess, and a friendship that ran thicker than blood.

The two walked arm-in-arm along the garden path behind their country home, moving at a slow pace in deference to Angelina's frail health. Her constitution had been in decline for months. The doctors their parents had consulted offered no hope. Angelina was wasting away from a disease too vague to fully explain and too little understood to treat, let alone cure.

"The London Season will begin soon." Angelina had frequently spoken of the annual social whirl. Of late, her tone was wistful whenever she did. "If only Father and Mother had permitted me to make my bows last year. I was strong enough last Season."

Their parents were overly cautious in regard to anything at all connected to Society. Mother had spent the weeks leading up to last year's Season in a near-panic over the possibility that someone in the family would misstep should they go to London and, as a result, the lot of them would be ostracized. She and Father had felt Angelina inadequately prepared to navigate the shoals of an unforgiving world. After *this* year, though, there would likely be no more opportunities for wading into social waters. There might very well be no further opportunities for Angelina at all.

It was so utterly unfair!

"Why should you not have your Season now?" Felicity wondered aloud. "At nineteen, you cannot be accused of being too childish for the endeavor."

"Considering the current state of my health, one might argue the opposite: that I lack the youthful energy for it."

Felicity shrugged as if unconcerned. "Every Season needs an aged dragon or two. Adds a bit of danger to the undertaking."

Angelina smiled. "I could sit with all the cranky dowagers, offering unflattering assessments of gowns and dancing abilities. Further, I could be excused from dancing at balls, which I wouldn't have the strength for anyway."

"Sounds ideal." Felicity pulled her features into an earnest expression. "You, of course, will not expect me to join the Row of Ancients. I am not nearly at so advanced an age as you."

"Only if you understand you will not be immune to our biting criticisms."

"I should think not!" She allowed a laugh. "Would that not be a great deal of fun? Spending a Season simply being ridiculous?"

Angelina sighed. Even facing the short future before her, she seldom grew discouraged, but she sounded it now. "I would be infinitely pleased if I could spend the Season doing anything connected to it. Instead, I will be here, waiting and wishing."

She didn't have to say *what* she would be waiting for; they both knew with heartbreaking clarity.

"Why not go?" Felicity asked. "Why not have a Season?"

Angelina shook her head. "You know perfectly well that I haven't the endurance for that endless social whirl."

"Then take on only a portion of it," Felicity insisted. "A bit of a spin would be vastly enjoyable, I daresay."

But, again, Angelina shook her head. "The purpose of a Season is to make a match. One in my situation hasn't that option."

Felicity stopped their slow meandering, faced her sister, and took her hands—carefully, on account of Angelina bruising very easily of late. She looked directly into her sister's dark-circled eyes. "Then let us give it a new purpose. Just this once, let the purpose of the annual Season be a young lady enjoying herself."

"That is very un *ton* of you," Angelina said with a wry twist of her mouth.

"Do you know what is even more un *ton* of me? I don't care."

Angelina laughed. How grateful Felicity was that her sister yet had the strength to do so.

"Mark me, Angelina. You and I will find ourselves in the traveling coach bound for Town before the Season is out. You shall have all the entertainments you can endure, and the *ton* won't have the first idea what to make of these two mad sisters and their uncouth interpretation of the Season."

She received an indulgent smile. "If you can manage that, I will declare you a sorceress."

They stepped through the terrace doors and inside the house once more. Angelina was handed over to her waiting lady's maid to be whisked off for a much-needed rest.

"Be thinking of an appropriately awe-inspiring sorceress name for me, dear sister," Felicity called after her. "I intend to work a great deal of magic."

"We cannot possibly present Angelina given her current circumstances," Mother insisted, looking alarmed. "Half of Society would assume we were trying to trick someone into marrying her by pretending her situation is less dire than it is."

"But we would not be dishonest about that," Felicity said. "And we certainly wouldn't be pushing for a match."

"And, thus, we hit upon the objections of the *rest* of Society." Father entered the discussion with his usual stiff logic. "To present a young lady who has no intention whatsoever of seeking a match is to turn up one's nose at the reason the *ton* has made the journey to Town."

Reason and logic was her best approach with Father. "Those already wed or widowed participate every year, and no one is put off by their presence. Gentlemen, particularly those with parliamentary duties, attend the social whirl year after year without being in pursuit of a wife. That is considered not merely acceptable but expected."

He lifted his brows. "Expectations are different for gentlemen than for young ladies. You know that perfectly well."

"I am also keenly aware that, beyond making matches, a purpose for the Season is to foster beneficial connections. We would be in a position to do precisely that."

Mother wrung her hands. "We would also be in a position to undermine what little standing we have by missteps and misspeaking. One cannot be too careful."

Felicity might have argued that being "too careful" was a significant part of their difficulty. Too many years of caution so great the family had avoided London rather than risk a single misstep had left them with few friends in the *ton* and very little standing.

"Society might look askance at Angelina's being part of the marriage mart, though we do not intend to thrust her into it," Felicity said, "but surely they would not object to *my* participation. I am of age and unwed and have every expectation of long-term health."

Mother and Father shook their head in perfect unison.

"The younger daughter cannot be out before the older is wed," Father insisted. "It is a very nearly unbreakable rule."

"We will not so much as entertain the idea of even bending rules," Mother said. "We will not take such a risk."

That put paid to Felicity's plan to convince her parents to undertake a Season for *her* and, by so doing, secure one for Angelina. She very quickly chose a different tack.

"I hadn't meant that I would go to London in order to make my bows, only that if we are in Town and have the opportunity to make a few beneficial connections and, with heaven's blessing, make a good impression on Society, it would be a very fine thing indeed. I will eventually make my come out. Laying a bit of the groundwork now would not be a terrible thing."

She could see she had given her parents something to ponder. Her next few moves needed to be delicate ones. If she pushed too hard, they would begin to worry she was too forward to be trusted in Society. If she pushed not at all, they would likely dismiss the idea she had planted in their minds.

"It is not at all unusual for families to travel to London for at least a portion of the Season," she said. "We needn't put ourselves forward at all, nor make appearances at particularly significant gatherings." She doubted they had the social cachet for that anyway. "No one will think either Angelina or I are making our debuts if we do not undertake any of those things that clearly mark us as doing so. We can be very careful on that score. I have my doubts Angelina would be equal to such a thing, regardless. We will be seen as nothing more than a family wishing to enjoy Town for a time."

Mother did not immediately object. That was, in Felicity's experience, a very good sign.

Felicity looked at Father. "Renewing acquaintances will ease our way when, in a couple of years, we return to Town for the traditional reason. We can think of this jaunt as nothing more than that: a brief family holiday in London and an opportunity for you and Mother to see a few friends you haven't in some time. Not even the greatest sticklers would object to that."

Father looked at Mother. "She is not wrong on that score. It is possible to journey to London during the Season without participating in the marriage mart. Angelina, I am certain, has no expectations of being Society's darling. She will be perfectly content to limit herself to quiet, unexceptional expeditions."

"But will Felicity?"

Here was her opportunity. She met her parents' gaze with earnest sincerity. "I will forgo *any* event or activity in London you find the least bit objectionable. I will make no effort to be part of something if it would give even the slightest impression that I am attempting to make a backdoor come out. I give you my word. This journey ought to be a joyous one for Angelina and a pleasant one for both of you. If that means remaining at our London house for most of our time in Town, I will happily do so. You have my word."

A few minutes more were required, in which she reiterated her vow, but in the end, her parents agreed to make the journey to London to allow Angelina to fulfill a few of her wishes. It was an opportunity for her sister that Felicity did not mean to waste.

Chapter Two

London

WILLIAM CARLISLE HAD SPENT five years mastering the art of self-distraction. Endless balls and fetes, races and pugilistic bouts, country house parties at the homes of his many friends, jaunts to the continent. He knew perfectly well how to free his mind from the pull of home and the pain that awaited him there.

He'd lost his parents at the tender age of eighteen. The vicar had finished his graveside rites, the local mourners had offered William their condolences, and then he had returned to the empty house, packed a trunk, and left. He hadn't been back to Sussex since.

The Season was usually the easiest stretch of months in which to find adequate distraction. This year, however, he was struggling. He had no desire to return home; that much had not changed. He simply found no pleasure whatsoever in the social whirl.

"We could always declare ourselves ancient grumps and take up lives of hermitry in an abandoned corner of the kingdom." His closest friend, Leonard Whitehall, made the suggestion as they completed a circuit of the small enclosed park near William's rented rooms. "We can attend the local assemblies and complain vociferously about all the noise the young people are making."

"I would be exceptionally good at that," William said.

Leonard's mouth twisted in thought. "We could always do that *here*, no need to find a distant corner."

It was tempting, but foolish. "London loses what little charm it has when one has offended the dragons."

"Would it be so tragic if the patronesses revoked your voucher to Almack's?" The dryness of Leonard's tone indicated not the least doubt in his assessment of William's lack of enjoyment of that social establishment.

"For me, no. For all the ladies denied the opportunity to dance with me, a tragedy of unspeakable proportions."

They both laughed at that. Pretending to be quite arrogant in matters regarding their romantic appeal had been a favorite jest between them since their days at Cambridge. Truth be told, William didn't imagine Leonard felt any less out of his element among the fairer sex than William did. It wasn't that either of them feared the ladies or were entirely inept at social interaction, they simply knew themselves to be lacking in that certain swagger and confidence that the Corinthian set possessed in spades.

They passed a group of nursemaids looking over their rambunctious young charges. The maids curtsied. William and Leonard dipped their heads. The children took no notice. Turning a corner on the path brought the men to a long, straight stretch without a soul in sight—a rare thing in London.

"Then allow me to invite you to my vast country estate for a bit of isolated grumpiness," Leonard said.

William eyed him narrowly. "You don't have a country estate."

"Ah, well, then I suppose you will have to invite me to yours."

The thrum of William's pulse immediately pounded in his temples. The vague light-headedness that always accompanied the mention of home washed over him once more.

"Apologies, Will." Leonard was entirely in earnest once more. "I was trying to be humorous. I didn't even think before I said it."

William tried to wave it off but knew he likely didn't succeed in appearing casual.

"Do you think— Do you think you'll ever go back?" Leonard posed the question hesitantly but with genuine curiosity.

"I'll have to eventually, I suppose." He whacked at a nearby bush with the end of his walking stick, setting off a tiny cascade of green leaves. "Unless, of course, I find myself a wife who prefers to be a vagabond."

"We could take out an advertisement in the *Times*, see if any fish take that particular bait."

The quip restored some of William's good humor. "'Wanted: one wife with no desire for a home of her own nor a permanent residence. Must enjoy never knowing from one month to the next where she will lay her head. A severe dislike of Sussex would be to advantage. Inquire anywhere except Carlisle Manor.'"

"Bang on the mark," Leonard declared.

They'd nearly completed their walk around the park. It was not so invigorating as usual. Nothing seemed to be lately.

"William!"

The sound of his name called out in a lady's voice stopped him, Leonard as well. Both took to searching about.

"William!"

Nearer this time. And then he spotted the source.

A young lady, her dark hair peeking out from beneath her poke bonnet, waved at him whilst the older lady at her side tugged desperately at her arm. A few of his school chums,

Leonard included, called him William, but no one else did nor had since he was very young.

He moved toward the mysterious lady, curiosity tugging him ever faster.

"Someone you know, I assume," Leonard said, keeping pace with him.

"I assume the same, though I don't know—" And suddenly he was close enough to see her clearly. "Felicity."

That brought Leonard's widened eyes to him once more. "You are acquainted on a Christian-name basis, after all."

William shook his head. "We grew up in the same neighborhood. I haven't seen her in years. We used given names between us when we were small."

"You are using given names *now.*"

William needed to take greater care. Such liberties were not permitted among unwed ladies and gentlemen.

"Mrs. Banbury," he said with an appropriate bow. "Miss Felicity." The formal address stuck a moment in his mouth. She'd been no more than thirteen when he'd last seen her, and far younger than that when he'd left for Eton. "May I make known to you Leonard Whitehall. Leonard, this is Mrs. Banbury and Miss Felicity Banbury."

All the required bows and curtsies were exchanged.

"We are well met," Felicity said, smiling as broadly as he remembered her doing as a little girl. "We've not seen you this age, Mr. Carlisle."

"It has been a while since I was"—he couldn't force out the word *home,* so he opted for a different ending—"in Lindsworth. What brings you to London?" He addressed the question to *Mrs.* Banbury, as was proper.

"The girls are older now, and we thought it wise to make certain they are known to Society and acquainted with Town and the whirl."

That made perfect sense. He did not, however, see the older Banbury sister. "Has Miss Banbury come to Town as well, then?"

"Of course," Mrs. Banbury said. "The younger sister cannot be out if the older sister is not."

"Has she made her bows, then?" Based on age, Angelina ought to have had her first Season a year or two ago, but he hadn't seen the family in London before.

Quite to William's surprise, Mrs. Banbury grew visibly panicked. Over so innocuous a question?

Felicity answered on her mother's behalf. "Angelina's health is poor, I am afraid. We have not come to Town for a *formal* Season."

"Her condition is nothing too serious, I hope."

Though the ladies smiled, the strain in their eyes told a different story. His memory of the older Banbury sister was that of a quieter, more fragile version of the younger. They'd ever been two very devoted peas in a pod.

He indicated the ladies ought to continue down the park path. He kept to Felicity's side. Reliable friend that he was, Leonard walked at Mrs. Banbury's side, making quiet conversation.

"How ill is Angelina?" William asked Felicity in a quiet voice. "Your mother seemed intent on downplaying the situation, but I suspect it is of greater concern than she let on."

Some of Felicity's characteristic optimism faded. "She is quite ill, I am afraid."

"Is she to see a doctor while she is here?" It was one of many things he wished his parents had done when they'd grown unexpectedly and seriously ill.

"She has been seen by six doctors already, and they are all in agreement about the direness of her situation." Felicity took a slow breath, the sound and gesture filled with both worry and determination. "Angelina longed for a Season. She hasn't

189

the strength for a true one, but I mean to see to it that she is able to do as many of the things she dreams of as possible."

There was a bleakness to the explanation that worried him. Though he'd not been home in years nor interacted with the Banbury sisters in all that time, he still cared for them. His heart dropped thinking of Angelina so ill and Felicity, no doubt, weighed down by worry.

"If I can be of any assistance, please tell me. I have a great deal of experience with the Season. I might be able to help you make arrangements for whatever Angelina wishes to do or help you gauge how taxing it might be."

Felicity smiled up at him. "Thank you. I want to make this special for her, but I know so little of the social whirl."

Her smile warmed him. He'd nearly forgotten what a sweet friend she'd been when they were young. He'd missed those connections in the years he'd been away. Few of the things he associated with home this past half decade weren't painful. Yet seeing Felicity again proved entirely pleasant.

After they parted ways with the Banbury ladies, Leonard wasted not a moment before peppering William with questions. "Why have you never mentioned these particular neighbors? Do you mean to see them again during their time in Town? Do you suppose they will join us in our nefarious plans to offend all the unforgiving dragons of Society?"

William nodded firmly. "If Miss Felicity is unchanged from the time I knew her, she would join in a heartbeat. Her older sister would likely struggle to say an unkind thing about anyone but would find tremendous humor in watching her sister be ridiculous."

"You are fond of these sisters."

"I am. It is good to see them again." He found himself eager about the coming few weeks, something he would not have thought possible a few hours ago.

He had this tiny connection to the home that felt so distant—a safe and comforting connection, one that didn't require him to face more ghosts than he was ready to stare down. He was grateful for it.

Chapter Three

THE FATES WERE SMILING on Felicity two days later when she accompanied Angelina to Gunter's. A table sat empty near the shop windows, affording them a view of Berkeley Square and the various pedestrians passing by. They were comfortable, entertained, and experiencing the famous tea and ices shop at its best.

Angelina had not stopped smiling since their arrival. Mother looked utterly terrified, as she had from the moment the traveling coach had dropped them in London. Felicity was able to worry less about her mother's displeasure because she took such delight in Angelina's happiness.

"This is just as lovely as I'd hoped," her sister whispered, eyeing their spread of victuals with excitement. "And to see everyone passing by and the park in the distance . . . I feel almost as though I am having a ride through Hyde Park as well."

A ride in Hyde Park. Felicity made a mental note. She already knew her sister longed for that very traditional part of the Season, but to hear her mention it again reinforced the need to make that arrangement soon.

"William Carlisle is in Town," Felicity told her sister. "He likely has a carriage. Perhaps he would take us for a ride during the fashionable hour."

"After your display," Mother said, "I have my doubts he will wish to be seen with any of us."

Angelina turned to Felicity with a look of alarm.

Felicity assumed her most unconcerned expression. "I was, perhaps, more familiar than I ought to have been when I first saw him. Old habits are difficult to shed, after all."

"And we haven't seen him very much since he first left for Eton," Angelina said. "It is sometimes difficult to remember how much older he is now—how much older we all are."

"*You* are nearly twenty years old," Felicity said. "Ancient, really."

"I can take some comfort in knowing I am unlikely to grow even more ancient." Angelina had the sometimes relieving, sometimes disconcerting tendency to jest about her illness and the expected outcome.

Mother always seemed to appreciate it. She would smile and squeeze Angelina's hand. Though Felicity wasn't entirely certain why, that response always surprised her. She would have assumed Mother would not have found the macabre humor to her liking.

"Some of us simply choose not to acknowledge the passing of the years," Mother said. "In case you are unsure, I would far prefer you avoid growing ancient by refusing to count beyond nineteen."

"I would prefer that as well," Angelina said.

"As would I," Felicity added with emphasis. "And I would also prefer if *I* were permitted to eat all six of these petits fours and not share a single one with either of you."

She reached for the tiny confections.

"I have seen woodcuttings of pugilist bouts," Angelina said. "I feel I am quite capable of fighting you over this."

"At your advanced age?" Felicity asked doubtfully.

Amid their quiet laughter, a shadow fell over the table. All three looked up at the same time.

"William." Felicity didn't catch herself quickly enough to prevent the slip in propriety. "Mr. Carlisle," she corrected too late.

Mother, predictably, looked utterly mortified.

"Ladies." William dipped his head, then turned his full attention to Angelina. "Miss Banbury. I was so delighted when your sister told me you had come to Town as well. It is, indeed, a pleasure to see you again."

"And I you. Lindsworth has been lonelier without you these past years."

His eyes dropped, and his mouth pulled, not in anger or frustration, but in what looked like sadness. "I have missed Lindsworth. We had a great many happy days there, didn't we?"

Angelina's smile was tender. "We did, indeed."

"Do join us," Mother said, indicating the empty chair at their table.

"I believe I will." He sat with every indication of pleasure.

"I should warn you," Felicity said. "Angelina has threatened us bodily if we take more than our share of the petits fours. If you prefer your bones unbroken, I suggest you not set your heart upon overindulging."

With a silent laugh, he looked at Angelina once more. "You wouldn't pummel me over a dessert, would you?"

"I most certainly would." She lifted her fists in an impression of a pugilist, though the picture was rendered less than threatening by the weakness apparent in the shaking of her arms.

"I shall have my obituary sent to the *Times* forthwith, though I intend to leave out any information about the cause of death. One mustn't go to one's grave having been brought to that state over pastries. How humiliating."

Felicity had all but forgotten how humorous William could be. The three of them had spent a good amount of their childhood laughing together at each other's ridiculousness.

He would make a very welcome addition to the miniature Season Felicity was attempting to provide for her sister.

They spent a pleasant quarter hour speaking both of childhood memories and the diversions of London. William was quick to redirect the conversation at any suggestion of his taking up residence at Carlisle Manor. Did he prefer London so very much?

"Which of London's amusements have you indulged in thus far?" he asked them after yet another diverting of the topic.

"We walked in the garden square a few times," Mother said.

That was hardly a pleasure unique to Town.

Felicity took up the topic. "We visited a dressmaker and are each to have a new, fashionable gown made."

"Excellent," William said. "What else?"

"We are enjoying tea at Gunter's," Angelina added. "I have always wished to do precisely this."

"What else have you wished to do?" His gentle tone told Felicity he had not forgotten the state of Angelina's health.

"Several things," Angelina said. "We thought perhaps to go to Hyde Park and join the crush there, but I haven't enough stamina left today for anything else."

William looked at Mother. "Would you object if, on some future day when Miss Banbury is feeling well enough, I offered to fetch your daughters in my carriage for a ride in the park during the fashionable hour?"

Mother's brow pulled. "Felicity is not out. We would not wish to give the impression that she was."

He nodded. "I appreciate your care for propriety. I assure you, her being in the carriage for a ride, along with her sister, will not give the impression you fear."

Relief touched Mother's eyes. "We do not wish anyone to think we are scandalous or worthy of being cut."

"If it would set your mind at ease, I can use the carriage that seats four and you can come as well."

Mother shook her head. "I do not believe that will be necessary. Both girls together in an open carriage will not be seen as inappropriate. If you feel no one will assume we have permitted a younger sister to be out before the elder is married, then that eases my concerns."

"You need only have your father send word when you are feeling equal to a drive," William told Angelina. "I am entirely at your disposal."

"Thank you," she said. "It will truly be a dream come true."

He shook his head. "You might change your assessment after you experience my stodgy driving. I am not one of those Corinthians who drives neck or nothing."

"My only requirement is that you not overturn us," Angelina said.

"That I can promise you."

Mother monopolized Angelina's attention after that, discussing the appropriate clothing choice for a drive in the park, whom she might see, and how to appropriately address those she might speak with.

Felicity leaned toward William. With her voice lowered, she said, "Thank you for your generous offer. Riding in the park with Father would have pleased Angelina, but riding alongside a dashing young gentleman will certainly be closer to what she had envisioned before . . . before this illness."

"She is more hale and hearty than I'd expected based on what you said before."

Felicity sighed. "She hides it well, but look at her eyes. You can see the illness there."

"It is certain, then, that she will not recover?"

"Quite."

True regret touched his face. She had known William as a convivial boy. She was pleased to be meeting the compassionate gentleman he had become.

"Thank you, also, for inviting me to join your drive. I so wish to be part of Angelina's time in London."

"Of course," he said. "And I meant what I said when last we met: if there is anything else I might do to assist your efforts at bringing your sister a bit of joy, do tell me. I wish to help."

"She mentioned last evening that she wished to attend a ball. I cannot imagine she would have the energy for a true crush, and I do not think she could actually participate in the dancing, but I would love for her to go to one. Can you think of any balls that might not exhaust her, ones that we might manage to secure an invitation to?"

He didn't immediately respond. His mouth pulled to one side. His eyes narrowed though he didn't appear to be looking at anything in particular.

"If any come to mind, do let me know. I am too unacquainted with London Society to have the first idea."

"There is one at the end of the week that fits your description," he said. "I know the host relatively well. I believe if I ask, they will be quite happy to include your sister and parents."

She nodded despite her disappointment. How she wanted to be there for Angelina's longed-for ball, but she understood. She was not yet out socially. To attend a ball would be an impermissible flouting of Society's rules and expectations. Mother would never allow it. And Felicity didn't wish to cause difficulties for her sister during so delicate and important an undertaking.

Chapter Four

MR. BANBURY CHOSE NOT to attend the Crawfords' ball. When William secured the family an invitation, he hadn't planned on accompanying Mrs. Banbury and Angelina personally, but he could not shake from his heavy mind the illness that had been apparent in his dear friend's eyes nor the heartbreak he'd seen in Felicity's face. This ball would be a quieter one, perfect for Angelina's limited endurance. He could not deny her the opportunity to fulfill such a simple wish.

"This is lovely." Angelina hadn't stopped smiling since their arrival some thirty minutes earlier. She certainly had not perfected, nor seemed the tiniest bit interested in, Society's preferred appearance of boredom at such events. "Thank you again, William, for bringing us."

As only they were privy to this comment, even her mother being occupied with a conversation elsewhere, he felt no need to correct her informal address.

"It is my very real pleasure, Angelina. I only wish Felicity could have come as well." He meant it sincerely. "Not only would she enjoy the ball, I believe she would prove quite entertaining. I am, of course, assuming she hasn't changed too drastically since we were children."

Angelina laughed lightly. "She no longer climbs trees but otherwise is not fundamentally changed. She has more energy than anyone I have ever known. She dearly loves to laugh, is never intimidated by a challenge, and is the most loyal of friends."

That was, indeed, the Felicity he remembered. "It must be difficult for her to be left behind while you participate in the whirl."

A look of pondering crossed her features. "I suspect it is more frustrating than she lets on. But I also believe she is genuinely pleased I am having these little adventures. Mother and Father wouldn't agree to any of it unless she vowed not to make the slightest foray into Society."

"And she agreed to that?" He wasn't surprised at her willingness, simply at the requirement. While, generally, a younger sister didn't come out before the elder, some exceptions were made. Angelina's circumstances would certainly warrant it.

"You know how she is," Angelina said.

"I know how she *was*," he answered. "Forever wanting to be in charge. Shockingly funny."

Angelina smiled. "She is still quite funny. And assertive when she needs to be."

"You do not still find her overbearing?"

"That is difficult to say. I can take charge of so little anymore. Mother is unaware of so much. Father keeps himself distant. I don't know how much of Felicity's dictatorial tendencies is a matter of character and how much is a matter of necessity."

The musicians struck the opening notes of a country dance. Angelina had not danced since their arrival. No one had asked, though he wasn't certain that was the reason.

"Would you like to stand up with me?" he asked.

"I would very much like to," she said, "but I know my lack of endurance too well to believe for even a moment that I could."

He had feared that was the case. "Do you feel equal to a turn about the room?"

"In all honesty, I am not certain I am equal to anything other than remaining seated right here where I am." Her shoulders drooped. "Indeed, I would be very much surprised if I am able to postpone my departure for home much longer."

You can see it in her eyes. Felicity's words repeated in his mind. He could indeed see there what Angelina kept so well hidden: exhaustion.

"My dear friend," he said gently, "do not feel you must remain on my behalf, neither do I think your mother would begrudge you an early departure."

She laced her fingers, resting them on her lap. Hers was a posture of calm serenity, but once more, her eyes revealed her. Disappointment and frustration had joined the weariness there. "I am finally attending a ball—something I've dreamed of for ages—and I haven't the energy to dance or remain for supper. I am trying very hard not to feel defeated."

"Consider it from this perspective: against the odds stacked so high against you, you have come to a ball and participated in the social whirl. Perhaps your time at this ball was shorter than you'd like and you did not do as much as you wished, but you came. That is not defeat, Angelina. That is triumph."

She closed her eyes as she took a deep breath, then another. "If Felicity asks, will you tell her that the evening was lovely and I was pleased the entire time?"

"She worries about you." He had seen the truth of that for himself.

"She wants to make everything perfect for me while she can." Angelina opened her eyes once more and met his gaze. "And I want her to have the comfort of believing she has."

"You have my word, as your one-time honorary brother, she will hear nothing but positives from me."

Angelina reached over and squeezed his hand. "You

always were a welcome coconspirator. I am pleased to know that hasn't changed."

"We did land ourselves in the suds more often than not, didn't we?"

"We did, indeed." She sighed, her hands interwoven once more. "We've missed you at home, William. I do wish you would come back."

He was grateful to be reunited with his childhood playmates, but he was not the least ready to return to his parents' home and the painful loneliness of being there without them. "Do let me know when you are ready to depart the ball. I will happily summon the carriage."

A sad sort of smile tugged at the corners of her mouth. "I believe I am ready now, more's the pity. I can feel myself wilting by the moment."

William sought out Mrs. Banbury, sending her to fetch her daughter while he sent word to the stables to send his carriage around. In less than a half hour, they were at the door of the Banburys' rented London house. Angelina leaned heavily against him, her strength quickly disappearing. Mrs. Banbury looked on with an unsurprised sadness.

Felicity appeared on the landing above. "You are home sooner than expected. Is something amiss?" she asked as she hurried down the stairs.

"I am only a little tired." Angelina somehow managed to sound less exhausted than William knew her to be.

Felicity reached her sister's side. "Was it a nice ball?"

"Lovely," Angelina said. "It was just what I always imagined a *ton* ball to be."

Felicity embraced her. "I am so happy for you. Next, we'll take that ride through Hyde Park, and I'm certain William will help us find a musical evening and a theater to attend that you will enjoy as well."

"Of course I will," he assured them.

Mrs. Banbury slipped her arm around Angelina. "Time to rest, dear. You have had a tiring night."

Angelina was led away, she and her mother moving slowly up the stairs. Felicity remained behind, watching their ascent.

"She looks worse tonight than usual." Felicity rubbed at her face. "I hope it is simply the exertion."

"She was in very good spirits throughout the ball. I believe she is only tired."

Felicity turned away from the stairs, pacing in the entryway. "She still has so much on her list of wishes. How are we to fulfill them all if she grows tired so quickly?"

"I believe you would do best to let her decide what she does and when."

She waved that advice off. "I want only to make these things *possible*. She can actually do whichever she decides upon."

"Unless she feels so much pressure to follow through with your plans that she takes on more than she ought."

That brought Felicity's gaze back to him once more. "I have placed no pressure on her."

She likely didn't realize how much Angelina wanted Felicity to feel she was being helpful and thoughtful. The two sisters were participating in a self-turning wheel of over-whelming expectations. Angelina had asked him not to say anything that would dampen Felicity's spirits where she was concerned, and he meant to keep his word.

He was enjoying spending time with the Banburys and reclaiming this bit of his past. But the deeper he involved himself in their lives, the closer it would pull him to home. Angelina had already suggested more than once that he ought to return, and that suggestion had, for one terrifying moment, proved tempting for the first time in five years.

No. He needed to keep his distance.

"Do let me know when Angelina is ready to take her ride in the park." He had made that promise already and didn't intend to break it. "I am at your disposal."

Felicity did not prove ready to leave their discussion on that note. "I need help finding her a musical evening, as I said, and we haven't a box at the opera or theatre or know anyone who does. And she has spoken more than once of wishing to attend Almack's. That last wish I have absolutely no ability to make happen. None." Franticness touched her tone and posture. "What am I to do? Mother might manage to cultivate connections sufficient to secure vouchers, but that could take years. Angelina doesn't have years. She has six wishes for this Season. Only six. I've managed two—three with your offer of driving through Hyde Park. How am I to make these last three come true?"

He was being pulled in again. How could he help it? She loved her sister. Her sister loved her. Theirs was not to be the typical tale of two sisters growing old together, being aunts to each other's children. And they were his childhood friends. He'd missed them and cared about them, and they needed his help.

Ah, lud. He couldn't turn his back on them.

"I will do what I can," he said with a quick bow. "A good evening to you, Felicity."

He would help, but he would guard his increasingly fragile wall. Home was not a happy place for him; he couldn't afford to be pulled back into that emotional purgatory. What, then, was he to do?

Chapter Five

"YOU LOOK SIMPLY HEAVENLY," Mother said, looking over Angelina with maternal regard.

"Not yet," Angelina said with a wink in Felicity's direction.

Mother shook her head, nudging them both toward the door of the bedchamber the sisters shared. "Mr. Carlisle will be here soon."

"He has been so very kind," Angelina said. "We could not have done so many things as we have without his assistance: the ball, the musical evening he has recommended next week, this ride in the park."

"He always was a sweet boy," Mother said. "It is a shame he has stayed away from home since his parents passed on."

Felicity hadn't thought of it in quite that way. He had been gone often since leaving for school, but now that Mother had pointed it out, the last five years became clearer. William hadn't been back since the late Mr. and Mrs. Carlisle had died. Not even once.

Poor William.

He arrived within mere moments of them reaching the entryway. Angelina would not be required to expend her energy standing about waiting for him. William was wonderfully felicitous, offering Angelina his arm and walking with her on one side, Felicity on the other, out to his waiting high-sprung carriage.

He handed Felicity up first. "If you will slide to the end

of the bench, Angelina can place herself between us. That should provide her a shield from the wind and save her the added effort of moving to the far side."

They were quickly situated.

William set the carriage in motion. "I did warn you, did I not, that I drive like an octogenarian?"

"You did," Felicity answered, "and we are fully prepared to be both bored and unimpressed."

"That *is* my goal for the afternoon." He drove at a sedate pace but not so slowly that anyone would actually find it frustrating. "And would you care to be introduced to anyone in particular should we pass him or her?"

"I don't know about Angelina, but I would very much like to meet someone who is both boring and unimpressive."

"I believe we already have," Angelina quipped.

William laughed out loud. They had done so much of that when they were children. It was good to know it still happened so easily between them all. As Angelina's health continued to deteriorate, they would need more reasons for cheer.

The carriage reached Hyde Park, and their speed changed from calm to stationary.

"Heavens," Angelina said, breathless. "I've never seen so many carriages in one place."

William leaned closer to her and lowered his voice. "There is a reason it is called 'a crush,' my friend."

Angelina set her hand on his arm. "I cannot tell you how relieved I am that the term refers to the number of carriages, not the result of reckless driving."

He smiled back at her. "I am not only an unhurried driver; I'm also a careful one. The others here can crush each other all they wish. We will return home safely."

"But not truly *home*," Angelina answered quietly.

William instantly grew more tense, his posture more rigid. Just as he had at Gunter's, he quickly changed the topic of discussion. "I am hopeful that my friend Mr. Whitehall will be among the throng this afternoon. I would very much like to introduce him to you, Angelina. Felicity has met him on one occasion."

Felicity answered. "If you can assure me that Mr. Whitehall will tell us embarrassing stories about you, I will be quite pleased to see him again."

"He knows a great many," William acknowledged with a smile.

"Lest you've forgotten," she said, "so do I."

He glanced at her before returning his gaze to the very busy road once more. "What stories?"

"There was that time when we climbed the elm tree behind the vicarage, and you caught your trousers on a particularly thick limb and rendered yourself unable to descend without tremendous embarrassment."

Angelina grinned at the memory.

"I distinctly remember you laughing instead of helping," William said.

"It was funny."

"As was that time you took strawberries from the conservatory and hid them in your pinafore pockets."

Felicity couldn't hold back her amusement. "Is it my fault I forgot they were in my pocket? It was a busy day."

"Even busier after my father's dog bumped into you and crushed the berries, convincing everyone that he'd desperately wounded you."

"I thought your mother was going to swoon."

William shook his head, smiling in amusement. "Years passed before she could laugh about that. Father, on the other hand, was in a fit of hysterics within minutes."

Angelina leaned toward Felicity and whispered, "It is good to hear him speak of his parents."

"What are the two of you gossiping about?" he asked.

"You," Felicity said. "What else?"

"What else, indeed."

A gentleman on horseback rode up next to them. "Well met, William."

"I had hoped to cross paths with you," William said. "You have made Miss Felicity Banbury's acquaintance, but you have not yet met her sister, Miss Banbury."

He managed the appropriate dip of the head whilst maintaining full control of his mount. "A pleasure, Miss Banbury."

"Angelina, this is Mr. Leonard Whitehall. He and I have known one another since our days at Eton."

Angelina smiled and offered an expression of pleasure. "We were promised embarrassing stories about our mutual friend should we cross paths with you, Mr. Whitehall."

"Were you?" Mr. Whitehall turned his gaze on William. "You wish me to humiliate you in front of your friends?"

"*They* wish you to humiliate me." He leaned forward enough to look at Felicity seated on the other side of Angelina. "Is that not correct? A bit of humiliation heaped upon your friend would, no doubt, set you up for life."

"You will convince Mr. Whitehall that I am a horrid person."

"I could never manage that, as no one who is at all acquainted with you would ever believe you were anything other than delightful."

His kind words and warm smile sent the oddest shiver over her. Her heart leaped about in her throat. Very unexpected.

"I understand you attended the Crawfords' ball, Miss

Banbury," Mr. Whitehall said. "I am sorry not to have been there so we might have conversed."

"It was a lovely evening," Angelina said. "I am so pleased to have been invited."

"The Banburys will be attending the theater in my box the evening after next," William said. "You ought to join us."

"You should," Felicity said. "Then we needn't spend the night with only William for company."

She looked at William out of the corner of her eye. He was grinning just as she'd expected he would.

"Your sister told me you were as playful now as when we were children. I am discovering she is correct in that."

"Is this a pleasant discovery or a disappointing one?" Felicity asked.

"Relieving."

She hadn't expected that answer and didn't quite know what to make of it.

"I will not detain you any longer," Mr. Whitehall said. "Until the evening after next." He tugged at his hat brim, then rode off.

"I like him," Angelina said. "And it is lovely to meet a friend of yours from your years away."

"Don't tell me you missed me?" he asked, laughing.

Felicity had most certainly missed him—more than she'd realized before crossing his path in Town. As they continued their slow circuit of the park, she could not stop her mind from slipping back to the many days she'd stood at the end of the drive leading to Carlisle Manor after William had left for Eton or during his half-decade absence following his parents' passing. She'd longed for him, worried about him, wished he were there still.

Her excitement at seeing him in the little park near their rented Town house ought to have told her how much her heart still longed for him. Other friends from Lindsworth had left, some taking up residence at other family holdings, but she could not imagine being as pleased to see them as she had been at the unexpected sight of dear, kind William.

"I think Hyde Park might be a disappointment to our Angelina." William's voice cut into Felicity's thoughts, pulling her back to the present. "The poor dear is done in."

Angelina's posture was slumped. Her eyelids had grown heavy.

"She hasn't the stamina she ought," Felicity said. "I only hope she'll be equal to the remainder of her wish list."

Angelina's head nodded as she attempted to keep herself awake. This happened more often lately. Felicity feared her sister's endurance was nearly gone. What if they had to return home before she could accomplish all six of her wishes for the Season?

"We had best cut our time in the park short," Felicity said. "She should rest."

William expertly moved around the crowds and stopped carriages until he reached a road branching off the main one. They were soon free of the crush of carriages. Angelina had slumped entirely, leaning against William's shoulder, quite asleep.

"I worry about her," Felicity said.

"I am beginning to as well. She is breaking my heart."

Those words returned to her long after Angelina was home and sleeping soundly in her bed. Angelina was breaking William's heart. He had shown her great kindness and was clearly fond of her. He had always been something of a brother figure to them. His absence from home since his parents' passing spoke of continued mourning. He couldn't cope with loss and grief. Felicity's inclusion of him in Angelina's final Season would simply bring him more pain.

Chapter Six

"THOSE BANBURY SISTERS ARE rather stunning," Leonard said two evenings later at the theater as they awaited the arrival of the Banbury family.

"They were darling as little girls." How well William remembered. "I confess, until seeing them here in Town, I generally thought of them as they were all those years ago. It has been a little jarring coming face-to-face with them so grown."

"The elder Miss Banbury appeared quite content seated beside you in Hyde Park the other day." Leonard wiggled his brows. "A fellow could grow accustomed to that, I'd imagine."

"I think you mean *a lady* could grow accustomed to being cozily situated beside *me.*" Again, he assumed his feigned mien of arrogance.

"Have you considered hiring out your Hyde Park accompaniment services?" Leonard asked dryly.

"Should I amass overwhelming gambling debts, I will consider that as a solution to my financial woes." He pretended to ponder deeply. "Do you suppose Miss Banbury would be willing to serve as a reference?"

"I suspect she would, though that Miss Felicity is more likely to laughingly dissuade people. She seemed to rather enjoy needling you."

It was true. "Felicity and I are good friends. We have been all our lives."

"She wasn't as sweet toward you as her sister, though.

Either the two are very different people or they have very different views of you."

He hadn't really thought of that before. The sisters weren't actually so very different. Both had clever senses of humor; both liked to tease and jest. Angelina's poor health had rendered her quieter and more subdued than her sister, but not fundamentally different. Was Leonard correct, then? Did Felicity think poorly of him? The possibility struck him with greater force and disappointment than he'd expected. Hers was a friendly teasing, a fondness. Wasn't it?

He hadn't time for answering that unexpected question. The Banburys arrived. Even Mr. Banbury had joined them that evening—something he'd not yet done. All the expected bows and curtsies were exchanged.

"I have so missed the theater." Mrs. Banbury pressed a gloved hand to her heart as her eyes cast about the expanse of the house. "What a treat."

An idea formed on the instant in his mind, and he seized it. "Why do not you and Mr. Banbury and Miss Banbury sit at the front of the box," he suggested. "Your view will be so much better."

"Oh, how generous of you." Mrs. Banbury then turned to her husband, eyes wide. "What an evening this will be for us and Angelina." She dropped her voice. "Were we wrong to bring Felicity, do you suppose? We will not be judged poorly for a young lady not out coming to the theater?"

"No, dear," Mr. Banbury assured her. "Families attend the theater and opera quite regularly, even the daughters who've not yet made their bows."

She looked at William, clearly still worried.

"I concur with your husband, ma'am."

"As do I," Leonard added. "You needn't fear being judged poorly."

That set her mind at ease. She slipped her hand through her husband's arm and, with a hand at Angelina's back to guide her forward, moved to the front of the box.

William turned to look at Felicity, fully expecting her usual laughing smile or at least a look of relief at seeing her sister and parents happily situated. Her expression, however, was filled with heartache. An answering pang sounded in his heart.

"Felicity?" He spoke in little more than a whisper as he stepped to her. "What is the matter?"

She took a shaky breath. "She is so ill, William. She grows worse every day."

Angelina had seemed paler. She also hadn't spoken since arriving.

"I am afraid for her," Felicity added in a pained whisper. "I do not know how much more she can endure, but we've not finished her list. How can she bear to return home with wishes left unrealized?"

There was something more in her voice than disappointment on her sister's behalf, though William couldn't put a name to it. He knew only that his heart went out to her.

He took her hand in his, gently, kindly. "I am so very sorry for all you and your family are enduring. I do wish there was more I could do."

"You have helped so very much, William. What would we have done without you? We would not have managed hardly any of her wishes."

Had he offered nothing more than that? A resource to accomplish their list of undertakings? A one-time chum to tease?

He, Felicity, and Leonard sat in the second row of seats as the performance began below. William struggled to focus. His thoughts spun over Felicity and Angelina and the contradictory things he thought and felt. He had, at first, happily agreed to help the sisters tick items off their list, finding it a welcome diversion from the boredom of yet another Season in Town, but that didn't ring true any longer.

Not ten minutes into the program, he heard the tiniest, almost imperceptible sound of trembling breaths. He required only a moment to realize the sound, that of quiet crying, came from beside him.

He reached over and wrapped his hand around Felicity's. She held fast to him. Her breathing did not grow calmer. Though she was neither sobbing nor wracked with emotion, her continued upheaval was apparent to him at such close distance. He dared not say anything, suspecting she worked very hard to hide her struggles from her parents and sisters. All he could think to do was raise her hand to his lips and press a quiet, gentle kiss there, before joining his other hand to his first, enveloping her hand in both of his.

As the performance continued on the stage below and the other Banburys were distracted, William sat holding Felicity's hand. He hoped he was offering her comfort. He hoped she didn't pull her hand away, as he was finding in the simple touch a reassurance he didn't even know he'd been longing for.

Felicity shifted to the side of her chair nearest him and rested her arm against his. He tipped his head enough to nearly rest it against the top of hers.

"I am so sorry," he whispered.

They sat that way as the first act continued on. William hadn't the first idea what occurred below. His every thought was for his dear friend, of her sister and her struggling family, of the almost-forgotten feeling of home he experienced with Felicity nearby.

The curtain fell, marking a brief intermission. Felicity sat up straight on the instant and, though he thought he sensed reluctance, slipped her hand free. Angelina turned back, looking at her sister over her shoulder.

William took a sharp breath when he saw Angelina's face. She looked beyond exhausted. She looked more than ill; she looked nearly desperate.

"You must get her home," he said to Felicity.

In a flurry of activity, the family gathered their wraps and overcoats and made a mad rush from the box. Felicity looked back at William in the moment before stepping out. A single tear dropped from her eye.

"I fear it is growing all too apparent what that family is shortly facing," Leonard said.

"I ache for them."

"And for yourself?" Leonard pressed. "You care about them. Losing Miss Banbury will be painful for you as well."

"I fear home will only ever be a place of mourning," he said. How could he ever return there, knowing even more grief awaited him? Yet how could he sever the growing connection he felt to Felicity? Without her, he feared his grief would forever be attached to this heavy, heartrending loneliness.

Chapter Seven

William,

Forgive my impertinence in writing to you, but I desperately need to speak with you. I would not ask if the situation were not dire. I will be taking turn after turn this morning in the little park where I first saw you weeks ago, hoping you can meet me there. Please come and speak with me. I need your help.

— FB

WILLIAM DRESSED QUICKLY AND rushed directly to the peaceful little green. She was not making the endless circuits she'd said she would be but sat on a bench, back bent, head in her hands.

He sat beside her. She'd struggled with her composure at the theater the evening before. He'd assumed upon spotting her in a posture of such dejection that he would find her in the same state of emotional upheaval, but when she looked up at him, it was not tears he saw, but the dark circles of one who'd not slept.

"Angelina?" he guessed.

"She is very ill. We do not know of a reliable physician here in Town who might look in on her and help us decide what is best to be done. You have been here every Season for years. Might you recommend one?"

Though the request was phrased quite calmly and logically, she did not entirely hide her fear.

The park was empty. He felt safe in reaching out to her a moment. He wove his fingers around hers. "I do know an excellent man of medicine and will gladly send him to look in on your sister."

"Thank you." She breathed the words out in a whoosh of incomplete relief.

He kept her hand in his. "What else can I do?"

"I haven't the first idea. At the moment, we are focused on discovering if we would do best to take her home directly or remain here and hope she can regain her strength." Her grip on his hand tightened. "I hadn't thought she would worsen so quickly."

He swallowed against the lump that formed at the all-too-familiar words. His father had said precisely that in the hours before his mother had passed away, to be followed by him mere days later. The quick descent into illness and sudden anticipation of loss dredged up a great many heavy memories.

His mind screamed at him not to put himself through another experience like the one he'd endured a half decade earlier. A servant could be sent to fetch the doctor. Word could be sent in a day or two to see how Angelina was faring. He could keep his distance.

He would do well to do precisely that. Yet he remained as the minutes ticked on, unwilling to abandon her.

"I should probably return home. I do wish to be with Angelina, but . . ." She sighed.

"You are worn thin. A moment's respite is more than justified."

She smiled tremulously up at him. "You are very kind."

"I have been where you are," he said quietly.

"With your parents?" Redness rimmed her eyes, and she took a shaky breath.

"Perhaps Angelina's outcome will be different from theirs." He offered the reassurance, though he doubted she truly believed the empty hope he offered her.

"How have you endured it?" she asked.

"Not very well, I'm afraid. I haven't been home in years."

Felicity's brow pulled low. "Because of them?"

"Because they are everywhere at Carlisle Manor, everywhere in Lindsworth. Being there without them is agonizing." He'd never told anyone that.

"I wish you would come back."

That set him on his feet once more. "You are asking more than you realize. I cannot endure it. I can't."

She stood as well, calmer than she'd been since he'd found her on the bench. "I've missed you these past years, but I understand. I'll not press you to return." Her shoulders set, and she assumed once more the resolute posture he'd come to recognize as hers. "Thank you for sending us your recommended physician, and thank you for your kindnesses these past weeks. You have given us, Angelina especially, a tremendous gift."

"You are speaking as if I won't be seeing you again." The idea left him as uneasy as the suggestion of returning home.

"I do not imagine we will be in London much longer, and you are never home." Her smile was sad but not accusatory.

"I cannot," he repeated.

"I know." She reached out and set a kind, tender hand on his face. "Think of us now and then. And please take care of yourself, William."

Before he could tell her that he worried more over whether or not *she* was taking care of herself, that he thought of her more and more often of late, she slipped away. He watched her go, his heart aching at the sight of her leaving him behind.

What could he do? He knew avoiding home was not logical or likely healthy, but was grief ever rational?

Dr. Benton called on William that night. His heavy expression told William all he needed to know, but he asked for details anyway.

"I've advised the family to return to their country home. Miss Banbury needs rest more than anything else."

"Will resting improve the state of her health?"

"For a time."

That was not very reassuring. "Then you concur with the evaluation of the other physicians with whom they have consulted."

Benton nodded. "It is a wasting illness. Her coloring is poor, her energy fearfully low. She bruises far too easily, and those bruises do not fade as quickly as they ought. Though we haven't a name for her condition, we do know what comes of it."

Poor Angelina. "Is there anything I might do for her or her family?"

"I have made suggestions for ways they might make Miss Banbury more comfortable: obtaining the services of a maid to look after her, repurposing a room on the ground floor to serve as her bedchamber so she needn't traverse the stairs in order to participate in family meals and such while she is able."

"Her time is short, then?" His parents' time had been so short, there'd been no opportunity for those arrangements and discussions. He wished he could have done more to make them comfortable and make their remaining time together less heavy and difficult.

"It is difficult to say just how short," Benton said, "but, yes. I would be very surprised if Miss Banbury lives to see the end of the year."

Emotion immediately clogged his throat. No matter that he hadn't been back home in five years and not often before that, he considered Angelina a dear friend, something of a sister. He cared about her and her family. He knew all too well the pain of losing a loved one.

"Thank you for calling on them," he said.

Dr. Benton stepped to the door. "I only wish there was more I could do."

"A sentiment I understand well."

Long after the doctor had left, William's mind fixated on that. What more could be done? Surely there must be something. He couldn't save Angelina from the fate that awaited her, but he wished he could at least offer comfort or ease some of the family's burdens. But which ones and how?

He was still sitting at his desk, mind spinning, when Leonard called.

"Yours appears to be a heavy mood."

William rose for the first time in an hour and paced toward the windows. "Dr. Benton has been to see Miss Banbury. His prognosis is a grim one."

"I am sorry to hear that." Leonard joined him at the window. "And the family?"

"They are being stalwart, no doubt. They will be returning to Sussex shortly."

Leonard didn't say anything further, but he watched William with a look of expectation. After a moment, William returned the expression with one meant to encourage his friend to speak his mind.

"Will you be returning as well? I have no doubt having you nearby will be a reassurance to them. You can offer assistance and pay calls so they need not feel so isolated. And it will set your mind at ease, being able to see for yourself how the family, and the young lady in particular, is faring."

William shook his head. "I know how Miss Banbury is likely to be faring. That will be heartbreaking to watch."

"She is not the young lady to whom I was referring."

There was no mistaking his friend's meaning. "I am deeply worried for Felicity. She and her sister are as close as twins. I suspect neither has a single memory that does not include the other. Losing Angelina will fracture her tender heart."

"And having you nearby will help her hold the pieces together."

William stepped away quickly. Leonard did not understand what he was asking. "I cannot go home."

"I think it is time you did—not merely for Miss Felicity's sake, but for your own. Those ghosts loom larger every year you're gone."

"I can't—"

"You *won't*." He held his hands up and forestalled the objection William was about to make. "I am not attempting to discount the enormity of stepping foot once more in your memory-filled home. I am only saying that I know you, and you are stronger than you think you are."

How he wished that were true.

"You could not bring yourself to make that pilgrimage for your own sake," Leonard said. "Make it for hers."

William rubbed at his sore and stiff neck. "I cannot walk through those doors alone. I know I can't."

Leonard sighed, the sound putting William firmly in mind of a person rolling his eyes. "So invite your best friend to go with you. I suspect he can work it into his schedule."

William looked back, hope warring with fear. "You would do that for me?"

"I helped you sneak out of that pub near Eton before the headmaster caught you, and you are questioning my loyalty?" Leonard's look of censure was ruined by the laughter lurking in his eyes.

William found he could smile. "We've had a few misadventures in our time, haven't we?"

"Let's have one more," Leonard suggested. "We'll hie ourselves to Sussex, face down a few lingering ghosts, call on a local family of whom we're very fond, perhaps scout out a pub of questionable reputation. I daresay we'll enjoy ourselves more than we would if we remained in Town."

Perhaps it *was* time. "This won't be easy."

"No. I suspect it won't." Still, Leonard didn't sound as though he were backing down.

"Felicity will need support—her parents as well. Angelina, I'm certain, will appreciate having someone call on her. Wasting illnesses are often compounded with loneliness."

"All true," Leonard said.

William released a tense breath. "You won't let me talk myself out of this?"

"I absolutely will not."

With that, William committed himself to making the soul-shattering journey he'd sworn never to make.

He was going home.

Chapter Eight

ANGELINA WAS SLEEPING, COMFORTABLY situated in the repurposed east sitting room. They'd been home for three days, and all the family and staff were exhausted. Their one consolation was that Angelina seemed to have already improved. Her coloring was better. Her energy had increased. London had been taking more of a toll than they'd realized.

If only Felicity could feel more at ease. Her sister was better, but she would never be whole. The coming weeks and months would be beyond difficult. Enduring it all meant, in the end, she would lose her dearest companion and very best friend. Her parents were grieving as well. She couldn't add her burdens to theirs, yet she didn't know how much longer she could carry this weight alone.

She put on her spencer, bonnet, and gloves and slipped from the house, needing some time away. Everything they'd done the last three days had been focused on preparing for Angelina's deterioration. Felicity's heart needed a respite, however temporary.

Tears threatened as she walked the familiar paths of their neighborhood. She'd wanted so badly to give Angelina the Season she'd wished for. She wanted to be strong and unwavering in the face of their coming struggles. She wished she could save Angelina from what was coming. She was failing on all three counts.

Her feet took her where they had so many times these past years: to the front drive of Carlisle Manor. How often she'd stood there, wishing William were home, willing him to step out and join her for a walk or a ride or simply talk with her. How deeply she had needed his friendship in the years he'd been away.

She leaned her shoulder against the tall brick column that made up one side of the arch under which carriages passed on their way up the drive to Carlisle Manor. The iron gates were closed, as they had been for five years. Through their foreboding bars, she could see the grand house, so dark and forlorn.

"Oh, William," she whispered. "I wish you would come home."

He'd been such a wonderful mixture of friend and older brother when they were children. She'd fully expected that to continue being the case while they were in London, but something had changed between them. Her heart had grown far more tender toward him, attached in a far less brotherly way. She could not, however, fully decide if his sentiments had changed.

If ever a lady was confused about a gentleman's regard, she was. Yet she would happily endure that emotional upheaval if only he would return.

"I miss you."

There was no answer, not even the quiet whisper of a breeze.

Felicity would permit herself only a moment more to wallow in self-pity. She sighed dramatically and allowed her shoulders to slump more than was ladylike. She did not, however, indulge in what would, no doubt, have been a very satisfying bit of foot stomping. She was lonely and confused and worn to a thread, but she was not a child.

With one final glance at the empty house, she turned and stepped away from the gated arch. Not two steps away, however, she stopped. Were her ears playing tricks on her or did she detect the sound of carriage wheels? This stretch of road led only to Carlisle Manor. Any carriage traversing the path had to be bound for that location.

She turned back. Her mouth dropped open in shock. A carriage was, indeed, coming directly toward the gate she had only just abandoned. She pressed her hand to her suddenly pounding heart. Dare she hope?

The carriage rocked and swayed as the driver reined in the horses. They stopped a close distance from the gate. It would, after all, have to be opened.

Felicity stood rooted to the spot, hardly breathing, hardly blinking.

The carriage door opened. A figure emerged. For a moment, she could not see who it was, her view obstructed by the large conveyance, but then he stepped around it, the sun shining on him at last. He looked at her, the light illuminating his look of soul-deep uncertainty.

Joy and excitement surged through her with such force she could not contain it. "William!" She ran to him, all thoughts of decorum gone in an instant.

Just as she had time and again when they were little, she threw her arms around his neck. He was much taller than she was. He set his arm around her waist as he stood straight once more, pulling her feet off the ground.

"And here I thought I would sneak home with no one the wiser for a time." He smiled as he spoke, alleviating any concern that she'd offended him with her overly familiar greeting.

"Oh, William. You're home at last."

"Almost." He lowered her back to her feet. His smile faded as he turned his gaze on the house. "I am beginning to suspect these last one hundred feet will be the most difficult."

She slipped her arm around his middle, just as she'd done when they were little. "We can walk those one hundred feet together."

"Would you?" His tone was both hopeful and pleased.

"Of course."

He turned back to face the carriage. Felicity glanced in that direction as well. For the first time, she realized that she and William had a most attentive audience. Through the windows of the carriage, Mr. Whitehall grinned quite unabashedly at their continued close quarters.

"How likely is your friend to whisper it about the neighborhood that I acted like a regular gudgeon when I saw you? My parents are particularly sensitive about propriety and the things people say about us behind their hands."

"Leonard is as dependable as the sunrise."

"But is he as good at shedding light on things?" she asked with a raise of her brow.

To her delight, he smiled again. Knowing how difficult returning home was for him, seeing any degree of pleasure on his features was reassuring.

"Let us go inside, William. I think it is time."

He pushed out a breath and took her hand in his. To Mr. Whitehall, he said, "Miss Felicity means to walk with me to the house. You are welcome to join us now or after the carriage sets you down."

"Go on," Mr. Whitehall said through the open carriage door. "Miss Felicity has a history with this house as well. I can think of no one better to take those first steps with you." He pulled the door shut.

The driver had opened the large iron gate and returned to his perch atop the carriage. William led Felicity through it, his hand still in hers. She hoped the connection was proving a comfort to him. The feel of his warm hand around hers set her

225

heart fluttering. She did her best to keep her expression light and free of the uncertainty she felt.

They moved slowly up the walk. The carriage passed through the gates but made for the stables, leaving William and Felicity alone on the path.

"How is your sister?" William asked.

"She is better now that we've returned home. London, I fear, was too taxing for her."

"And you worked so hard to make certain she experienced all the things she wished to."

Felicity set her free hand on his arm, her other hand still in his. "Perhaps I should not have. Her strength would not have been so quickly depleted."

He met her eyes. "It is my understanding that her strength would have grown depleted regardless. Without her exploits in Town, she might have remained in London longer, but she certainly would not have been happier."

"I think she did enjoy what she was able to do."

They continued onward, the house drawing nearer.

"I never was able to arrange for her to go to Almack's," Felicity said. "I do regret that. She mentioned her hope for that more than any other activity of the Season."

"I am sorry. I know I could have obtained vouchers from any of the patronesses if you'd remained in Town a bit longer."

She squeezed his hand. "You were very good to us, William. I cannot thank you enough."

"It was my absolute pleasure."

They'd reached the front steps of Carlisle Manor. William stopped, eyes fixed on the tall doors as they pulled open.

"You did warn the staff, did you not?" Felicity asked.

"I did. They are expecting me."

She slipped her hand from his. "Then perhaps it is best you go in without me. Mr. Whitehall's silence may be depended upon, but nothing remains a secret between the servants in neighboring homes."

A hint of panic touched his eyes. "Could you walk in with me if we do not do so hand in hand? They know we are friends and neighbors. If ours is a friendly interaction and nothing more, perhaps . . ." The sentence dangled in a peninsula of desperate hope.

How could she turn her back on him now? "I suppose it would not push the boundaries of propriety should I step inside briefly. I can offer my greetings to your housekeeper. Mr. Whitehall will join you shortly, so you needn't continue your return alone."

"Thank you."

The staff filed out of the door, fanning out in both directions. William dipped his head to them as he passed toward the door. Felicity walked slightly behind him, careful not to give the impression of anything more between them than friends who happened to have crossed paths.

The butler bowed, and the housekeeper curtsied.

"Mr. and Mrs. Johnson," William said, emotion in his tone. "Thank you for caring for the estate while I've been away."

"Our pleasure, sir," Mr. Johnson said.

"And a very real pleasure to have you home again," Mrs. Johnson added.

William stepped to the open door but didn't step inside. He looked back at Felicity.

"Go on," she said. "You've strength enough for this."

He squared his shoulders and crossed the threshold.

Mrs. Johnson turned briefly to Felicity. Her expression rang with gratitude. They understood the strength of the emotion that had kept William away. Felicity felt better about his situation in that moment. These two dear people would look after him and cherish him. He had Mr. Whitehall as well. William would soon feel at home again here.

As the staff followed their master inside, Felicity turned her steps back toward the iron gate and brick arch. She moved away from his home and toward her own. For so many years, she'd longed for her dear friend to return home. Now that he had, her emotions were decidedly mixed.

He needed to be home again for his own sake, and she was happy for him.

The demands on the time of the master of so grand an estate, however, meant she would likely have less of his company than she'd had in London, and she was a little sorry for herself on that score.

The moment of self-pity would only be permitted to last as long as it took for her to reach home. Angelina needed her, and she would not leave her sister without support.

Life asked a lot at times. She had to find the strength to answer.

Chapter Nine

"YOU HAVE AN IMPRESSIVE pile of stones here, William." Leonard sat on his horse, looking out over the expanse of the estate from their vantage point atop a low hill in the east meadow. They'd ridden out that morning—William's first after arriving in Sussex the afternoon before.

"I'd only ever thought of it as *home*," he admitted. "I hadn't expected to inherit it for decades yet. I suppose that kept me from seeing it as anything other than the place where my childhood memories reside."

"And where your childhood friends reside," Leonard added. "The neighborhood, at least."

"It was fortuitous that Felicity was at the gate when we arrived yesterday."

Leonard eyed him sidelong. "There is a difference between 'fortuitous' and 'a sign from heaven itself.' Don't confuse the two."

"You think Felicity's arrival yesterday was an act of divine intervention?" The laughter with which he asked the question slipped a little at the seriousness of Leonard's expression. "You're in earnest."

"The moment you spotted her, you changed. The worry that had been crushing you eased. No one has ever done that for you except Miss Felicity." Leonard set his mount to a walk.

William caught up to him. "She's my friend."

"So it would seem."

William knew that dry tone well. Leonard reverted to it

when he thought William was being particularly dense. "I will confess, seeing her at Carlisle Manor was as near to a miracle as I've ever experienced. She is one of the happiest memories I have of this place. Having her with me gave me something less heavy to think about."

"Her mind was most certainly heavy, though," Leonard said. "Her sister's health is not likely much improved."

"She spoke of Angelina, actually." He thought back on that conversation as they rode slowly toward the stables. "Their time in London was meant to have been a substitute Season for the elder Miss Banbury, but they weren't able to fulfill all six of her wishes for the Season. Though Angelina likely feels some regret over that, I think it weighs more pointedly on Felicity. Finishing that list matters a great deal to her."

"What remains on it?"

He took a minute to think back on what she'd told him in Town. "'Attend a musical evening' and 'attend Almack's.' We managed all the rest."

"A shame." Leonard had a good heart. His disappointment on the Banbury sisters' behalf was genuine.

"Her family could likely arrange for a musical evening in their home." William had given that some thought the night before. He hadn't been able to sleep. "It could be a small affair—only a handful of people and a very short list of performances."

Leonard nodded. "And Almack's?"

William pushed out a deep breath. "That one cannot be fulfilled. Angelina isn't strong enough to return to Town."

"And Almack's isn't mobile enough to come to Sussex."

They dismounted, handing the reins to a waiting stable hand. William didn't generally neglect to offer some greeting to the staff, but his mind was suddenly spinning so quickly that he couldn't manage much beyond a nod and a vague word of thanks.

Almack's can't come to Sussex. But what if . . .

He looked at his friend as they made their way back to the house. "How much do you remember about Almack's?"

"Judgmental patronesses. Barely edible food. Not nearly as much of a crush as it used to be."

William waved that off. "I mean, how much do you remember about the place itself? Colors and such?"

"I can't say I took a great deal of note of the decor," Leonard said. "Are you thinking of redecorating the old place?" He motioned to the manor house with a quick twitch of his head.

"Temporarily." He stopped their forward progress, a plan forming quickly and haphazardly in his mind. "If we can recall enough details of Almack's, we could recreate it here in the ballroom. We could invite a few local people, not so many that it would be overwhelming, but a few. And Angelina could come and have her night at Almack's." Would it work? It had to. What else could be done for her? "The evening would not be quite the same as actually spending an evening at Almack's, but surely it would be enough to offer her a bit of joy."

"And her sister a bit of relief."

Were he entirely honest, William would have to admit Felicity's feelings held the greatest sway for him. The worry and disappointment in her eyes the afternoon before had nearly erased his own concerns upon returning home. She bore too great a burden for one person. If he could relieve any part of that, he would. Gladly.

"Who do we know that is still in London and is in possession of vouchers?" he asked.

Leonard's gaze narrowed on him. "You mean to send spies into Almack's?"

William kept his chin at a self-assured angle. "Without hesitation."

Leonard held his hand out, clearly meaning to exchange a handshake. William obliged but made no effort to hide his confusion.

"It is a fine thing seeing you again, William Carlisle. It's been a long five years."

William sat at the small writing desk in his bedchamber, the room he had called his own from the time he'd outgrown the nursery. He was now master of the house and likely should have taken possession of his father's room. Doing so felt far too final, an inarguable acknowledgment that the man he'd idolized and loved and assumed would be present for so much more of his life was truly gone. It was hardly rational, but he couldn't step through that threshold and extinguish that reality-defying flame of hope.

His childhood bedchamber wasn't a significantly easier place to be. He'd enjoyed many a tender conversation with his mother within these walls. He could so easily picture her sitting on the window seat, motioning for him to join her there.

"You remember Felicity Banbury," he said to his absent mother. There was some comfort in speaking to her, though he knew she could not hear nor respond. "She is likely to lose her sister before year's end. I'm worried about her. I care about her."

He swore he could see her scolding and disbelieving expression.

"I am falling in love with her," he admitted. "I don't know that she thinks of me in terms other than friendship, but it is a close friendship. She has trusted me to help Angelina and has told me of her worries. She is the reason I have returned home."

He paced to the window seat where he had sat so many times before. Its emptiness prevented him from doing so now, though he did continue his one-sided conversation.

"Ought I to tell her that? Would I be ill-advised to admit what is in my heart when I know with such clarity how much is weighing on hers? I do not want to add to her burdens."

What he wouldn't have given to have heard his mother's voice in that moment, to have received her encouragement and advice.

"I intend to host a recreation of an evening at Almack's. Felicity wanted to take Angelina to the actual Almack's, but her sister's health failed before she was able." He pushed out a breath. "I have never hosted anything beyond an informal gathering of former schoolmates. To take on something this significant so soon after arriving home for the first time in a half decade . . ." He rubbed his hand over his forehead. "I don't want to make a mull of the whole thing, not when it means so much to her—to both of them."

He paced away, lowering himself into his desk chair once more, though he sat facing the window.

"You would have made it perfect; you always did." William blinked a few times, bringing himself under control once more. "Perhaps I might ask Felicity to help with the planning. That would likely ease some of her regrets over the sudden end to her London efforts. She would also do a fine job of it." A fleeting smile tugged at his mouth. "And I would have an excuse to spend time with her. I would like that bit."

He sat for long minutes, debating. Were he to involve Felicity, she would have an unobscured view of him being utterly inept, something he'd rather avoid. However, the evening would be far less likely to prove a failure if she helped in the execution of it.

In the end, what convinced him was the inarguable fact that having her in his house would make it feel like a home again. He needed that, and he felt certain she would not begrudge him that longing.

He would make his Almack's proposal to her the next day when he called at Banbury Hall and then pray with all his might that he didn't come to regret that decision.

Chapter Ten

FELICITY SAT OVER HER embroidery, though she'd not accomplished anything in the thirty minutes she'd been in the sitting room ostensibly toiling over her needlework. Too many questions hovered in her overburdened mind. Ought more to be done to make Angelina comfortable? How much longer would this improvement in her sister's health last? How was William holding up under the grief that had met him when he'd returned home? Was there more she might do to help these people she cared for so deeply?

Beneath those questions lay the undeniable loneliness she felt, the longing in her heart for a moment of William's time. How quickly he'd gone from childhood friend to the gentleman who had captured her affections. How could he not have? All she'd known of him as a boy—his good heart and fun personality—hadn't disappeared, but he'd added to those admirable qualities—compassion and kindness and, she suspected, a willingness to undertake a lark now and then. He was, in a word, lovely.

Who would have guessed I would go to London and lose my heart to the boy next door?

The housekeeper stepped through the threshold of the sitting room, drawing Felicity's attention there. "Mr. Carlisle to see you, miss."

William was here? Her heart leaped even as she shakily rose to her feet. "Show him in, please."

A mere moment passed—a moment in which she didn't

235

even breathe—and there he stood, that familiar smile greeting her. Was she managing to hide how surprisingly over-whelmed she felt? Perhaps fear of discovery was a common affliction in those who had only just realized their feelings for someone.

Mrs. Green slipped out but left the door open as was proper. A maid would likely arrive soon to provide an added layer of propriety.

"William." Felicity allowed herself the intimacy of so personal a greeting during this brief moment of privacy. "How are you faring? I know you anticipated your return home would be difficult for you."

"It has been," he admitted. "Some aspects have been easier than I'd expected; some have been harder."

"Do have a seat." She motioned to the cluster of chairs and sofa nearby.

They moved to the gathered furniture. She sat a mere breath before he did the same. And there they remained for a long period of awkward silence. She felt the discomfort of the moment acutely. Never before had conversation with her dear friend been anything but easy and natural. Love, it seemed, had the unnerving ability to empty one's mind and tie one's tongue.

"I am attempting to discover a means of introducing a topic without doing so too abruptly," William said, "but I find myself at a loss. Therefore, I will simply dive directly at the heart of my purpose here."

A topic he found difficult to introduce? An aching sort of hope rose in her chest. She, too, had a secret and withheld declaration. Could his topic be the same one she felt horribly reluctant to introduce? Could newly discovered feelings for her be tying his tongue?

"I want to host a ball."

Her heart dropped at those five words that would have, mere days earlier, been a source of delight. She'd let herself hope for a more personal confession. Still, it was not in her nature to be easily devastated.

"I think that is a wonderful idea," she answered, proud of the calmness in her voice. "Though that is a great deal to take on while your burdens are not precisely light. I don't imagine you have ever put on an event of such magnitude."

"I have never put on an event of any magnitude." That he could laugh at that admission told her clearly he was not truly overwhelmed at his undertaking. "That, my dear friend, is why I am here. I am hopeful I might find some assistance at Banbury House."

Warmth tiptoed over her at the tenderness in his tone. She would allow herself to believe that regard was for her in particular. "I am certain we will do all we can."

His posture visibly relaxed. "My vision for the ball is 'An Evening at Almack's.'"

"Almack's?"

He nodded. "I hope to recreate, to some degree, the look and feel and experience of that famous London landmark. It will not be an exact replica, of course, but I hope it will be near enough the real thing to be an acceptable substitute."

In an instant, she understood. "You are helping Angelina tick one more wish off her list."

A touch of sadness entered his eyes but did not erase his smile. "I am. Your parents can likely arrange some kind of musical evening with the local families. Between that and my Almack's offering, Angelina will have had the Season she'd hoped for."

Felicity reached across and took his hand in hers. "Thank you, William. I don't know what I would have done without you these last weeks."

His fingers wrapped more firmly around hers. "I know enough of your capability to believe you would have managed the thing."

"Managed, perhaps, but not enjoyed nearly as much."

Was that a hint of a blush she saw steal over his features? A good sign, it seemed to her. Whether or not he felt the same heart-tug she did, he was, at least, not entirely indifferent to her.

A maid slipped into the room. Felicity pulled her hand from William's and resumed her proper distance once more.

"I will convey your suggestion of a musicale to my mother. I believe she will enjoy planning it." No one listening could fault the propriety of Felicity's tone or words. "Do let us know what we can do to assist you in your endeavor."

"As this is meant to be a particular treat for your sister, I would appreciate knowing what aspect of Almack's in particular she would wish to experience, as well as how long of an evening she would be able to endure. I would very much wish for those things she longs for to occur at a point in the evening when she would be able to enjoy them."

Her William, always so thoughtful. "The earlier in the evening the better. Her energy lasts longer than it did those last few days in Town, but it is certainly not boundless."

William nodded. "And would she prefer we recreate the less-than-satisfactory food and beverage offerings Almack's is so famous for, or ought I to allow my cook to create something edible? In other words, which matters more: accuracy or palatability?"

The maid in the corner barely managed to stifle her laugh.

Felicity allowed her own smile to spread. "I suspect everyone, and their stomachs, will forgive you the deviation from precision."

"Do you know, I harbor the same suspicion." He winked at her.

He'd never done that before. She would have remembered the way it sent her insides fluttering about.

"The other aspect of this I need assistance with is the choosing of a date on which to hold this Evening at Almack's ball. I would appreciate your parents informing me of any conflicts they anticipate in the next few weeks."

Considerate of him, but unnecessary. "With Angelina's health what it is, we have no immediate plans to travel or be away from Lindsworth. I will, of course, have my father send word to you of anything I am not aware of."

William nodded and rose but made no immediate move to exit. "Would you— Would I be asking too much to ask if we might take a turn about the knot garden?"

"I would enjoy that immensely."

He offered his arm as she rose. The maid didn't look at them as they passed, but Felicity felt certain she saw a smile tug at the girl's mouth. Perhaps the hope she felt at William's kind and unexpected offer was not entirely unfounded.

The weather was everything pleasant: bright, cheerful, warm without being hot, a cooling breeze that didn't hold an uncomfortable chill. She kept her arm through William's, something he did not object to.

"You seem in better spirits than last I saw you," she said.

"That is, in fact, the reason I wished to have a private moment of conversation. I want to thank you for your presence as I made my return home. The weight of my grief was less crushing with you beside me."

"The fates were smiling on us both that afternoon. I had been standing at the Carlisle Manor gate, wishing you would return."

He looked down at her. "Have you missed me?"

"For years, William."

His gaze returned to the path in front of them as they continued their meandering walk. "Leonard said much the same thing, though he and I have been in company with one another often in the years since I left home. I didn't think I was so absent as all that."

She leaned her head against his arm, reveling in the warmth of him so nearby while simultaneously hoping he derived some pleasure, or at least some comfort, from her touch. "The vicar once said that grief is like a fog from which one struggles to emerge."

"I have been fighting that fog for far too long, Felicity." She felt him take a deep breath. "I am ready to find my way back into the light."

She stopped walking, so he did as well. Slipping her arm free, she turned to face him directly. "You can make that journey far better, William, if you are here, if you are home. London holds many diversions, and I am certain there are many other places you might go, but being here, no matter how difficult, will help. I know it will."

To her great surprise, he reached for her, brushing his fingers gently along her face. "Being here has already helped."

She closed her eyes and simply breathed through the moment. "I've missed you." She'd made the admission before but did not attempt to stop herself from repeating the feelings of her heart.

His hand slipped from her cheek to her back, holding her closer to him in a tentative embrace. She rested her head against his chest, and his other arm joined his first, embracing her fully.

"I didn't understand until recently how much I was missing being away from home," he said. "I had cut myself off from your friendship, your support, your company."

It was not quite the admission of love she would have preferred, but it tiptoed close enough to give her hope. That he was holding her so affectionately added to the reassurance she felt.

"Then you mean to stay for a time?" She stood very still in the circle of his arms, awaiting his answer.

"I do. I have a great deal of time to make up."

That was enough for her. He had held her, expressed a longing for her company in particular, and he meant to remain. Love could easily grow on such a sturdy foundation. She would do all she could to nourish it.

"I likely shouldn't push the bounds of propriety much further." He sounded genuinely regretful as he dropped his arms away and took a step backward. "I know your parents worry a great deal over decorum."

She opened her eyes once more, letting the lightness she felt show in her expression. "Our scandal-free weeks in Town helped ease a lot of those worries."

He nodded. "Then I will do nothing to diminish the confidence they feel as a result." He offered a small dip of his head. "Do have your parents send me word of any evenings that won't be convenient for your family to attend the ball and see if you can't finagle for me an invitation to a musicale evening here at Banbury House."

His teasing tone inspired an identical one in her. "It may be difficult to procure, but I will manage the thing somehow."

"As difficult as vouchers to Almack's?" he asked with a twinkle in his eye.

"Have you not heard? We need not plead for entrance to that famed establishment; Almack's is coming to us."

"Aren't we fortunate?" He offered one final bow, then turned and made his way back toward the house, no doubt on his way back to Carlisle Manor.

Felicity's sigh echoed inwardly. "We are fortunate, indeed."

Chapter Eleven

"You, William, are a milksop." Leonard's declaration, dropped as it was without warning during their carriage ride to Banbury Manor while William was making a difficult admission of discomfort at the prospect of seeing Felicity again, prompted a momentary silence between them.

"What has inspired this observation?" William asked at long last.

"Ten minutes of you bemoaning your uncertain situation with Miss Felicity." Leonard eyed him with humor-tinged annoyance. "The lady allowed you to embrace her, embraced you in return, and expressed a longing for your company. Those aren't exactly reasons for discouragement."

The man wasn't entirely wrong, and yet some uncertainty was warranted. "I hadn't intended to lay bare so much of what I feel and still didn't admit to all. She said she missed me and was grateful I'm back, but she didn't say she loved me, or was beginning to, or—"

"In the words of the Bard, 'Where love is great, the littlest doubts are fear.' You love her, and I am very nearly convinced she returns your regard. Don't let doubts convince you that you've reason to be afraid of pursuing that love."

William let his shoulders slump. "When did you grow so wise?"

Leonard shrugged. "It is easy to be wise when advising someone in a crisis that the advice-giver need not pass through."

"In other words, someday, when you are rendered a mass of spineless jelly by love, I can lord it over you as you are doing now to me."

Leonard laughed. "I give you full permission to do so, though I will likely not thank you at the time."

The carriage stopped at the top of the drive at Banbury Manor. It was the night of the musical evening Mr. and Mrs. Banbury had quickly arranged. Owing to Angelina's continued poor health, the evening was to be an abbreviated one. William hoped it was successful, for the entire family's sake, and relatively private, for his own. Though he was nervous at the prospect, he was in need of time with Felicity in which to determine where things stood between them and how best to proceed.

Mr. and Mrs. Banbury greeted their guests in the generous entry hall. Leonard and William took their place in the short but slow-moving line, awaiting their turn. The longer they stood there, the more nervous William grew. Perhaps Leonard was correct, and he truly was a milksop.

By the time they reached the head of the reception line, he felt entirely tongue-tied. He stumbled through his expression of gratitude at the invitation, offered an awkward bow, and only just managed to prevent himself from blurting out his desire to see and speak with Felicity. Knowing the Banburys were particularly concerned with exactness of propriety, he wished to be careful in that regard.

He and Leonard slipped into the formal drawing room where the musical evening was to be held. Familiar faces filled the space—a few years older than he remembered, yet still well-known. He was greeted with very real pleasure, most expressing great delight at his return to Lindsworth. William found himself able to return the sentiment sincerely.

At long last, he made his way far enough through the

gathering to spot Felicity sitting beside her sister on a sofa nearest the pianoforte. Angelina appeared to be in good spirits. Her coloring, while not ideal, was not so worrisome as it had been the last time he'd seen her in Town. Being in the country was proving beneficial for her, and he was glad of it.

His gaze did not remain long on her, though. Felicity pulled his attention, as had happened with increasing fervency each time he was near her. She was watching her sister, both enjoyment and concern touching her features. While he did not wish to distract her from her purpose, he did hope she would look at him, even if only a glance. He hadn't the first idea how she looked back on their unexpectedly intimate moment walking in the gardens of Banbury House. Her eyes, no doubt, would tell him a great deal. Felicity possessed the most expressive pair of eyes he'd ever encountered.

A couple approached the Banbury sisters, offering their greetings. Then an area family. And another. William was undeterred. He remained nearby, watching his sweet Felicity easily converse with whoever approached, all while maintaining a noticeable awareness of her sister.

How did I not realize before what a gem she is?

In his defense, she was only thirteen when he'd last been in Lindsworth, and he'd been mired in grief.

"I've never seen you so patient," Leonard whispered to him, more than a hint of amusement in his words.

"Some moments are worth waiting for."

"As are some people?"

William didn't look at Leonard; he didn't have to see his friend's face to know the man would be silently laughing at him.

"I will find us a place to sit," Leonard said. "You can wait here and pine."

He didn't bother correcting the description, though he didn't feel he was "pining." He preferred "patiently hoping."

His patience, however, did not pay the dividends he'd have liked. Before he had even a moment of Felicity's time, the evening was called to order. Everyone moved to his or her chosen spot. The younger gentlemen, himself included, were required to stand along the edges of the room, allowing the ladies and the aged to occupy the sofas and chairs gathered around the pianoforte.

From his position, William was able to see Felicity. Perhaps, if he were fortunate, he would manage to catch her eye at some point. He was not near enough to see the tiny nuances that might be there, but at least he ought to be able to differentiate between horror or pleasure at the sight of him. He likely could even identify indifference, should that be the emotion written on her face.

The music began. All eyes were on the musician. William tried not to be too obvious in his differently directed focus. He didn't wish to embarrass her, but neither did he want to pass the entire night without even a momentary connection.

Watching her as she listened to one musical offering after another proved a treat. Her mouth settled into a captivating whisper of a smile. Her eyes unfocused, all her attention on the notes floating about the room. He found himself less frustrated at the distance between them. A gentleman would count himself fortunate to spend his years finding ways to bring just such a look of contentment to her face.

Just as he was allowing himself to imagine that very future as his own, she turned her head, and their eyes met. For the first time in his life, he fully understood what the poets meant when they spoke of having one's breath stolen by a glance.

A hint of color stole across her cheeks. Her smile didn't fade. That seemed to him an encouraging sign. As he'd assumed, he couldn't see her eyes in enough detail to ascertain anything further.

If he managed nothing else that evening, he would make certain she knew how he felt at seeing her again. He offered a soft and tender smile and the smallest upward twitch of his brow. She responded with a tiny increase in her own happy expression.

He would accept that as encouragement.

It was the extent of their interaction that evening. As soon as the last performer completed her piece, Felicity rose, her arm around Angelina, and the two slipped quickly from the room, leaving their parents to make the necessary farewells and expressions of regret.

The carriage ride back to Carlisle Manor was quieter than the one they'd made to Banbury House. Leonard allowed him silence in which to contemplate his situation.

He was no wiser tonight than he'd been the previous evening, but he was more determined. His mind had filled with the vision of a future he could not easily let go of, one he found himself eager to pursue. If Felicity shared any of his feelings, if she would consider having him in her life, he would do all in his power to prove himself worthy of any bit of her regard.

"Was it a mistake to plan such a tiring evening?" Felicity worried not only about her sister's recovery from that night's festivities but her ability to attend the Almack's-inspired ball at Carlisle Manor. The family had decided to keep the ball a secret—both because Angelina would enjoy the surprise and to save her from disappointment should her health decline too quickly for her to attend.

"The evening was heavenly," Angelina assured her. She sat in her bed, propped up by an abundance of pillows. Her coloring was poor, but her smile was genuine. "Though I knew with perfect clarity we were at our home in the country, I could easily imagine we were in a London drawing room. I can, with confidence, mark as completed 'attend a musical evening' on my list of wishes for the Season."

Relief wrapped itself around Felicity's heart. They had not been mistaken in their efforts. "I thought all who performed this evening made a good showing. Such lovely music."

"Yes, and the music added such ambience to the true performance of the evening." Mischief hung in Angelina's words. It filled her eyes as well.

"Which was?" Felicity could not begin to imagine her sister's meaning. The musical offerings *were* the evening's true performance.

"I daresay you did not see what was plainly before us, no doubt because your eyes were closed—in more ways than one."

Felicity, who had been occupying a chair beside her sister's bed, moved to sit on the thick blanket, facing Angelina directly. "I suspect I am being accused of being thick, but I cannot begin to imagine what I have done to earn such a denouncement."

Though the amusement remained, Angelina's expression turned sympathetic. "I suppose all people are a bit bacon-brained in these matters."

"*What* matters?"

Angelina patted the bed beside her. Felicity scooted across, placing herself directly beside her. They had often sat thus as children, reading stories or imagining adventures. There was comfort in doing so again.

"Are you aware, dearest Felicity, that William is in love with you?"

Felicity would have been equally as surprised had her sister announced that the queen herself had requested to be hired on as their chambermaid.

Angelina laughed lightly, though not unkindly. "Do not be so shocked. You are worthy of the highest regard, and he, I discovered during our time in Town, has grown into a very wise and discerning gentleman."

"He has made no declaration of partiality," Felicity protested even as a flip of her heart betrayed her attempt at being logical.

"I watched him tonight." Angelina leaned more heavily against her pillows. "He could not keep his eyes from you. When you would smile, he would smile. When you turned even slightly in his general direction, his posture would straighten and hope would enter his expression. When you spoke to me or Mother or Father, the longing on his face could not be mistaken."

A surge of unexpected hope flooded over her. She'd known herself to have grown partial to him during their weeks in London, but she'd not allowed herself to believe anything could come of it. "He is likely fond of me—of *us*—because we were children together, and he was remembering those times."

"He was not looking at you with the eyes of a child, I assure you."

"He didn't hold me like one either," she whispered.

In an instant, she had her sister's full and rapt attention. "When did he hold you?"

"A couple of days ago, when he called here." She'd been mulling that moment over in her mind ever since, though she'd told no one of it. Sitting there, with her closest friend and confidante, her beloved, darling sister, next to her, she heard the entire story spill from her lips, complete with her own recounting of hope and disappointment, uncertainty and intrigue, pounding heart and spinning thoughts.

"But he pulled away so suddenly and simply left. I hadn't the first idea what to make of it."

"I would wager he didn't either." Angelina tucked her hands under the blanket. She grew cold more easily than she once had. "He likely wonders about your feelings as much as you appear to be wondering about his."

Perhaps. "Our friendship means so much to me—to him as well, I suspect. I couldn't bear it if I lost that by confessing to feelings that are neither reciprocated nor welcome."

She received a look of such deep empathy from Angelina. "Many people would tell you to lay your entire heart bare, no matter the enormity of that risk, no matter the potential for heart-shattering agony. People always expect others to do what they themselves would likely not undertake were the roles reversed."

"Is that your way of saying I ought to tell him of my regard but also acknowledging that you understand why I might not manage to do so?"

Angelina nodded. "I believe it to be both the correct course of action and the most difficult."

"Those two are often one and the same," Felicity said on a sigh.

"Yes, they are."

Felicity pulled her legs up toward herself, hugging her knees. "You have grown very wise in your old age, sister."

"Wisdom does seem to expand as one's time shrinks." Sadness Angelina didn't often allow in her expression snuck across her face. "Do not waste the time you have been given, Felicity. It is so very precious." She looked at her, earnestly, almost desperately. "You have a future laid out before you. Seize it. Not everyone is granted that gift."

Chapter Twelve

MRS. BANBURY STOOD IN William's ballroom, eyeing his efforts at recreating what was, arguably, London's most famous dancing salon. She had, after all, been in attendance in the hub of *ton* exclusivity, though not for decades. Further, that night's ball was being held for her daughter's benefit. Would it meet with her approval?

"It is not an exact replica," William acknowledged. "Repainting was certainly not an option, but we thought hanging straw-colored silk against the white would at least call to mind the colors of the Almack's ballroom."

She didn't answer but continued slowly turning, looking over their surroundings without a word. He could not ascertain her impression of it all.

"We also replaced the draperies with blue. I am told by the wife of a good friend of mine that it is almost precisely the shade that hangs in the windows there. My housekeeper has converted the formal dining room to a relatively close replication of the Almack's tea room, where we will host tonight's supper. We've identified a room to be used as an antechamber. I chose not to recreate the card room, however, as I did not wish to detract from the true purpose of the evening."

Her continued silence worried him greatly. Was she disappointed? He did not wish for her to be. Though the evening was being held for Angelina's benefit, he knew it meant a lot to Mrs. Banbury as well.

"I know it is not the same as obtaining vouchers and attending the actual Almack's, but I hope it is something of a joy to you and your daughters. I do hope that it is."

She turned to him at last. "Oh, sweet, darling William." To his utter shock, the lady set her hands on either side of his face, just as his own mother had been wont to do. "What a miracle you have wrought here. You are giving my poor Angelina the final wish of her Season."

The gesture deeply touched him. How he had longed for a moment of maternal comfort. "Your daughters have been my dear friends all my life. This is the least I could do for them."

Mrs. Banbury wove her arm through his and walked with him toward the ballroom door. "This will be a comfort to Felicity as well. My heart has ached for her as much as Angelina throughout this ordeal. She will be lost without her sister. I do wish I could save her from the pain that awaits her."

"As do I," William acknowledged.

"But you will stand by her as her friend," Mrs. Banbury said. "At least she will not be entirely alone in her grief."

"I will stand by her whatever her struggle. I care deeply for her."

Mrs. Banbury looked up at him. "How deeply?"

That was certainly a direct question. "Deeply enough that I considered repainting my ballroom."

She laughed. "The evening is for Angelina, but the effort is for Felicity."

"That is not an incorrect statement." How was it he had confessed, to one degree or another, his tenderness for Felicity to nearly everyone except her? "Though I am sorely tempted to press you for any insights you might have as to the state of your daughter's heart, I have too much respect for you as her mother as well as for her privacy to do so. I only hope I will have the opportunity tonight to spend a few moments with her—something I did not have the night of the musicale or any evening since."

"You are the host tonight," Mrs. Banbury said. "If you are granted more than a moment of *your own* company, I will be greatly surprised."

He hadn't thought of that. She was correct, though. He was hosting a grand ball, the first at Carlisle Manor since before his parents' deaths. Every issued invitation had been answered in the affirmative. He would have little time to breathe, let alone find a private moment with Felicity to speak even a portion of what lay in his heart.

By the time the guests began arriving, he still hadn't sorted the question of how to claim even a brief conversation with Felicity. He would make the evening a pleasant one for the Banburys and his other guests and resign himself to delaying, yet again, the essential yet risk-riddled confession he knew he needed to make. Losing his parents had taught him that a person does not always receive second chances to say things he wished to say.

She arrived in the midst of the influx of guests. Despite her position behind the rest of her family—her parents stood on either side of Angelina, supporting their increasingly fragile daughter—William saw *her* first. Had she always drawn his eye this way? Had he simply not realized?

She wore a simple gown of pale green, a thin gold chain about her neck. He didn't know the term for the way she had styled her hair, but he liked it. A ribbon tied the thick locks up high off her neck, while loose wisps hung long over one shoulder.

William took a deep breath, forcing himself to swallow, to keep his composure. She utterly overset him at times, in the best sense.

"Mr. Banbury. Mrs. Banbury." He dipped his head. "Miss Banbury." His eyes moved to Felicity. His veneer of strictly decorous host cracked. He allowed a more personal smile than he ought. "Miss Felicity."

They all offered the expected bows and curtsies. Felicity's gaze returned immediately to him. He could not be certain, but he thought he saw an added bit of warmth in her gaze.

The evening was for Angelina; he could not neglect to make it so. "Miss Banbury, it is my very real pleasure to welcome you to"—he motioned through the open ballroom doors—"Almack's."

Her brows raised even as her mouth dropped open. She looked through the doors. "Almack's?"

"He has recreated it," Mrs. Banbury said. "The same colors, same draperies."

Angelina turned her gaze to him once more. "Almack's—the last item on my list."

He answered with a bow of acknowledgment, admiration, and welcome. "I hope the evening is all you've dreamed it would be."

The Banburys escorted their oldest daughter inside. Felicity lingered a moment. A shimmer of a tear hung in one eye. "Thank you," she whispered. "Thank you, again and again."

He knew she couldn't remain long without drawing undue attention from the others waiting to enter the ballroom. He had but a moment.

"Am I foolish to hope you might save a dance for me, Miss Felicity?"

The softness of her expression nearly crumbled his composure. "No one has claimed my supper dance."

It was a forward suggestion, but one he did not mean to waste. "I would be honored if I might claim your supper dance."

She dipped a tiny curtsy and followed in her parents' wake.

He had been granted her supper dance, a position of significance. Being her partner during the nighttime meal meant he'd have her company longer than he would otherwise. This, he knew full-well, was the chance he sought.

The Evening at Almack's ball was everything Felicity could have hoped for her sister. Angelina never stopped smiling as the musicians played tune after tune. Her health was too fragile for joining in the dancing, but she watched with real delight. Their neighbors, kind and attentive as always, kept her company, giving every indication of being pleased to sit out a set or two talking with her. Mr. Whitehall even secured permission to take a brief and necessarily slow turn about the room with her, something he and Mother both agreed was done with great regularity at the actual Almack's.

Felicity could not have been happier for Angelina.

When William pulled himself away from the demands of being the evening's host to claim the supper dance she had granted him, she could not have been happier for *herself.*

"Thank you again for this evening," she said in the moment before the musicians struck their opening notes.

He hadn't time to offer so much as a "You're welcome" or "My pleasure." He moved with a light, bouncing step, his gaze returning to her the moment he had taken his place in the line opposite her. Happiness shown in his eyes, but his smile was subtle, as if kept between the two of them. How she hoped she was not allowing her own longing to color her perception of his.

The movements of the dance pulled them together long enough for a brief clasp of hands, a momentary brushing of arms. At one point, they were permitted enough proximity for a quick, whispered exchange.

"I believe the evening can be counted a success," he said. Not the personal remark she'd hoped for, but still encouraging.

"I agree," she said. "And your dancing skills are proving you an excellent partner for the supper dance."

"Wait until you witness my talent for eating, then you will truly be impressed." He winked.

Again, the requirements of the dance pulled them apart. She contented herself with watching him from the opposite line, cherishing the glances she received, allowing her pleasure to show in her expression. She was, no doubt, laying bare her feelings for all to see, but she couldn't hide what she felt. It overflowed from her.

By the time the set concluded and the doors to the dining room opened to the guests for the much-anticipated supper, Felicity's heart was pounding with pleasure and racing with the promise of William's company at last. Beneath that lay a healthy dose of uncertainty; she meant to make a confession that night, after all. Despite the encouragement she'd felt at the discernible warmth of his glances and the tingle of his fingers brushing hers, love seldom allowed logic to temper all emotion. She remained nervous.

He walked with her arm through his into the dining room, leading the guests as was customary for the evening's host. The warmth of him so near settled her nerves considerably. Father walked near them with Angelina on his arm.

"This room was decorated to closely resemble the tea room at Almack's," William told them. "I thought it an important addition to the evening."

Angelina looked over the elegantly arranged space with the same sparkle of joy that had lit her face all night. "You have thought of everything."

"Anything at all for my two favorite people." He looked from Angelina to Felicity, winking again.

"Why do you keep doing that?" Only after the question spilled without warning from her lips did she realize how potentially accusatory or rude or displeased she might sound.

William didn't appear offended. "Keep doing *what*?"

"Winking at me."

He laughed quietly. "If you aren't sure, I'm likely not doing it correctly."

That was all the explanation she received before the demands of hosting pulled his attention in dozens of directions. He still managed to fill a plate for her and make certain she was well fed while he saw to his duties. He even made time to speak with Angelina, telling her more than once how happy he was to see her enjoying herself. His was a good heart. Felicity would count herself fortunate to have a claim on any part of it.

"Have you spoken with him?" Angelina asked in a whisper after William was pulled away by yet another guest.

"I've hardly had time for more than two words with him at any one time," she said.

"But ample time for warm glances between the two of you."

Felicity bit back a smile, though she felt certain her blush was obvious to anyone watching. "He has been winking at me."

"Has he?"

She nodded. "And he insists I ought to know why he's doing so. I know the 'why' I would like to be true, but I am hesitant."

"The time for hesitancy has past, Felicity." Angelina motioned with her head toward William, making his way with frequent interruptions back to where she sat. "Seize your future, my dear. It is a surer thing than you realize."

He reached her and took his seat. "I am proving a horrible partner for supper, I'm afraid."

"You are making me doubt your self-professed talent for eating."

He chuckled. "I am beginning to doubt it myself."

She leaned the tiniest bit closer. "I had hoped to speak with you, William. I am rather anxious to, in fact."

Worry tugged at his brow. "Is anything the matter?"

"No." At least she hoped not.

"I suspect our only hope of an uninterrupted conversation is to make an escape," he said. "That, however, would bring down on our heads the judgment of essentially everyone here."

That was a delicate aspect of their situation. Should they both slip out, whispers would be unavoidable. She didn't wish to mar the evening or either of their reputations.

"Perhaps tomorrow, then. Of course, Angelina will likely be entirely exhausted and in need of assistance. In a day or two, she should, I hope, regain her strength. Perhaps we might speak then." Her heart dropped. Two or three more days without seeing him or speaking with him. Not only would she struggle to keep her courage up, but she would also miss him. "Perhaps you might call on us, provided Angelina is equal to having visitors."

He dipped his head to someone across the table, offered another silent acknowledgment to someone else, then, under his breath, said to her, "After supper, do you think you could quietly slip out to the east terrace?"

She had spent enough of her childhood at Carlisle Manor to know the small balcony he referred to—one off the family wing. It was a public location, but an isolated one.

"I could," she said. "We would have to be very careful."

"We will be."

Enough winding and weaving ensued as the guests returned to the ballroom that Felicity was able to easily slip away down a corridor to a family staircase. The wing was dim, but she knew the area well. Arriving on the terrace was not overly difficult.

She did not have to wait long. William joined her on the terrace, arriving from a seldom-used room in the family wing. The full moon provided enough light to faintly illuminate him. Though she was nervous about the conversation that awaited them, the sight of him brought her comfort and a feeling of deep contentment.

Their eyes met. He didn't look away, neither did he speak. The tiniest smile tugged at the corner of his mouth.

"William." It was all she could say. Too much filled her heart and spun about in her mind. "William."

He closed the distance between them. "I've been anxious for a moment with you. I'm glad you suggested it."

"Angelina says I need to stop being a ninny." It was not the sophisticated beginning to this all-important conversation she would have liked, but it was sincere.

"Leonard has been telling me much the same thing." He took her hand and, to her pleased surprise, raised it to his lips. "Fate, I am told, would not have crossed our paths in London if it hadn't intended to bring us together." He brushed a soft and tender kiss over her knuckles. "But Fate can't do everything for us." He kissed her fingers once more before enveloping her hand between his. "Have I reason to hope, my dear friend, that there might someday be more between us than friendship?"

She set her free hand against his chest. "Clandestine meetings and stolen kisses would indicate there already is."

His arm slipped around her, even as he kept her hand warmly clasped in his other one. "Kissing your fingers is not as scandalous as you seem to think."

"Perhaps I was making a prediction rather than offering a summary."

She felt his laughter rumble beneath her palm. "I like this coquettish side of you, Felicity."

"*Like?*" Not merely a hint flirtatious, she found herself shockingly bold.

"I haven't the talent for pretty speeches I wish I did," he said quietly.

"I don't need speeches, William. I don't need poetry or Shakespearean wordplay. I simply need to know if you—if you love me the way . . . the way I love you."

Shock, joy, and hope filled his face in an instant. "You love me?"

Felicity had promised Angelina she wouldn't lose her courage, and she didn't mean to break that vow. "I do love you."

William rested his head against the top of hers, both his arms now wrapped around her. "I came here prepared to plead for some hope that you might, one day, learn to love me, ready to offer my heart with no promise of being granted any bit of yours."

"I spoke the words, William. You needn't offer them elegantly, but I do need to hear them."

He kissed her forehead. "I love you, Felicity. I love you deeply, with all my heart."

She bent her neck, looking up into his eyes. "If only you'd come home sooner, darling. We might've managed this moment without breaking so many rules."

His smile blossomed. "Where would be the excitement in that?"

"I believe we could find a way of making the moment sufficiently exciting."

He arched an eyebrow. "I am certain we could."

She slid her hand from its place on his chest, over his

collar, along his neck, and cupped his jaw. He tightened his arm around her, bringing her flush with him.

"We truly are breaking rules tonight," she whispered.

His voice equally quiet and husky in its breathlessness, he said, "Let's break one more."

Their lips met without a hint of the hesitancy that had marked their arrival on the terrace. She folded her arms about his neck, clinging to him and the moment. He held her with equal amounts of tenderness and earnestness.

A perfect and wonderful moment.

Epilogue

CARLISLE MANOR HAD NOT hosted a wedding breakfast in thirty years, not since the day William's parents were married. How grateful he was that Felicity suggested the festivities be held at his home rather than hers. The house needed every bit of happiness and joy it could be granted. Too many years had passed in mourning.

"Why do you keep looking at me that way?" she asked with a smile from her seat beside him.

"What way?"

"As if you were . . . a little shocked to see me here, but pleased at the same time."

"Perhaps because I am yet perplexed at my undeserved good fortune and also unspeakably happy at this morning's events."

She leaned her head against his shoulder. "If your fortune holds, I will not come to my senses any time soon."

Oh, how he adored her. She made him laugh, brought him joy and comfort. If he hadn't stubbornly remained away in the years since his parents' deaths, he might not have been consumed by his grief for so long.

"Thank you for being so understanding about the wedding trip," she said quietly. "I am certain you would have preferred more time to ourselves."

He kissed the top of her head. "There will be time for that, my dear."

His gaze slid to Angelina, seated nearby between her

parents. Her health had taken a turn for the worse. The doctors did not believe she had much time left. Felicity, understandably, wished to remain close. William had no desire to take from her the last remaining weeks or months she had with her sister.

"You have only just begun emerging from the cocoon of your earlier grief," she said. "Are you equal to facing even more?"

"Together, I believe we can face anything at all." He meant the bold words. Yes, there would be sorrow; there would be difficulties ahead for them. But neither of them was alone.

She looked up at him, happiness evident in her eyes despite the heaviness of their topic. "There is one destination I would like to formally request we visit."

"Anywhere in all the world." He waited to hear what place could mean so very much to her that she would request it specifically. Europe? The Americas? Someplace farther afield?

"Almack's. The *real* Almack's."

He laughed, as he so often did with her. "I fear you will be sorely disappointed."

"Never fear, my love. Together, I believe we can face anything at all."

No matter that half the neighborhood was watching, no matter that doing so was likely to be met with shocked whispers, he kissed her. He kissed her fully and wholeheartedly, filling the gesture with the promise of years to come—years filled with laughter, with strength.

With love.

Sarah M. Eden is the author of multiple historical romances, including the two-time Whitney Award Winner *Longing for Home* and Whitney Award finalists *Seeking Persephone* and *Courting Miss Lancaster*. Combining her obsession with history and affinity for tender love stories, Sarah loves crafting witty characters and heartfelt romances. She has thrice served as the Master of Ceremonies for the Storymakers Writers Conference and acted as the Writer in Residence at the Northwest Writers Retreat. Sarah is represented by Pam Victorio at D4EO Literary Agency.

Visit Sarah online:
Twitter: @SarahMEden
Facebook: Author Sarah M. Eden
Website: SarahMEden.com

Made in the USA
Middletown, DE
03 April 2023

28166282R00156